D1744230

Nicole lives with her family in a rural town in the Victorian Central Highlands. She's a full-time writer and a fan of happily-ever-afters.

Nicole HURLEY-MOORE

McKellan's Run

ARENA
ALLEN&UNWIN

For Christopher

First published in 2015

Copyright © Nicole Hurley-Moore 2015

All rights reserved. No part of this book may be reproduced or transmitted in
any form or by any means, electronic or mechanical, including photocopying,
recording or by any information storage and retrieval system, without prior
permission in writing from the publisher. The Australian *Copyright Act 1968*
(the Act) allows a maximum of one chapter or 10 per cent of this book, whichever
is the greater, to be photocopied by any educational institution for its educational
purposes provided that the educational institution (or body that administers it) has
given a remuneration notice to the Copyright Agency (Australia) under the Act.

Arena Books, an imprint of
Allen & Unwin
83 Alexander Street
Crows Nest NSW 2065
Australia
Phone: (61 2) 8425 0100
Email: info@allenandunwin.com
Web: www.allenandunwin.com

Cataloguing-in-Publication details are available
from the National Library of Australia
www.trove.nla.gov.au

ISBN 978 1 76011 384 1

Set in 12/18 pt Sabon by Midland Typesetters, Australia
Printed and bound in Australia by Griffin Press
10 9 8 7 6 5 4 3 2 1

The paper in this book is FSC® certified.
FSC® promotes environmentally responsible,
socially beneficial and economically viable
management of the world's forests.

This is a work of fiction. Names, characters, places and incidents are products of the
author's imagination or are used fictitiously. Any resemblance to actual events, locales,
or persons, living or dead, is entirely coincidental.

Prologue

Cradling her newborn daughter in her arms, Violet felt her heart swell with so much love she thought it might burst. 'Holly Eliza Beckett, you are the most beautiful baby I've ever seen,' she whispered, gently kissing her daughter's head and breathing in her gorgeous new-baby scent. As Holly stirred, a wave of protectiveness washed over Violet. She would move heaven and earth to make sure her precious baby was always kept safe and loved.

Tearing her gaze away from Holly a while later, she felt a pang as she caught sight of the birth registration papers. All she needed to do to complete them was write Jason's name in the blank space provided for the father.

Careful not to wake Holly, she slowly lowered her into the hospital bassinet. Then, steeling herself against the pain, she shuffled over to the window.

It was late morning and the sun was filtering through the slatted curtains, throwing shadowy lines across the room. Though desperately tired, she knew there was no way she would get any peace until she came to a decision. Yet again she remembered the night she'd told Jason she was pregnant with his baby and how he'd made it absolutely clear that since getting his first job he needed to consolidate his career. Settling down with a partner and baby at such a young age just wasn't part of his plans.

Well, Jason had made his decision the night she turned up on his doorstep looking for help and now she had to make hers.

Do I have the right to deny Jason the knowledge of his child, despite everything, she wondered. Perhaps I don't, but he didn't want a child and he said that she should get on with her life without him. She'd done exactly that, managing to keep herself and Lily afloat since moving to Melbourne. Somehow she'd make things work, even with a baby. Picking up the document and placing it on the hospital side table, in the blank space under 'Father's Name', Violet wrote 'Father unknown'.

Chapter 1

Violet pulled up outside the solicitor's office, her heart beating hard. Ever since she'd crested the hill into Violet Falls she'd felt fearful and uneasy.

Looking in the rearview mirror, she put on some lipstick, twisted her hair into a knot at the nape of her neck and then turned around. 'Are you ready, sweetie?' she asked Holly, trying to hide her unease with a smile.

'Uh huh,' said Holly, her face serious.

'Great, come on then, let's go and get the key to our new house,' said Violet.

'Mummy, are we ever going back to the city?' asked Holly.

'We'll definitely visit Aunty Lily whenever we can, but we're not going to live there anymore,' said Violet. 'We have a new home now, here in Violet Falls. And very soon, I'll have a new business as well.'

Holly remained quiet, her expression troubled, as Violet opened the back door for her.

'It'll be great,' said Violet, leaning over and kissing Holly's forehead as she unbuckled her seatbelt. 'You're going to have a new house, a new school and lots and lots

1

of new friends. We're going to have a great adventure, just you wait and see.'

'I'm really hungry,' said Holly, taking Violet's hand.

'After we pick up the key, we'll stop at the local super-market and grab some groceries before we head over to our new house.'

Holly looked uncertain as they walked hand in hand up the old stone steps and into the building.

* * *

After greeting Violet and Holly, Mr Taylor, who had been Violet's grandfather's solicitor, asked his secretary to take care of Holly for a few minutes while he spoke to Violet.

Closing the door to his office he walked over to his desk and handed Violet an envelope and a key before briefly explaining the terms of her grandfather's will. Violet thanked him, but couldn't trust herself to say anything more. She'd always believed that one day she'd be reconciled with her grandfather—but time had run out and now the words she'd practised saying to him in her head a hundred times would be forever unsaid.

Mr Taylor looked as if he wanted to say something more but the moment passed and there was just an awkward pause.

'Was there something else?' Violet asked.

'I know that you and your grandfather had your differ-ences but I thought you'd still like to know that in the end he didn't suffer.'

'That's good,' said Violet. 'What happened?'

'I was at a council meeting with him and one minute he was laying down the law to the other council members—you remember how passionate he could get—and the next he's fallen on the floor. It was that quick. We called an ambulance straightaway but he was gone before they got him to the hospital.'

Violet reached over and briefly touched his hand, realising no matter what she thought about her grandfather, Hugh Taylor had lost a friend. 'I'm glad it was so fast and he didn't linger. He would have hated that.'

'You're right,' said Mr Taylor after a pause. 'He would have wanted to go out during a fiery exchange rather than have his health decline.'

'Well there was nothing he liked better than a fiery exchange.'

'Quite right, quite right. You'll find the house untouched. Other than organising for the fridge to be emptied and the electricity turned off, I left everything as it was when Silas set off for the council meeting.'

'The electricity should have been reconnected by this morning.'

'So you intend to move back?'

'I do. I'm going to open a party planning business,' said Violet, sounding braver than she felt.

Mr Taylor's bushy brows drew into a frown. 'I see. I'm afraid that other than the house, the funds left by your grandfather are rather meagre.'

'It'll be enough,' Violet said. It would have to be, she thought.

'Right then, very good,' Mr Taylor said before lapsing back into another uncomfortable silence.

'Well, thank you again, Mr Taylor,' Violet said. 'I'd better get going. It's a big change for Holly, and I need to pick up some groceries and get to the house before the removalist arrives with all our stuff.'

'Yes, yes of course. Welcome back to Violet Falls, Miss Beckett. Please give me a call if you need anything.'

'It was nice to see you again,' said Violet as he showed her out.

* * *

As Holly was getting back into the car, Violet caught sight of her old English teacher, Mrs Wardley, who waved to her from across the street and then started crossing the road. Violet watched as Holly snapped the seatbelt to her booster seat shut, and wondered if she had enough time to jump in the car and take off before Mrs Wardley reached her.

'Violet, my dear, it's so lovely to see you,' called Mrs Wardley.

Ah well, so much for the getaway plan.

'Mrs Wardley, how are you?' said Violet.

'It's been a long time. Why it must be almost six or seven years,' she said, looking past Violet into the back of the car.

'Yes, something like that,' Violet replied vaguely. She'd forgotten that the one thing Violet Falls loved most was gossip and Mrs Wardley was renowned as a master of it.

'Are you back now, to stay I mean?' asked her old teacher.

'Yes, I am,' said Violet, smiling nervously, desperate to get away.

'Good—and who is this?' said Mrs Wardley, bending down at the window and smiling in at Holly.

Violet repressed a sigh and opened the back door. 'This is my daughter, Holly. Holly, say hello to Mrs Wardley. Mrs Wardley was one of my teachers.'

Holly gave the older woman a shy smile.

'She looks just like you, Violet,' said Mrs Wardley, straightening up. 'Are you by yourself?'

'Yes, it's just Holly and me,' said Violet with a tight smile. 'Now, if you'll excuse me, I'd better get to the supermarket.'

'Of course, dear. I'm so glad you're back.'

'Thank you, Mrs Wardley,' said Violet.

* * *

Violet felt a tumult of emotions as she pulled into the driveway of the large white weatherboard house she and Lily had once shared with their grandparents. Memories from the past—many happy but most of the latter ones were not—threatened to overwhelm her.

'Wow, is that all ours?' said Holly from the back seat.

'Sure is,' said Violet, smiling.

'It's so much bigger than our flat.'

'Yes, there'll be plenty of room for you to have friends over to stay,' said Violet.

'It's got a garden!' Holly exclaimed, her face alight.

As she parked, Violet recalled how as a kid she'd sort of taken for granted the acre or so of land around her grandparents' house, but for a city kid like Holly it would be a revelation to have so much space.

'Yes Holly, it has a garden.'

'It's as big as the park! Can we get a dog?'

Violet popped open the door. 'Hmmm, I'll have to think about that one.'

Holly held up her thumb and forefinger. 'But it could be just a little one, Mummy.'

'I think it would need to be a bit bigger than that,' Violet said with a laugh. 'We'll see, okay?'

'Okay,' said Holly, grabbing her bright pink backpack and clambering out of the car. 'Maybe we could have a cat instead.'

Violet started up the verandah steps. 'Why don't we get inside first before we start filling the house with pets?'

Holly tramped behind her and Violet waited until she made it to the top before she put the key in the lock and undid the bolt. They were here, they were home and ready to start their new life.

The seconds ticked by as Violet stood with her hand around the doorknob. She took a deep breath but somehow couldn't find that last scrap of courage to turn the knob and push the door open.

'Aren't we going in, Mummy?' Holly asked.

'Yes, yes, of course. Mummy was just thinking about the last time I was here, that's all,' Violet replied, smiling at Holly to hide how emotional she was feeling.

When she finally opened the door everything was just as she'd remembered it—dark, silent and oppressive. She tried to appear cheerful for Holly's sake, making a big show of opening up the windows to let in cleansing air and sunlight as well as talking about how much fun they'd have painting and redecorating their new house. She even promised Holly she could choose the paint colour for her new bedroom.

Hugh Taylor had been right about the place being the same as when her grandfather had set off to his council meeting. Other than a layer of dust it still looked as if her grandfather had just popped out and was expected back at any moment. Violet's heart lurched as she wandered into the kitchen and glanced at the table—an empty mug sat next to a half-finished crossword.

As Violet walked through the house she felt sad as she saw her grandfather's jacket slung over the back of the couch and the book he'd never finished reading next to his bed. She did her best to push away the melancholy feeling, rolled up her sleeves and tried to eradicate the ghosts of the past.

* * *

For the first two nights after their arrival, Violet and Holly slept on a mattress in the almost bare lounge room. Holly thought it was a great adventure and said they should always sleep in that room; Violet was just too tired to argue.

In the week and a half they had before Holly started school, Violet hired a skip bin, donated most of her grandfather's furniture to Vinnies and threw out lots of ancient belongings, including piles of newspapers. She quickly discovered the Hummingbird Café had the best coffee—and child-friendly staff—in town and made sure to take Holly there when they both needed a break.

After deciding impulsively to rip up the house's fifty-year-old carpet in its entirety she encouraged Holly to spend time exploring the huge backyard while she got on with the sweaty, dirty, tiring job of tearing up carpet. When it came time to start painting (she swore like a trooper when she realised it would have been better to do it before ripping up the carpet) she began with Holly's room, savouring Holly's delight when she walked into her freshly painted room for the first time to see all her furniture from Melbourne set up, and the little desk that Lily had bought for her, positioned in the corner, with all her pencils, textas, paints and paper set out on it.

Another special moment occurred when they came home from a treat at the Hummingbird Café, after days of Violet painting from the crack of dawn each day, to find the swing and slippery dip set that Violet had secretly bought had been delivered and assembled in the backyard.

Bit by bit the house started to feel lighter, airier and more 'theirs'. Violet couldn't wait to get someone to sand and polish all the wooden floors, but she'd do that when Holly started school. Meanwhile, all that was left to decide on was the main bedroom—the one that had once belonged to Violet and Lily's grandparents.

The room was austere with not a picture or a throw pillow to soften it. Violet ran her fingers along the foot of the large wooden bed. Its legs were carved in thick, barley sugar twists and it had been in the family longer than anyone could remember. There was no way she could bring herself to sleep in it but she couldn't give it away either. Maybe she'd buy a new mattress and set up a guest bedroom at the back of the house. She cleared out the room, but when she started sorting through the bedside table she found something that made her take a breath and pause. At the bottom of the drawer was an old-fashioned tin with a picture of a castle on it. She lifted the lid to find a stack of letters and immediately recognised her own handwriting.

Violet sat down on the floor and picked up the letters. The first was the note she'd sent her grandfather just after Holly was born. She hadn't asked him for anything—it had been a quick note to let him know he had a great-granddaughter and that the baby was perfect and beautiful. She'd enclosed a photo of Holly swaddled in a bunny rug and looking angelic. Though Violet had never received a reply, Holly's picture showed signs of being looked at many times.

There were another half a dozen letters, all of them written by Lily. She opened one and a couple of photos fell out. One was a picture of Lily standing next to a sample of her dress designs and the other was of Holly's fourth birthday. In the second photo, Holly, Violet and Lily were all crowded around a pink birthday cake which was covered in candles and sparklers.

Violet looked back at the letters, which all appeared to have been well-read—the pages creased from being folded over many times. The tragedy was that Silas Beckett had cared enough for his granddaughters to re-read their letters and keep them safe but he'd never been able to bring himself to get in contact with either of them. His stubborn pride had robbed him of the family he could have had.

Violet wiped away her tears with the back of her hand and stood up, still holding the tin close to her chest. Walking out of her grandfather's bedroom in a daze she went to find the letter that Mr Taylor had given her which she hadn't been able to muster the courage to read. She riffled through the suitcase and found the letter but she still couldn't bring herself to read it.

* * *

Outside the Violet Falls Public School, Violet bent down and wrapped Holly in a hug. The old school—which Violet and Lily had also gone to—was a pretty, Victorian-era red brick building set in an established shady garden. But its beauty was lost on Violet today, as her whole attention was centred on her daughter.

'Have a great day.'

Holly gave her a broad smile. 'I will.'

'You're excited aren't you, about meeting the other kids?'

'Ah-huh. Mummy, stop worrying. I'll be alright.'

Violet gave her another squeeze. When had Holly become so perceptive? It seemed like only yesterday when she started to talk.

'You'll be having fun while I'll be stacking up the last few boxes in the spare room before starting on the floors. Are you sure you don't want me to walk you to your new classroom?'

Holly shook her head. 'Nope, I'll be fine.'

The bell sounded and Holly gave her mother a peck on the cheek. Reluctantly Violet let her go and watched as she skipped up the steps at the front of the school.

'I'll see you later then. I'll pick you up from here,' Violet called out as she pointed to where she was standing.

Holly looked over her shoulder and waved before she disappeared into the building.

Violet stood there a while longer, staring in the direction Holly had gone. Her stomach was knotted. Lord, she was more nervous about Holly's first day in a new school than her daughter was.

'Are you okay?' came a woman's voice from behind her.

Violet turned to see two women smiling at her. One was a little shorter than Violet and had a warm friendly face and deep russet-coloured hair that fell around her shoulders. The other woman was taller, thinner and had her blonde hair dragged back into a ponytail.

'Oh, yes I'm fine. Thanks,' said Violet.

'I'm Meg Laragy,' said the redheaded woman, offering her hand, 'and this is my friend Sally Ford,' she added.

'Hi, I'm Violet Beckett,' said Violet, shaking her hand and nodding to Sally. 'It's my daughter's first day. We've just moved up from Melbourne.'

'What grade is she in?'

'Um, grade one with Mrs Henshaw.'

'Oh our girls are in that class! I'll tell Amber to keep an eye on . . .'

'Holly, my daughter's name is Holly.'

11

'Right then. We'll make sure Amber and Kylie help her find her way around.'

'Thank you—that's very kind,' said Violet, smiling.

'Not at all. If there's anything you need just let me know. Even if it's just a coffee and a chat,' Meg said.

'So where are you living?' asked Sally.

'I'm over on Black Jack Road.'

'Oh, it's pretty over that side of town, although I always thought it odd that they called the road after a card game,' Sally said with a frown.

'Um, actually it was named after a notorious bushranger who lived in this area during the gold rush. According to legend "Jack" wore a black mask every time he robbed and raided and that's how he got his name.'

'Really, I didn't know that,' said Meg, shaking her head. 'Did you say your name was Beckett? Are you any relation to the Councillor Beckett who died not that long ago?' she asked as the three of them fell into step together as they made their way towards the car park.

'Yes, he was my grandfather.'

'My condolences. He was a bit of a character I hear,' said Sally. 'Of course, I know your place—it's a great house. I run past it every morning. Are you doing it up?'

'Yes, it needs a lot of work but I can only afford to do a bit at a time,' said Violet.

'Oh, you're so lucky to be able to restore a wonderful old house like that,' said Meg. 'I bet it still has all its original features.'

'It sure does,' said Violet.

'I love old houses,' said Sally, 'but Jim insisted on opting for a new build. I'm over on Prospect Way if you ever want to come over for a coffee.'

'We're around the corner from each other,' Meg said, leaning against the fence beside her friend. 'And you're more than welcome.'

'Thanks,' said Violet, smiling. 'That's very sweet of you both.'

***

If anyone else told Violet how lucky she was to be restoring an old house, she might lose it. The romantic notion she'd had about just how lovely it would be to bring the house back to life had been totally obliterated. The culprit had been a belt sander and what seemed like endless kilometres of wooden floors. Okay, she was exaggerating—but not by much.

Her rapidly decreasing funds had prompted her into one of the most stupid ideas of her life—namely to sand and polish all the wooden floors by herself. So she'd hired the sanding machine from the local hardware store and been slightly indignant when the shop assistant suggested the names of a couple of local tradies who specialized in floor restoration. In hindsight it would have been a much better idea to have used one of them.

It was the dust that almost did her in. It was in every nook and cranny of every inch of the house. Despite taping off rooms and wearing protective gear, the dust seemed to have invaded everything. To make matters worse, no matter how hard she cleaned, the dust lingered well after the initial job had been completed. For almost two weeks after she finished the sanding, Violet swore that she could taste the grittiness in every cup of coffee she made.

The only bright spot had been the night she and Holly camped out in the backyard, which Holly had loved. Violet had pulled out some long-forgotten camping equipment from the spare room and pitched the tent beneath the plum trees. They had eaten barbecued sausages wrapped in fresh bread and stared at the twinkling night sky for well over an hour.

Holly had thought it was a great adventure to have her mother reading her a story by flashlight and telling her about how she and Aunty Lily would sometimes camp out in the bush. Holly's joy had been infectious and somehow before she fell asleep, she extracted a promise from her mother that they would go camping again.

Two weeks after Holly's first day of school and after more hard work than Violet had ever imagined, she sat back in her office chair and admired her newly polished floors.

She had decided that financially and practically it'd be best to run her business from home and had turned her grandmother's sewing room into a home office. The room had good bones: a high ceiling, and plenty of light streaming in from the large bay window. After several coats of white paint her office felt light and airy.

Everything seemed as if it was finally beginning to fall into place.

Chapter 2

Violet braced herself against the scratched wooden counter, the heavy weight in her stomach refusing to budge.

'So, Mr Ogilvy, exactly how much would all the repairs cost?'

'I'm afraid it's pretty steep. Because you've blown the head gasket it means we have to replace the engine. It's an old car, perhaps you should think about upgrading it? Anyway,' he said, looking down at his paperwork, 'it all comes to $3352.'

Violet blinked as the enormity of the number sunk into her brain. 'I'm sorry, how much did you say?'

'I'm sorry, but it all comes to $3352, even if I source the cheapest parts possible,' said Ned Ogilvy, looking over his glasses and giving her a reassuring smile. 'Listen Violet, your grandad was a loyal customer and well, hell, you were raised here. I can shave a bit off the price, let's call it three thousand dollars-even and you can pay it off over a few months if you want.'

Violet felt numb and sick inside. Where on earth was she going to get three thousand dollars? She'd put all the money she had into getting her business off the ground and even though she was getting some bookings, putting on parties, and building a name for herself as an events planner, there was no way she could just pull that sort of money out of thin air. Being able to pay it off gradually would help but it still put her in a tight spot.

'Um . . . thanks, Mr Ogilvy, that's um . . . very kind of you.'

'Nah, no worries. So, you need to have a think about whether to go ahead with the repairs or put the money towards a new car.'

Violet knew she didn't have an option. She needed a car so she could do the handful of parties she'd been hired for. There was no way she could borrow enough to buy a new car.

'How long will it take?'

'A week or so. If I can get the parts from Bendigo, I'll hurry it along.'

Violet's mind whirled. A week! How was she going to organise and then put on the Freemans' thirtieth anniversary bash?

'I know how much you depend on that car,' said Mr Ogilvy. 'You can use one of ours for free until yours is fixed if you like.'

'Really?' A surge of relief ran through her. 'That would be fantastic, thank you so much.'

He waved his hand as if to swipe away her thanks. 'It's fine. Now, the car we can lend you isn't much to look at but it's safe and reliable. I'll get my grandson, Sam, to give it a once-over when he gets back and then he can drop it over to your place after work.'

'Thank you.'

'So, does that mean I go ahead with the repairs?'

Violet took a breath. She was caught between the devil and the deep blue sea and there was absolutely no way she could get out of it without dropping thousands of dollars.

'Yes, please. That would be great.'

* * *

No matter how hard Violet stared at her computer there was no way she could get her bank balance to remain in the black. It was already flatlining but now with the car repairs it was going in the wrong direction. She pulled up her events calendar. Other than the Freemans' anniversary party, she had a meet-and-greet for a local businesswoman who was preparing to run for council and two birthday parties. She'd started up the Violet Falls Parties & Events as soon as the last suitcase had been unpacked. So far she'd been pleasantly surprised at how well the town had taken to it. Violet had poured everything she had into setting it up, to the point that even now the spare change jar she kept on top of the fridge was looking a little low.

Violet had plans for her business. Lovely, expansive plans that would one day draw in parties from not just the local area but as far away as Melbourne. The potential was there and maybe, as time went on, she would consider doing bigger events, perhaps even a wedding or two. But that was a little way down the track.

Violet Falls had a lot going for it. Other than the old Levine mansion that had been converted into a high-end bed-and-breakfast, there was the ornate neo-Gothic bluestone church in the middle of town, a beautiful botanical gardens, an old theatre (tiny but perfectly formed), a lavender farm and the Gold Dust Vineyards lay on the outskirts. There were also a couple of great restaurants and an old church hall. As a result, the possibility of organising fantastic, elegant parties was there but she needed to embark on things carefully while she got Violet Falls Parties & Events up and running.

The next couple of weeks were going to be tight, but once she was paid for the upcoming events she'd thought everything would fall into place. Now with the whole car drama she would have to try and book some more events as quickly as she could, just so she and Holly could eat.

She reached over and flicked on her answering machine. There were three messages and she prayed that one might be about a job. The first was from Lily just saying hello and asking how she and her favourite niece were, the next was from Ned Ogilvy to say they wouldn't get the parts for two more days and the third was from Sarah McKellan.

Violet had to listen to Mrs McKellan's message twice before the words properly sank in.

'Hi Violet, it's Sarah McKellan. I'm so sorry that you've already been back in town for a few months and we haven't caught up. I've been meaning to come around and see you as it'd be good to talk about a couple of things. I've been hearing some great reports about the events you've been doing and, well, err, I have an event I need help with.

18

It's short notice but I want you to help me with Jason's wedding—I hope you'll consider it. Give me a call. Bye.'

Violet shook her head. There was no way that she was going anywhere near Jason McKellan—hell would have to freeze over first. She'd call Sarah and tell her that even though she'd love to catch up, she couldn't plan Jason's wedding.

She looked down at the desk, overwhelmed by emotion, only to see the Ogilvy and Sons bill taunting her.

No, there's no way she could go through with it. Jason was part of her past and that's where she needed to keep him. Besides, she'd already heard some of the rumours about her and Holly circulating around Violet Falls. All sorts of stories from wild and funny to some that were just plain vicious. But there was one question that was being whispered all over the place—who was Holly's father? She couldn't go anywhere near McKellan's Run if she wanted to keep Holly safe. Besides, she'd never planned a wedding on her own. She'd assisted at a few and they were invariably hard work.

Then again, this job could be the answer she was praying for—couldn't it?

'Mummy,' Holly called out from the hall.

'Yes, sweetheart?'

'Mummy, I can't get the bathroom tap to turn off. I turned the handle really hard but the water just keeps coming.'

'Okay, sweetie, I'm coming,' said Violet as she pushed back her desk chair and stood up. Great, the car blows up and now the plumbing . . . what else could possibly go wrong?

The plumber gave her a nervous smile and offered some inane comments about old houses and plumbing as he handed her the dreaded bill.

'Thanks,' said Violet as he headed out the door. Then, glancing down she saw that the bill was for $230. The damn tap had run all night and she shuddered to think what the water bill would be like. Great, just great.

She'd spent most of the afternoon waiting for the plumber to turn up. Unfortunately it had given her more time to mull over her finances. There was nothing for it; she needed an influx of money as quickly as possible. Unfortunately, the only sure bet she had was the McKellan wedding and she just didn't feel up to taking that on.

Guilt washed over her. She wanted to help Sarah, she really did, but the thought of going to McKellan's Run kind of terrified her. Maybe she should ring Sarah and give her some advice? Sarah just might need some direction—there wouldn't be any harm in lending a hand—just as long as it was from a distance.

Violet grabbed her handbag and phone. She had to pick up some supplies for the Freemans' do and stop at the supermarket before picking Holly up from school. She locked the door behind her and hurried down the steps to her borrowed car. But as she slid behind the wheel she felt an overwhelming urge to ring Sarah McKellan. It wasn't like her to put off anything, even when it was unpleasant, and she couldn't settle with this wedding hanging over her head.

She pulled her phone out of the bag and before she could chicken out she punched in Sarah's number, then sucked in a breath and braced herself.

'Hello?'

Violet instantly recognised the warm voice on the other end of the line.

'Hi, Mrs McKellan, it's Violet Beckett. Sorry I didn't get back to you sooner.'

'Violet! Oh, Violet—it's so lovely to hear from you.'

'Thanks, it's good to talk to you as well.' Violet's heart beat a little faster as old emotions of warmth, happiness and belonging swirled inside of her.

'Are you well?'

'Yes.'

'Good. Oh, Violet, I've missed you so much. I've kept meaning to drop by and say hello.'

'Me too,' said Violet. 'So, I gather you need a bit of help with Jason's wedding.'

'Yes, I'd really love it if you could plan it. I feel completely out of my depth.'

Violet's stomach knotted as she clutched the phone. 'Seriously, Mrs McKellan, I don't think this is a good idea.'

'Of course it's a good idea. You're an events planner and I'm planning a wedding.'

'I'm more of a party planner really, Mrs McKellan, and I've never done a wedding on my own.'

'Oh please, Violet, weddings are just glorified parties after all. And please start calling me Sarah. I feel like I'm a hundred when you call me Mrs McKellan.'

'Okay, Sarah,' said Violet, laughing, 'I don't want you to feel old. But I don't think I should—'

'Please say you'll help, Violet. Celine is, shall we say, "determined". And for some reason she's hell-bent on the marriage taking place at our home—which I was a bit surprised about because the two of them could afford to have a swanky do in Melbourne. I really need someone to take charge of the planning, otherwise Celine will hijack the whole place with an army of helpers, assistants and coordinators. Mac will be beside himself. I had to do some fast talking to get him to agree in the first place. If Celine is allowed to run amok, well, I really don't know what he'll do.'

Violet couldn't help but smile. The usually unflappable Sarah McKellan was slightly ruffled. 'I'm sure it won't be that bad. Mac has always been a sweetheart. Surely Celine can be reasoned with?'

'Oh really? Last night she called and asked what was my opinion of painting over the original wallpaper in the great room. You know when part of the wall was damaged years ago, Mac spent months and a small fortune tracking down original rolls of the paper so the whole thing could be restored. He ended up having to get it from London. Well, you can imagine his response when I relayed that conversation. I swear one of Mac's eyes started twitching when I told him about it.'

An image of the great room popped into Violet's head. From what she could remember it was huge, with high ceilings and French doors which opened out into a courtyard. It had once been called the ballroom, though that was a long time ago—balls were pretty few and far between these days in Violet Falls.

'Oh,' Violet said.

'And she wondered if she could pay a gardener to pull out a section of the rose garden and put in a huge wrought-iron rostrum.'

'Ah.'

'Ah, indeed. That rose garden was planted by Mac's great-grandmother. I really need you on this, Violet, please.'

'Hmmm, but wouldn't it be a little awkward?'

'That you and Jason were an item when you were in high school? Believe me, Celine wouldn't be fazed by that at all. But of course if you—'

'Oh no, not at all,' Violet said quickly. 'That was a million years ago. I just wouldn't want to upset the bride. From what I've seen, some of them can be highly emotional when it comes to planning their weddings.'

'So you'll help me then? Please, Violet, please. We only have a limited time to pull this together. I don't understand the urgency, but Celine is insisting on having the marriage at the end of this month. I need you on this, Violet, I really do.'

Violet's hand tightened around the phone. 'Did you say *a month*?'

'Yes, that's right. Please, Violet, help me. Money isn't an issue as Celine's father is taking care of the cost of the wedding and he's quite well off apparently.'

'Um, er, I'm not so sure,' said Violet, closing her eyes for a moment and wondering why she always found it was so hard to say no. Though the money would be welcome it was more about not wanting to disappoint Mrs McKellan.

'Please,' said Mrs McKellan.

'Oh, alright, I'll help.' There, the deed was done and she couldn't take it back.

'Oh thank heavens! Thank you so much, I just knew I could count on you,' said Mrs McKellan.

'No worries, Sarah. I'm happy to help out.'

'So you'll come over now?'

'Oh, I'm just about to pick up my daughter Holly from school.'

'Even better, bring her with you. I'd love to meet her. I've just made a batch of sugar biscuits.'

'Are you trying to bribe me, Sarah?'

'Absolutely, sweetheart,' she answered with a laugh. 'So, I'll meet you at Mac's.'

'Sorry, I don't understand? Don't you live at McKellan's Run?'

'Oh no, not for years. I have a little place on the edge of town and that's the way I like it. No, it's just that Mac has been gracious enough to have the wedding at his place, I thought you'd want a walk-through, just to refresh your memory.'

'Oh, I see. Yes, a walk-through would be great,' Violet said. 'Okay, we'll see you soon, bye.'

'Thanks, darling, and I really do appreciate this.'

Violet dropped her phone back in her bag and slumped back in her car. *Why didn't I just say no?*

Chapter 3

The main street of Violet Falls was uncommonly wide. It had been designed that way so it could accommodate horses and wagons, carriages and the odd herd of cattle being taken to market. On both sides of the street were rows of Victorian-era shops; most were two storeys with verandahs that shaded the footpaths and were decorated with wrought-iron lacework.

As Violet drove along the street she thought back to the day she arrived in town with Holly, and how nervous she'd felt. Since then, she'd come to feel not only a familiarity, but also a comfort with the place. Shops had changed and new people had arrived but the backbone of the town hadn't really altered. The bakery which had first opened its doors a hundred and eighteen years ago was still operational—and was sandwiched between an antique shop and a bright new chemist. The bookshop had been under the watchful eye of the Andrews family for forty years, whereas the Hummingbird Café seemed to change hands every few months. Mixed in with shops she remembered, were new additions like Magpie's Shiny Home Wares and the Millstone, which was Dan McKellan's restaurant.

Violet slowed the car as she passed the only empty shop in the row. You could just make out the faded sign painted straight onto the second-storey wall, which said: *Beckett's Good Food Store and Supplies Est. 1883.*

Her family, the Becketts, had founded this town. Although back in the late-1850s it had just been known as The Falls, after the pretty waterfall situated on the outskirts of town. The Falls had grown out of a tent city in the gold rush. Her ancestor Michael Beckett had struck it rich and staked out almost a thousand acres. The other founding families, the McKellans and the Hartleys, had also lived in the Falls during the early gold rush days. But all three families saw the potential in the land rather than chasing gold. When the other prospectors moved on in the hope of finding richer goldfields, they stayed and put down roots, and worked hard for a bright future.

Over the following couple of generations the Beckett family were the richest and the most influential in the whole area. But the family's fortunes turned around when one of Violet's ancestors, the woman she'd been named after, drowned at the waterfall. Out of deference to the family and because of the tragedy, it was agreed that the town would be renamed Violet Falls. Sometimes Violet's own grandmother had wondered whether the death of their ancestor had put a curse on the family because, bit by bit over the years, the Beckett family lost nearly everything.

Now the vacant store and the family home were all that was left of what used to be the vast Beckett fortune. The money, the string of shops and land had all disappeared through bad business decisions and gambling.

Violet's estranged grandfather, Silas Beckett, had surprised both her and her younger sister Lily by bequeathing everything to them in his will. He had left Lily the shop and Violet the family home with the acre of ground it sat on.

Violet hadn't thought him capable of such a kind act. But then, Silas had probably been thinking about family pride and what the town would think, rather than doing what was right.

She really must talk to Lily about the shop. It seemed wrong that it should sit there empty. Maybe Lily could put it up for rent, it wasn't as if she couldn't use the extra money. Violet tapped her foot on the accelerator and continued on her way. She still had a few minutes to get to the school and pick up Holly before heading out to McKellan's Run.

* * *

Charlie 'Mac' McKellan stood in the home paddock, his eyes scanning the distant ridge. Taking off his Akubra hat he ran his hand through his dark brown hair and leaned back against a tree. It felt good to have the cool breeze on his face after digging fence posts all afternoon.

He filled his lungs with the sweet air and gazed around at the beauty that was McKellan's Run—twelve hundred acres of some of the best grazing land in the area. McKellan's Run had sheltered and sustained his family for almost a hundred and fifty years. It was in his blood and he'd been honoured when his father had charged him with managing and protecting it until it could be handed down to the next generation.

Mac put his Akubra back on and headed to the house to grab a bottle of water before he took the quad bike and went up to the ruins to do some more fencing—just another job to add to the growing pile. September had arrived, which meant the forty-two hundred merinos which roamed over the Run needed to be rounded up so the shearing could be done. It was a lot of work and he would probably have to hire in some casual workers as well as the shearers, to get it done in time.

It really shouldn't have come as any surprise that it was right at this moment that Jason, his high-flying and errant brother, decided he wanted to get married. Not that Mac had any problem with Jason tying the knot—it was just his decision to do it here. It seemed as if Jason never really thought about anyone else and what they might be in the middle of. He was always too focused on what he wanted.

Though Mac could hardly have said no. McKellan's Run might be his but Jason and Dan had both grown up here too. So he'd bitten his tongue and agreed to the wedding being at home, though he did warn his mother he didn't have the time to help, so if they wanted a wedding they'd have to organise it themselves.

His mother had assured him everything was in hand and she was hiring a professional events planner—whatever that was—to help. How hard could it be to throw a wedding together?

His mother had texted him earlier to say she'd arranged to meet this events person at the house this afternoon. All he needed was some damned stranger poking about the place and asking a whole lot of damn questions. He'd grab a drink and get the hell out of there before he could be roped into anything.

Mac let out a shrill whistle and Razor, his trusty blue heeler, swung around and ran back across the paddock.

'Come on, Razor! Time to go.'

Mac opened the gate and walked towards home, the dog trotting by his side. Daylight was burning and he had a hundred things to do before nightfall.

* * *

Violet stopped the car after she pulled into the gates of McKellan's Run and drank in the sight. The poplar-lined drive led down to an impressive two-storey homestead with a wide verandah which wrapped around the entire building. The woodwork was painted white and stood in dramatic contrast against the red brick. Most of the home had been constructed in the early 1870s and there was a bygone grace about it rarely seen these days.

It'd been a long time since she'd been here but the view hadn't changed much, apart from the trees being taller. There was something comforting about the reality still matching the picture she carried in her head. McKellan's Run was just as elegant as she remembered.

'It's a pretty house, Mummy.'

Violet looked across at Holly. 'Yes it is, but it's even prettier up close.'

At the bottom of the drive, Violet parked the borrowed car and took Holly by the hand.

'Come on, sweetheart, this way.'

With a smile she led Holly down the little path through the tunnel of wisteria and jasmine toward the side door which led to the kitchen. She hadn't forgotten that this was the entryway most people used when they came visiting. However with each step, Violet's stomach fluttered. Forget butterflies, this was more like a stampeding herd of wildebeest thundering in her tummy. Just being here was bringing up a slew of memories she'd rather forget. She drew in a deep breath and ignored the impulse to turn around and run away.

Violet leaned forward and gave a quick knock on the door before suddenly, without warning, it swung in. She heard a soft grunt as she stumbled and fell against Charlie McKellan's hard chest.

'Hey, I've got you,' he said as his arms tightened around her. 'Violet! Violet? I'd heard you were back but what are you doing *here*?'

She grabbed onto Mac's shoulders and tried to steady herself, feeling the warmth of his skin through the cool cotton of his shirt and the bulge of muscle beneath his sleeves.

'Sorry, about that, I didn't realise you were about to knock,' said Mac, with a hint of a smile. 'I wasn't expecting you. I mean, um . . . Why are you here?'

'It's fine, Mac. It's good to see you again,' said Violet. He looked the same as ever—lean, hard and handsome. High cheekbones, beautiful hazel-green eyes, squared off chin and a hint of a five o'clock shadow.

Mac stared back at her until heat crept into her cheeks and she forced herself to look away.

'Um, your mum hired me to help with the wedding. I'm a party planner these days.'

'Oh right, well, it's good to see you too, Violet. I've—'

'Are you going to let my mummy go?' said Holly.

Recovering her wits, Mac let go of Violet and she said, 'Holly, this is Mac. Mac, this is my daughter, Holly.'

'Hi,' said Holly, linking her fingers more tightly with her mum's.

Mac's eyes widened and he hesitated for a second before he squatted down. 'Hi Holly, it's nice to meet you. You're as pretty as your mum. Maybe later you and her could come and have a look at our new kittens.'

'You've got kittens?' asked Holly, her face lighting up. 'Mum can we go and see them now?'

'Maybe later,' said Violet with a smile. 'But first, we have to see Mrs McKellan.'

Mac stood up. 'She's in the kitchen. You remember the way?'

'Yes, yes I do.'

'Good,' said Mac, walking through the doorway before turning back and staring at her. 'I'll catch you both later and hopefully we can go and see those kittens. Oh and Violet, I'm glad you're back. I've . . .'

His sentence trailed off and hung in the air between them.

'You've what, Mac?' asked Violet.

'I've been meaning to come and say hello, but I wasn't sure if you were keeping to yourself,' he answered. 'You just

31

disappeared all those years ago and . . .' he started, before shrugging, taking a long last look at Holly, and continuing out the door.

Violet stared after him at a loss for words before Holly tugged on her hand. 'What are we doing now?'

Violet shook herself out of her thoughts. 'We're going to find Mrs McKellan in the kitchen so I can talk to her about planning a wedding. Hmmm, I do believe there was talk about lemonade and sugar biscuits.'

'Really?'

'Yep, let's go.'

Walking through the house they came to a large, bright open kitchen.

'Ah, there you both are!' said Sarah, standing up from a chair at a large table near the wall. 'I was wondering when you'd get here.'

Time had been kind to Sarah, thought Violet. With her trim figure and blonde hair cut into an elegant bob, she was as attractive as ever.

She hurried over and was soon wrapped in a tight perfumed hug. 'It's good to see you again, Sarah.'

Sarah gently pushed her back and held her by the shoulders. 'Let me look at you. Ah, Violet, I'd forgotten just how beautiful you are. Why, you haven't aged at all.'

'Not true, but thanks,' said Violet and then gestured Holly forward. 'This is my daughter, Holly.'

As Sarah bent down, Violet noticed her eyes soften, even mist up a little.

'Holly, well you're just as beautiful as your mummy aren't you?'

'That's what that man just said,' Holly replied.

Sarah gave Violet a questioning look.

'We just ran into Mac—literally—as he was heading out.'

'Oh, I see,' Sarah said with the hint of a smile before turning to Holly. 'Well, why don't you come over and sit up at the table and I'll get you some lemonade and something sweet to nibble on. Would you like that?'

'Sure,' said Holly, nodding.

'Holly, manners.'

'Yes please,' said Holly before wandering over to the table.

'Hmmm, better,' said Violet as she followed her daughter. Opening her bag she pulled out some pencils, stickers and a colouring book. 'I got you these, sweetheart.'

Holly grinned at her mother as she settled herself at the table. 'Thanks, Mum.'

'You're welcome,' Violet answered, ruffling her little girl's hair before she sat down next to her and took out her tablet. 'So Sarah, about the wedding. Have Jason and his fiancée given you any ideas about what sort of look they want?'

Sarah looked up from pouring Holly's lemonade. 'It's a fairly small affair. The guest list at the last count was about seventy. As for a "look", Celine did mention "timeless elegance",' she said, rolling her eyes.

'Okay, maybe we should work on an idea—"a vision" in party speak—for the reception space,' said Violet as she fired up her tablet.

'Celine and Jason were here last weekend and did a walk-through of the house and the different options for where the actual ceremony would be. She's quite a demanding girl. I'm not saying I don't like her, I'm just saying she can be a bit full-on,' Sarah said as she set down the biscuits and lemonade in front of Holly.

'Thanks,' said Holly, briefly looking up from her drawing.

'So why isn't Celine organising it all?' asked Violet. 'Generally brides like to plan every little detail.'

'Both she and Jason have pretty fast-paced lifestyles which involve a lot of travel. Everything about this wedding seemed to come out of the blue. Jase rang to tell me he and Celine had decided to get married in six weeks and I assumed at the time that they'd be doing it in the city. But he rang Mac the same evening to ask if he could have it here—though I'm not sure if it was really him or Celine who wanted to.'

'Why the rush?' asked Violet. 'Sorry, I don't mean to sound rude or anything. It's just, I mean, usually wedding venues are decided on a whole lot earlier than this.'

'I'm not really sure, but the short timeframe has really thrown a spanner in the works. Mac's busy with the farm and I've had to call in all sorts of favours and beg friends for help.'

'What about the catering, do we have to arrange that as well?' asked Violet.

'Oh no, thank goodness. Dan is doing that as his present to the bride and groom.'

Violet breathed a sigh of relief. She'd heard recently that Dan—Mac and Jason's younger brother—had spent a few years training to become a chef in France or Italy, she couldn't remember which. 'Great, I saw that he'd opened a restaurant in town.'

'He's doing very well,' said Sarah, smiling. 'I'm so happy for him. He's finally putting all his experience to good use.'

'So, am I right in thinking all you need me to do is dress and organise a ceremony space and the reception area?'

'Yes, that's about it,' Sarah replied.

Violet looked up from her tablet. 'Too easy,' she said, grinning as she took in the relief on Sarah's face.

Chapter 4

Mac strode away from the house and back out into the home paddock. He needed to put some distance between himself and Violet. It was surreal, that after all these years she'd fallen into his arms like a gift from heaven.

He stared at the rolling hills and the cluster of green-grey gums in the distance. The air was fresh and scented with eucalyptus, but all Mac could smell was Violet's soft floral scent.

She'd felt so good in his arms. It had been a perfect moment, just like he'd constantly imagined all those years ago when he'd been plagued with desires he knew he shouldn't harbour for his brother's girlfriend. Back then when they were still at high school, Violet had been with Jason. Later, after Jason finished uni and got his first job, Mac had felt helpless when he'd heard she and Lily had left town after Jason broke up with her.

The weeks had crept by and he didn't hear anything. He'd even gone to Silas Beckett's place to find out where she was, which had been difficult because of old Beckett's hatred for all McKellans. The old man had been cagey and vague with his answers, telling him that Violet and Lily had decided to go away for a while and stay with friends in Melbourne. 'And a good thing it is too,' he'd added. 'Better that than hanging around with a blasted McKellan.'

The old shit always had such a way with words.

When Mac had asked Silas for an address or phone number for Violet, he'd refused point blank to tell him either.

Months had passed with no sign of Violet and Lily coming back when Mac finally called Jason and asked if he knew what was going on with Violet and Lily.

'It's none of your business, Mac,' Jason had snapped.

'I know you've broken up with Violet, just tell me where they are,' Mac had asked.

'I don't know. Anyway, why do you care?'

'She's missing and so is Lily. No one has seen or heard from them for months now,' Mac had said.

'She hasn't been home for *months*?' asked Jason.

'No, she hasn't,' said Mac.

A long silence followed and he wished he could reach down the phone and throttle his self-centred brother.

'She came to visit me here a few months ago and we broke up,' Jason said. 'I haven't seen or talked to her since. I tried to ring her a couple of times, just to see if she was okay, but she didn't pick up and she hasn't returned any of my messages.'

'Why wouldn't she be okay?' asked Mac.

'She took our breaking up hard. I didn't want to hurt her but things are different now. I've got a full-on job with lots of opportunities and Violet, well, Violet would just hold me back.'

'*Please* tell me you didn't say that to her?' said Mac.

'Not in those words exactly. I wished her well. Hell, I still care about her. But we'd been growing apart during my last year at uni and she's just not part of my world anymore. Oh, come on Mac, even you have to see that.'

'Damn you, Jason,' Mac had said before ending the call.

After that Mac had rung anyone he could think of who might know where she was. But everyone had just thought she'd moved to Melbourne with Lily to be closer to Jason. And the general consensus was that who could blame her for wanting to leave town, with old Silas Beckett trying to control her every move.

For years Mac had hoped and waited for news but there'd been nothing and eventually he'd realised he had to move on. Violet and Lily clearly didn't want to make contact with their friends from Violet Falls. Whenever their names came up in conversation no one had heard from either of them. They hadn't even returned for their grandfather's funeral—not that Mac held that against them. Silas Beckett had made their lives hell. But still, a part of him had hoped.

Then out of the blue a few months ago, he'd run into that old bat, Mrs Wardley, who'd told him that Violet had returned to town with a young daughter who was the spitting image of her. Mrs Wardley said she'd heard they'd moved back into Violet's grandfather's place. Since then he'd heard lots of people talking about her being a single mother, with lots of speculation about whether the father of the little girl was a local or had a father in the city. It was widely agreed that the child—Holly—looked just like her mother when she was the same age, an oval face with waves of long walnut-brown hair.

But it hadn't been until today when Mac knelt before Holly that he'd realised Violet had left town with a secret— and it was one she'd kept for far too long.

* * *

'Jeez Mum, you could have told me Violet was coming!' Mac said quietly as he followed his mother outside to her car.

'Where's the fun in that? Besides Mac, you said you didn't want anything to do with the planning of Jason's wedding,' said Sarah.

'Yes, but Mum—'

'Well, that is what you said. So as I can't plan the whole thing, I had to hire a professional. Violet was the obvious choice. Now, I'd better get moving and no doubt you still have a million things to do?'

Mac rubbed his chin. He'd been too distracted by Violet being at the house to stay away long and it was too late to ride to the old ruined cottage to start checking the fences now.

'I suppose,' he said. 'I just wished you'd told me, that's all.'

'Ah well, now you know. I hope it won't be a problem, you're bound to be running into her quite often,' said Sarah, giving him a questioning look.

'No, why would there be a problem? I like Violet,' he said.

Sarah reached up and patted his cheek before she got into the car. 'I know, darling, I know.'

Mac stood back, not really knowing how to respond and watched her reverse out. He gave her a wave as she drove past, before turning his attention back to Violet who was just emerging from the house with Holly and all her kiddie paraphernalia. For one little person, Holly sure travelled with a lot of bags, toys and God knows what else.

He watched Violet as she settled Holly into her seat and clicked the seatbelt into place. Violet hardly looked any different from the last time he'd seen her. The years had passed but Mac's reaction to her was the same as ever.

Her little white shirt kicked up at the back as she leant forward, revealing a creamy patch of skin just above her jeans. Mac swallowed hard. Her legs were long, lean and strong—and seemed to go on for miles.

He'd be damned if he didn't dream of her tonight.

'And the cat, her name is Mud, has three teeny, tiny kittens,' Holly said as she held up her thumb and forefinger. 'They're only this big.'

'Really, that little, huh?' Violet said, getting into the driver's seat and closing the car door. 'Mud. He named the cat Mud?'

'I wanted to hold one but Mac said I had to wait until they were a little bit bigger,' Holly nodded her head. 'Yep, he called her that because when he found her she was all covered in mud.'

'Ah, well that explains it then.' Violet could just picture Mac rescuing a muddy little cat, it's just the sort of thing he'd do. 'So where did he find her?'

'Someone left her in a box by the creek.'

'Well, in that case I should think she's very happy Mac found her and brought her home, even if he did call her Mud,' said Violet.

Holly nodded in agreement. 'Mud likes him and she won't let anyone else give her a pat.'

All of a sudden Mac filled the space beside her open window.

'Thanks so much for helping out. I know it's short notice and Mum really appreciates it.'

'It's my pleasure. I mean I'm happy to help,' said Violet, finding it hard to look him in the eyes.

'Mac?' called Holly.

'Yes, sweetie?' Mac replied, grinning at her.

'Next time when we come, can I visit the kitties again?'

'Of course you can, anytime you want.'

'Okay, well, we better be going,' said Violet.

Mac gave her one last smile before he stood back. 'Take care and see you soon.'

Violet nodded. 'Bye,' she said before reversing and starting down the long driveway, watching him disappear in her rearview mirror.

* * *

Resisting Violet Beckett was one of the hardest things he had to do. Jason had beaten him to asking her out when they were still in school, which was bad enough, but then he had to go and bring her home to McKellan's Run.

41

Talk about rubbing a guy's nose in it.

At first Mac had tried to put a wall up every time Violet arrived, but that lasted all of two days. The problem was that she was just so approachable, funny and sweet. Before too long he realised that somehow Violet had smashed through nearly every one of his defences and they'd become friends.

Which was the very last thing on earth he wanted. But what could he do? Nothing, absolutely bloody nothing. He had to wear it and pray to God that she never found out how he really felt about her.

With Lily's help, Violet managed to sneak behind old Silas Beckett's back and spend so much time at McKellan's Run that she almost became a permanent fixture. Which put Mac in a joyous sort of purgatory. He was happy to be able to spend time with her, but deep down he was in all sorts of hell because he wanted to be more than a friend.

It wasn't just Mac that had fallen under Violet's spell, but the rest of the family as well. His Dad had kept a fatherly eye on her, his Mum treated her like the daughter she'd never had and Dan had come to regard her as some sort of cool big sister.

And then one day after visiting Jason in Melbourne she just disappeared and left a huge gaping hole, not just in his life but that of the whole McKellan family. So much so that he'd battled old Silas and Jason and spoke to anyone who might know where she was before he jumped in his ute and took off to find her. But the problem had been he didn't even know where to look.

After a week or so in the city he returned to Violet Falls and prayed Violet would turn up—but she never had.

Home seemed a lonely and hollow place without her.

He missed her and the way they used to talk about everything and nothing at all, the way her chocolatey golden eyes would warm with laughter and her smile. Damn it, he missed that more than everything.

For Mac, time moved slowly in Violet Falls. The seasons blended with each other and still there had been no word or sighting of Violet or Lily. All he could do was to throw himself into the day-to-day running of McKellan's Run. With enough hard work, maybe he could purge her from his heart and mind.

Mac was meant to go to university like Jason, but he'd persuaded his parents to let him stay and work on the farm for a year. However, after Violet left he devoted himself entirely to the property and when the year was up, he refused to leave. His parents had argued with him, saying all they wanted was what was best.

It took them a little while to realise McKellan's Run was the best thing, that there was nowhere on earth he'd rather be. From that day on, they stopped harping at him about going to uni and gave him more responsibility around the farm.

Mac lived and breathed the land. Without Violet, it was all he had left.

Eight years had passed before she returned. After that long you'd think he'd have managed to push her aside and move on with his life. Well, he had until she'd stumbled into his arms and smiled up at him.

43

When she'd looked up at him and smiled, his world once again tumbled out of orbit. It was that same smile that caused him to catch his breath and remember what it was like to be a love-starved teenager. He should be over it but there was something in her eyes that made him want to pause and hold her a little closer.

Shit, Flynn would have a field day with this. He always said that Mac had never allowed himself to get over Violet and maybe he was right. Hell, when did his best friend end up being so smart? Maybe there is still a hint of something there. The question was, should he take notice of it or leave it buried and forgotten?

Mac rolled his shoulders as he headed towards the shed. He was going to do what he'd done for years—work as hard as he could until he forgot all about Violet Beckett and her sexy body and pretty smile.

Mac stood at the entrance of the shed, where there were a heap of hay bales to stack. A grim smile touched his lips.

Yeah, that should keep him busy for a couple of hours.

Chapter 5

Well, it serves me right for being over-confident, thought Violet, because I'm sure as hell eating my words now. She and Sarah had worked out some tentative styles and colour schemes and Violet had been pleased with their results. As time was so tight, Sarah had suggested they ring Celine for her input. She paced up and down; in fact she was surprised she hadn't worn a track in the floor of the old ballroom at McKellan's Run.

Violet had emailed through her ideas for the wedding's overall look and feel. But she'd been on the phone for almost forty minutes now and every single design, colour scheme or vague idea had been shot down by Celine.

'Really Ms Beckett, Sarah assured me you were a professional,' came Celine's haughty voice from down the phone.

'I am,' Violet answered through gritted teeth.

'Well, I have to say I'm disappointed,' said Celine. 'Our wedding needs to be perfect. Lots of the guests are from Melbourne's elite, including Jason's boss. This isn't a run-of-the-mill little bush wedding. It needs to be elegant. I may need to find a planner down here and send her up to McKellan's Run instead.'

'As I said—' Violet started to say but the phone had already gone dead. She stared at the phone for a second and blinked twice. 'I don't believe she hung up. Un-bloody-believable!'

She went through the notes she'd made while she'd been talking. Celine didn't like yellow. When she'd said she wanted white flowers she hadn't dreamed Violet would think of having camellias. The place settings were old-fashioned. The glassware looked cheap. She didn't like that particular shade of green and was not convinced about antique gold, ivory, dull pink or eggshell blue either. She wanted timeless elegance with an old-world feel—but not anything Violet suggested. Lace tablecloths reminded her of her grandmother, damask were too busy, plain white tablecloths were just too plain; oh, and too white; but she didn't want a colour.

Violet had never failed on a brief or event before, and she'd developed great relationships with all but one client in her years in the business. If she hadn't agreed to undertake the job as a favour for Sarah she'd be telling Celine what she could do with silver flatware with a shell motif.

She closed her eyes and took a deep breath, trying to gather herself and work out what to do with Celine's brutal feedback.

'Not going well?'

Violet opened her eyes to see Mac leaning in the doorway. He gave her an easy smile—she'd forgotten how infectious it was. She didn't want to smile back but somehow she just couldn't help herself. 'No, it's not. In fact I think we could call it a total disaster,' she sighed.

'It can't be as bad as all that?' said Mac. 'I had no idea it could be so difficult to organise a wedding.'

'I've only ever assisted at weddings but I've done lots of parties and things over the years and nearly every client I've had has been thrilled with the end result. But this time every idea I come up with, Celine shoots down. I'm running out of time to organise anything. At this rate there will be no flowers, and dinner will be served on paper plates with plastic cutlery,' said Violet, running her hand through her hair.

'Have you got a favourite design?'

'Well, actually yes.'

'Can I see?'

'Sure,' Violet said, reaching down and scooping up her tablet from the table. 'See, this was the seating plan I was going with in the great room. The colour scheme is dark cream, ivory and champagne with a touch of pearl and a slight hint of shiny pretty things.'

Mac leaned over her shoulder so she could show him her different designs on the tablet. Violet was acutely aware of his presence. They weren't touching but if she just moved a little . . .

'I like it,' said Mac.

'You do? Really?' she said, trying to ignore the sensations caused by the feel of his warm breath on her shoulder.

'Yes, really. It's beautiful,' he said.

Violet looked up and her eyes locked onto his. That was a mistake. Her stomach did a sort of squiffy thing as she saw his eyes darken. Why was she feeling like this? Mac had always been just Mac—Jason's nice, quietish younger brother. But as she looked at him, something shifted inside her. It was as if she was really seeing him for the first time.

47

How on earth could she have ever been so blind? Her gaze drifted down to the little line that appeared at the corner of his mouth when he smiled.

'Thanks Mac. That means a lot,' she said, looking back at the screen to try and hide the acute embarrassment flaring through her. She needed time to think about all the crazy ideas that were racing around her head. 'I thought I'd anchor everything with this deep green, but Celine said she doesn't like green; though I'm not sure if she meant particular shades or green in general.'

'Run with your idea, Violet. I'll sort things out with Jason and Celine.'

'But Mac, I'll have to get Celine's approval. It's her wedding, not mine.'

'Don't worry. You'll have her go ahead. Start ordering the things you need and stop worrying,' he said as he touched her faint frown line between her brows. 'I'm on it.'

'But Mac . . .'

But before she could say anything more he'd pulled his mobile out of his pocket and was strolling away.

***

The following day, Violet dropped Holly off at school and raced home. She was going to have a frantic day trying to pull the McKellan wedding together. Parking the car, she hurried up the old wooden steps to her front door, doing her best to ignore the creaking sounds they made as she climbed them. She turned the key and opened the door to her childhood home. It still felt weird, but after these past few months she'd finally stopped expecting to see her grandfather glowering at her every time she came through the door.

Silas Beckett had been a proud, hard and unforgiving man, who had tossed her out when she'd needed him the most. He laid the blame of every disappointment in his life at the McKellan's door. It was easier for him to howl at the moon and curse the McKellans than to accept that it was he who was lacking. He'd gnaw and rant at the injustices life had dealt him and the rest of the Beckett family. After the death of her grandmother, Silas had become more vicious and the bile he spat was even more toxic.

As much as she tried to shut them out, voices from the past swirled inside her head.

'I know you're pregnant with Jason McKellan's baby. All I can say is, I'm glad your grandmother is dead. At least she's not here to see the shame you've brought on our family,' shouted Silas Beckett, his dark eyes boring into hers.

Violet's hand tightened around the door handle until her knuckles turned white. 'There's no shame, Grandad. Jason and I love each other,' said Violet, feeling frightened as she looked up at her grandfather standing on the stairs, his face cold and furious.

'What do McKellans know about love? They're scum who have tricked and cheated our family out of land for the past four generations and now it looks as if one has even managed to take your good name.'

Violet felt like crying but she knew she couldn't break down in front of him.

'Do you deny it then?'

'No, I don't. I slept with Jason because I love him, Grandad, and we're not exactly living in the 1800s,' she said, standing a little straighter. 'And I'm not ashamed of what I . . . we did. Why would I be? Besides, it was our family that got into debt and lost the land. The McKellans didn't steal it.'

'That's a damned lie and you know it, Violet Beckett. You know they've taken everything from us. They've ruined us and now one of their pups has managed to ruin you. Of all the boys in this town why in God's name did you have to pick a bloody McKellan?'

'Grandad, let the past go. We could be happy if you'd just let us. Please, for the sake of your great-grandchild,' said Violet.

His lips set in a grim line as he squared his shoulders and Violet knew what his answer was going to be before he even opened his mouth.

'I can't. You ask too much.'

'Grandad, please.'

'No, if you want to side with that family you can't stay here.'

'What do you mean? There's nowhere else I can go.'

'You should have thought about that before. Hell will freeze over before I have a McKellan under my roof. Just leave girl, you and your child aren't welcome here. Not now, not ever.'

Violet shook herself, her grandfather's voice seemed to resonate through the empty house.

'You're dead and gone, Grandad, and you can't judge me or my child anymore. Besides, you were the one who missed out. Holly is kind, clever and wonderful,' Violet whispered as she walked into the large front room on her right which she'd turned into an office. It was time to put the past behind her and concentrate on the wedding from hell.

* * *

Violet slid into her chair and grabbed the phone off the desk. First things first, she needed to secure equipment for the wedding; she rang her go-to supplier and crossed her fingers.

'Hey Tony, I have a wedding I have to put together in a month and I need your help.'

'Hi Violet, are you serious when you say a month?'

'Yes, I am. I'm sorry there's hardly any notice but I'm so hoping you can help me out? I promise it's only a teeny weenie wedding.'

'Violet, define "teeny weenie",' said Tony.

'Smallish . . .'

'Violet, you're killing me.'

'But you'll do it?'

Tony gave a long and exasperated sigh. 'I'll do whatever I can, but only because it's you.'

'You're the best, Tony. Thank you, thank you, thank you!'

'Yeah, well I'll be asking for a favour.'

'What?'

'It's Jazzy's eighth birthday party in a couple of months. I expect you to plan it, decorate it and bring Holly.'

'Done, and I promise it will be every little girl's fantasy birthday party,' Violet said with a laugh. 'Thanks, I'll see you soon.'

'Bye Violet. Hey, and next time give me a bit more warning.'

Violet flopped back in her chair and let out a relieved sigh as she replaced the phone. With a little begging and the promise of a party, she'd placed an order to hire the glassware, extra tables, chairs and the damask tablecloths (even if Celine thought they were busy).

She rested her head on the back of the chair and stared up at the ceiling. If anyone had told her a month ago that she'd be planning Jason McKellan's wedding she would have said they were completely bonkers. But that was before her car engine blew up and the plumbing decided to start self-destructing. In the end she didn't have a choice about taking on the job but she still had to admit the whole situation was surreal.

The phone rang and Violet snatched it up 'Hello, Violet Falls Parties & Events.'

'Violet, it's Mac. You've got Celine's go ahead, just don't use yellow flowers or lace tablecloths.'

Violet's stomach did that annoying clenching, squiffy thing as she recognised his voice.

'But how did you—?'

'Doesn't matter, everything is sorted.'

'Thanks Mac, I don't know how I can thank you.'

'Dinner?'

'Sorry, what?' said Violet.

'Have dinner with me, Violet.'

'Sure,' said Violet, 'but can we wait until after the wedding? I need to concentrate or the whole damned thing will go to hell in a hand basket.'

Mac was silent for a moment or two. 'Does that mean I distract you?'

His voice was so soft, deep and beguiling, thought Violet. Funny how she'd never noticed before.

'Perhaps, or maybe I'm just flat out trying to organise a wedding,' she said.

'Okay, we'll wait until after the wedding but I'm holding you to it,' he said, his voice seeming to wrap around Violet, making her feel warm and tingly.

'Fair enough. Thanks again for getting Celine to agree,' said Violet, smiling.

'No worries. I'm so glad you're back. See you soon Violet.'

'Bye,' said Violet then sat for a long time just staring into space. Despite the feelings Mac stirred up in her, she was just re-establishing herself back in Violet Falls, she had a fledgling business and a daughter to raise. She needed to stay focused on her goals and not get involved with anyone, especially another McKellan, she told herself, a determined expression on her face as she picked up the phone.

'Hello, is that Mainstop Florist? Yes, hi, I know its short notice but I need to order some flowers.'

* * *

Violet closed her eyes and tried to go to sleep but the image of Mac kept creeping into her mind. He had taken her by surprise, appearing in the doorway looking so strong, handsome and sexy. It had been eight years since she'd seen him. In that time the gangly frame she remembered from school had, well, filled-out.

They had been in the same year at school but Violet had only really got to know him through Jason. Back then, she'd spent every moment she could at McKellan's Run. Other than the obvious allure of being at Jason's home it was also a good distance out of town and away from gossiping tongues.

Mac had always been quieter and more reserved than Jason or his best friend Flynn Hartley. But Violet remembered he had a kind heart and plenty of courage. She'd seen him step in and stop the bullying of poor Andy Ferris by a group of boys in their year who should have had more sense.

Violet had always liked Mac, though she'd grown to see him mainly as Jason's sweet and dependable little brother. Violet rolled over and wiggled around in an attempt to get comfortable. She needed to get some sleep because tomorrow was going to be a hectic day. Apart from the McKellan wedding, there were the other events she had to see to.

There was Rex Bottle—actor, poet and local eccentric— who had commissioned her to transform the small private dining room at Hedge's restaurant into a sumptuous feast for royalty (his words not hers). She still needed to track down the rest of the props as well as the centrepiece. Apparently the highlight of the evening would be his recitation of an ode himself, praising all the great food, good wine and all the women he once had, although not necessarily in that order.

Other than Rex's bacchanalia, she had a young couple coming to discuss throwing a surprise 'We're Engaged' party for their families.

So why did her mind keep going back to Mac? Violet snuggled down under the covers. Moving back home and running into old friends was bound to stir up some memories.

* * *

Violet pulled up to Mac's house in her newly repaired car. She smiled when she heard the sound of work boots crunching on gravel and watched as Mac made his way over to her.

'Hey,' he said with a nod.

'Hi Mac, I hope you don't mind but I really need a few measurements and I wanted to check how much natural light there is in the great room.'

'Whatever you need,' he said as he stopped in front of her. There was mud on his jeans, sweat trickling down his brow and a couple of nasty scratches on his forearm.

'Mac, what happened?' Violet asked looking at his arm. Blood was oozing from the scratches which looked deep and nasty.

'One of the ewes got herself wedged between some rocks and a big blackberry bush up at the top dam,' he said, glancing down at his arm.

'Would you like me to bandage it for you?'

'Nah, it'll be fine.'

Violet grabbed her handbag and shut the car door. 'I'm sorry I had to pull you away from your work.'

'Not a problem,' said Mac, taking off his hat and running his hand through his hair.

'Well, thanks anyway,' said Violet, thinking how strong and dependable his hands looked.

He gestured to Violet and they started walking towards the house.

'I figure you'll have to get into the house a fair bit to get ready for the wedding, won't you?' said Mac.

'Yes, but I promise next time I won't drag you away from work. I'm sorry I disturbed you.'

'You didn't,' said Mac. 'Do you remember where we used to keep the spare key?'

'Yeah, under that ugly garden gnome you and your brothers bought your poor mother one birthday.'

Mac grinned at the memory. 'It was a joke. You know how much she hates them. Besides, we got her a real present as well.'

'Good thing too.'

'Anyway, the key is still there. Mum accidentally-on-purpose forgot to take the gnome with her when she moved.'

'A very wise woman, your mother,' said Violet with a smile.

'Hmmm, so if I'm not here, just let yourself in.'

'You don't mind?'

'Not at all,' said Mac as they wandered over to a small herb garden. Nestled amongst the rosemary and basil was the ugliest garden gnome in all creation.

'I see age hasn't improved him,' said Violet.

'Shhh, you'll hurt his feelings,' said Mac, reaching over and picking it up to reveal the hidden key. 'So, here it is if you need it,' he added before replacing the gnome.

Mac walked over to the door and opened it. 'I'd better get back.'

'Thanks and sorry again for interrupting your day.'

'Nothing to be sorry about.'

There was a pause and Violet glanced up at Mac just in time to see him look away.

'Um well, if you're alright I'll get going. Just pull the door shut when you go,' he said.

'Sure and thank . . . I mean. I'll see you around.'

Mac hesitated as if he was going to say something else. Instead his eyes locked onto Violet's for an instant before he gave her a nod and headed back down the path.

Violet stood by the open door and watched him go.

Since when had there been awkward silences between them?

Chapter 6

On Saturday morning Violet sat in her office and stared at her bank balance on the computer screen. Things were going to be a bit tight until she managed to get a few more events booked. Still, she and Holly lived quite frugally and she'd certainly been in worse positions than this. At least now there was some work coming in and things were looking a bit better.

She looked up at the envelope Mr Taylor had given her when she'd picked up the key. It had been sitting on her desk since she'd organised the house, tucked between a glass filled with multi-coloured pens and her business card holder. Reaching over, she picked it up. *"Miss Violet Elizabeth Beckett"* was written on it in her grandfather's bold handwriting. Somehow she just couldn't bring herself to read it.

Violet put the letter back. It probably just said how disappointed he was in her and how she'd let down the entire family (both living and dead). She really didn't need to hear all that again, especially while she was so stressed.

It had been pretty grim when her grandfather had kicked her out all those years ago. Grim and scary, that was the only way she could describe it. And the whole situation had been made better and worse because Lily had insisted on going with her. Lily had made everything better by supporting Violet through every decision. The flipside was that Violet felt terrified because she was responsible not only for her unborn child but also for her little sister.

Long hours and two jobs had taken its toll on Violet. But they got by in a tiny rundown flat in a dodgy area. After Holly was born, Violet cut back to one evening shift. That way she could look after Holly during the day and then Lily would care for her at night.

After Lily finished Year 10 and began her fashion design course, life became a lot easier. Violet found a job as an assistant to an events planner. At first she was hired to just help set-up and then dismantle venues. But as she'd gained more responsibility, Violet had found the idea of helping people celebrate happy occasions in their lives made her feel fulfilled—something she hadn't been in a long time. Her grandfather would have told her she was wasting her life on ridiculous, frivolous nonsense but she didn't care. She'd found a job she loved and that kept food on the table.

She'd been so proud of Lily when she got a job with an up-and-coming fashion designer as soon as she left college. For the first time since they'd left home, Violet finally felt she could relax a little. She'd supported Lily while she finished school and been at college and now Lily could finally pretty much take care of herself. And Holly was thriving at her preschool.

She'd written to her grandfather to say Lily had done well at TAFE and got a great job, that she herself was also well and had a job she enjoyed and his great-grandchild was a bright little girl who was adored by all who met her.

She'd never received a reply to her letter, so it had come as a complete surprise several years later when his solicitor tracked her and Lily down and told them their grandfather had left them the family home and Lily the original Beckett shop in Violet Falls. Though Lily's life was completely tied up with Melbourne and the fashion industry and she had no interest in moving back to their home town, for Violet the news of their inheritance had seemed like pure serendipity. She and Holly would be able to live in the place she'd grown up in and she wouldn't have the pressure of expensive city rents anymore.

'Mummy, can we please go to the park now? You said we could go ages ago,' said Holly, jolting Violet out of her reverie.

She looked up to see her daughter leaning against the door with an exasperated look on her face. 'Of course we can, go put on your shoes.'

Holly did a happy twirl in the doorway. 'So we can play on the swings and the slide and . . .'

'Hmmm, and what?' said Violet with a mock frown.

'Maybe we could have an ice cream on the way home?' said Holly.

Violet stood up. 'Well that would depend on how fast someone gets her shoes on.'

'Yay!' Holly said as she did the 'getting an ice cream' dance down the hall towards her room. 'We're gonna get ice cream. We're gonna get ice cream.'

* * *

'What's the old saying?' said Flynn Hartley when Mac ran into him at the post office. '"There's always a Beckett in Violet Falls"?'

'Hey, Flynn. Yeah, something like that,' said Mac, leaning against the post office's wall and staring across the road at a line of parked cars. He and Flynn had been mates for as long as he could remember. They'd gone through school together, played football in the same team, chased girls and both ended up running their families' farms. 'Two peas in a pod,' his mum always said of them, with their dark hair, infectious smiles and an innate sense of mischief.

'So, what are you up to?' asked Flynn.

Mac's eyes stayed fixed on Violet who was getting Holly out of her car, across the street. 'Nothing much, just enjoying the view.'

Flynn followed Mac's gaze. 'Jeez, when are you going to do something *about* that?'

'Oh, fuck off Flynn,' said Mac, smiling. 'I'm just biding my time.'

'I think you've waited long enough, haven't you?' said Flynn. 'Ask her out or move on. There's a line of girls waiting out there for you to notice them.'

'I'm fine,' said Mac.

'You're a monk.'

'No I'm not, I'm just choosier than some people.'

'I'm wounded Mac, truly wounded,' said Flynn placing his hand over his heart and staggering back a step in mock distress.

'You're an idiot is what you are. Besides, I'm not

61

judging,' Mac replied with a laugh. 'It was an observation, that's all.'

'Sure it was. So what are you doing in town, other than stalking Violet?'

'Getting a new chain for the chainsaw. You?' said Mac, pretending not to have heard the last comment.

'Dropping off the ute for a service. So, as I have a couple of hours to spare, why don't we grab lunch?'

Mac looked back just in time to see Violet and Holly walking hand in hand into the bakery. For a moment the breeze picked up and blew against Violet, moulding her dark floral dress to her curves.

'Fuck, did you just sigh?' Flynn asked with a grin, his dark-brown eyes full of laughter.

'Oh shut up,' Mac snapped as he started to walk down the street. 'Come on, let's get lunch. And it's your shout!'

'Shit,' said Flynn as he loped after Mac. 'You just can't take a joke.'

* * *

Violet and Holly left the bakery and made their way to the Hummingbird Café. As they stood at the counter Violet bent down and asked, 'So what sort of ice cream would you like?'

Holly tilted her head to one side as she considered her options. 'Hmmm, strawberry, please.'

'Good choice,' said the waiter as he materialised behind the counter.

'Thanks,' said Violet. 'Could we have two strawberry ice creams please?'

'Would that be one scoop or two?'

Violet looked at Holly who held two fingers up. 'Oh, I think we'd better have two.'

The waiter gave her a grin. 'Coming right up.'

'Thanks,' Violet said again as Holly wandered over to a cane basket filled with toys and books.

'Don't look, but that's her,' came a whisper from a nearby booth.

'Who?'

'You know, the woman I was telling you about. Remember, she's just moved back here with her daughter.'

Violet tensed and moved away slightly, trying really hard to ignore them.

'The girl is a sweet little thing which makes it even more of a pity.'

'What?'

'You know Doris, the secretary at the primary school? Well, she said that there doesn't appear to be a father anywhere in the picture.'

'Oh that's sad. Well, good luck to her.'

Violet peeked over her shoulder and checked out the two women. One was super-thin with a blonde bob and sharp features, and she didn't recognise her from anywhere. The other woman had dark hair and a green dress, though Violet couldn't see her face because she had her back to her.

'She's started her own party business. I wouldn't have

thought there'd be much call for that, but there you go,' said the blonde.

'She must be the woman my boss used her for her daughter's birthday. She was really pleased with the end result.'

Violet turned her head so they wouldn't catch her staring. The one thing about this town that she could have lived without was the gossip. She sometimes missed the anonymity of living in a large city like Melbourne.

'Isn't it funny that after all these years she turns up just when Jason McKellan gets engaged?'

'Sorry, I don't follow?'

'Oh, of course, you moved here after she and her sister left. You see, years ago she and Jason were an item. They went out together for years . . .'

'There you go, two strawberry ice creams,' said the waiter.

'Thanks,' said Violet, forcing herself to smile as she took them, though she had a lump in her stomach and felt sick. Why didn't people just mind their own business?

'Here Holly, come and get your ice cream,' she called.

Holly skipped up to her and grinned. 'Thanks, Mummy.'

'You're welcome. Now, come on sweetie—let's get out of here.'

'Here's your change,' the waiter said as he offered her the coins.

'Oh, keep it,' Violet said with a tight smile before she grabbed Holly's hand and hurried to the door.

* * *

Flynn was wrong, thought Mac. He wasn't a monk. He'd gone out with his fair share of women. Well, maybe not in comparison with Flynn, but that was a whole other story. Sure, some of the women he'd gone out with had just been flings but some had lasted for some time.

Mac frowned as he tried to remember a relationship that had lasted longer than a year but couldn't think of any. Surely that couldn't be right?

Andrea Culpit. The image of a cute blonde shimmered in his head. They'd started going out two years after Violet disappeared. Andrea had been bright and sunny and a whole lot of fun to be around. But after ten months or so, Andrea got sick of waiting for Mac to make a commitment. 'It's not that I expect you to propose to me or anything,' she'd said. 'I just want to know there's a chance we can have a future together.' Mac had stood there like a statue, the words she wanted to hear caught in his throat. But he couldn't say them and Andrea walked away—smart girl.

After Andrea there had been a handful of women who'd slipped into his life with the changing seasons. But none of them had stayed. He'd never asked them to. Each and every one of them had wanted something he wasn't able to give— his heart.

Shit, he hated it when Flynn was right.

Chapter 7

Mac pulled into his mother's driveway. She loved her modern two-bedroom house on its large block which she'd transformed into the prettiest garden in all of Violet Falls within a year of moving in. The one thing his mum had always loved almost as much as her family, had been her garden at McKellan's Run.

Mac got out of the ute and looked for a second at the line of peach and plum trees that lined the front fence. White and pink blossoms covered the trees, their scent beautiful and delicate. There was the drone of bees buzzing from one fragile flower to the next and Mac could almost smell the honey.

He walked up the winding path and around to the back door giving it a quick rap as he walked in.

'Oh hey, darling,' Sarah said, turning around from the oven.

'Hi Mum, have you got a few minutes?' said Mac wandering over to lean on the kitchen bench.

'Of course I do,' she said, smiling at him.

Mac was silent, tongue-tied. He'd driven over so he could talk about Violet and now he was here, well, he couldn't seem to get the words out.

'Whatcha making?' he asked. How lame was that?

His mother studied him for a second. 'It's banana bread and it will be ready in about five minutes. You've got good timing.'

'Great,' said Mac.

'Okay, stop pussy-footing about. I can see you've got something on your mind so spit it out,' said Sarah.

Mac never quite knew how his mother managed to see right through him and zero in on a problem.

'I know that I promised to stay out of what went on with Jason and Violet all those years ago. But I can't, not anymore,' said Mac.

Sarah sighed and leaned back against the kitchen sink. 'I won't hold you to it. I was wrong, Mac. I always hoped that he and Violet would eventually sort out their differences and get back together. I didn't know until much later how badly he'd ended it. No wonder Violet didn't want to have anything to do with any of us. I completely understand Jason wanting to concentrate on his career but I just wish he'd let her down more gently.'

'Yeah, well he didn't,' said Mac.

'No Mac, he didn't, and though it pains me to say it, he behaved in an appalling manner. He should have been . . . Oh, I don't know . . . more understanding. Violet was . . . *is* a sweet girl.'

'Why did you ask her to get involved in planning his wedding then?' asked Mac. 'Wouldn't it have been better to hire someone else?'

'Maybe, but I thought it was time for the past to be the

67

past and for Violet to realise she'd turned into an extraordinary woman all by herself, without the help of my feckless son or any of us for that matter,' said Sarah.

'I don't understand,' said Mac.

Sarah sighed. 'Jason told me and your father that once he found out that Violet and Lily were on their own he'd tried to provide Violet with financial support but she'd refused to accept anything from him. We tried several times to make contact and offer her support via Hugh Taylor but she refused any help. After a while Hugh said she stopped responding to his phone calls and the letters he sent her came back with, "Return to Sender" written on them.'

'Why would Jason offer her money?'

'I guess that even though he didn't want a future with her, he still cared for Violet in a way. I think underneath all that sophisticated polish he's a good person, it's just sometimes I think he loses sight of it.'

'Why didn't you tell me any of this?' said Mac.

'Your dad and I always knew you felt an affection for Violet, but we just wanted you to get on with your life. Violet was Jason's girlfriend, and back then you could only ever be Jason's little brother to her,' said Sarah, taking Mac's hand. 'She'd made it clear she wanted to cut off her ties with everyone here, including us.'

'But I still don't understand why you asked her to help with the wedding,' said Mac.

'Because after I heard how well she was doing back here and how happy she and Holly were—a teacher friend of mine told me what a delightful, bright little girl Holly was—I wanted even more for Violet to know she'd done the sensible thing moving on from Jason. I also knew, and again it pains me to say this about your brother, that if she met Jason again and saw the sort of woman he was marrying it would confirm to her that she and Jason would never have shared the same values.'

'Then why didn't you warn me before she came to the house that first time?' said Mac.

'Because I'm not blind. I knew you always carried a torch for Violet,' said Sarah. 'I thought you'd move on from your crush but you didn't. You've had so many lovely girlfriends and though you've always been totally up front and gentlemanly with them, you've never really committed to anyone. So I thought, after all these years, it was time to finally clear the air. You're an adult, Mac, and no longer in Jason's shadow when it comes to Violet. So why not see what happens if that's what you want?'

'Maybe there's something in that. We just keep bumping into each other, and . . .'

'And there's a spark?' asked Sarah.

'Yes, I think so,' said Mac.

'Well from what I've seen I'd say she likes you. What I can't understand is that she's been back in town for almost four months and you're only getting around to asking her out now? What the hell is holding you back?'

Mac's eyes widened in surprise. 'I thought—'

Sarah shook her head. 'I made you promise not to chase her back then, Mac. You were all barely more than children.

Besides, Violet needed space, she needed time away from *all* of us McKellans. But now—'

'It burns me up, Mum. Just thinking of Violet and Lily in the city with no-one they could turn to. She should have been here, safe at home with the people who cared for her. How the hell could her grandfather have turned her and Lily out of their home?'

Sarah stepped forward and wrapped her arms around her beloved son. 'I know, sweetheart, but Silas Beckett was a hard and vindictive old man. He blamed everything from his family's bad fortune to the lack of rain on the McKellans. Violet and Lily probably had a hard time trying to live in the city at first but maybe staying here in Violet Falls would have been even tougher. Violet has grown into a strong and independent woman.'

'And stubborn,' said Mac.

'Yes, I suppose she can be that,' Sarah said. 'The truth is, I blame myself. I keep telling myself that I should have taught Jason to be more responsible; more like you. I want to say he's just like his father, but that wouldn't be entirely fair on my first husband Simon. It's not just his Prescott genes. I must have screwed up somewhere.'

'You were and are great, Mum. You turned an empty shell of a house into a home, not to mention a belligerent and angry six-year-old who didn't want a new stepmother, into a happy kid,' Mac said as he reached over and gave her hand a quick squeeze.

'You were never really belligerent, sweetheart.'

'Yeah I was,' said Mac. 'And Jason might have been

born a Prescott but when Dad adopted him be became a McKellan. Dad didn't bring him up to run away from what was expected of him and not to do what's right. There comes a time when we all have to take responsibility for our actions. The way I see it, Jase has never got to that point.'

'I think sometimes that could be true and I don't think Celine will change that. He's always been wrapped up in himself and never really registered the needs of people around him. I don't think he does it on purpose, it's as if it just doesn't occur to him. And Celine is pretty much the same,' said Sarah. 'That clearly doesn't matter too much in the corporate world, but it's different with family and friends.'

* * *

Violet stood outside her front door double-checking she had everything she needed in her huge handbag. Wallet, sunglasses, tablet computer, tissues, perfume, lipstick and keys. Damn, she'd forgotten her phone again. She raced back inside and grabbed it off her desk, glancing up at the old wall clock. It was already 9.17 a.m. and she had to drive to Melbourne and back in time to pick up Holly from school. The things she'd hired from Tony were going to be delivered to McKellan's Run, but there were still supplies she needed from other places, and the only way she was going to be totally sure of having them all was if she drove down to Melbourne herself.

Throwing her phone in her bag she hurried out and pulled the front door shut behind her. She was halfway down the front steps when the worn wood suddenly gave way beneath her. Violet grabbed the handrail for support but it collapsed under her weight. She fell awkwardly to the side, her ankle twisted and the broken wood badly scratching her shin.

It took her a second or two to gather herself. Her ankle throbbed, her shin stung and she was pretty sure her arm would be bruised from her tangle with the banister. Carefully extracting herself from the broken mess that had once been her front steps, she wiggled her toes and then gently rotated her ankle.

'Ouch!' The dull pain seemed to radiate and intensify.

She frowned and sucked in a breath. As far as she could ascertain she was sore and bleeding but nothing was broken. She picked up her bag and, heart beating, checked her tablet. The screen hadn't shattered, turning on immediately, thank goodness—if she'd broken her tablet it would have been an utter disaster.

Looking up, an equal measure of dismay and anger shot through her as she considered the steps. *Well fantastic, like my bank balance really needs this.*

'Ow, ow, damn it, ow!' Violet muttered as she hobbled around to the back door. She'd have to find some bandages, and reassess her wardrobe and find some trousers to cover up her bloody leg.

* * *

Mac slowed the motorbike as he approached the old stone cottage. Even from here it was clear that a dozen or so of his sheep had managed to get through to the wrong paddock.

A tall gum tree had come down on the old fence, the force knocking over a couple of the fence posts and pushing down the wire, leaving a large gap just big enough for a mob of rambunctious sheep to escape through.

He stopped the bike near the gnarled crabapple tree, told Razor to come, and walked over for a closer inspection. Besides cutting up the tree, he'd have to replace at least three of the posts and a section of the fence.

He looked over at the original McKellan's Run cottage, which had been the first home of Angus McKellan and his wife, Bridie. Angus McKellan had arrived in this area just over a hundred and fifty years ago and, from what Mac's father had told him, Angus had been a young man with an innate sense of adventure. In 1854 he'd left everything he knew in the small village of Gillocky in the Scottish Highlands, for the chance of a new life half a world away. He'd caught a fast clipper from Portsmouth and after nearly four and half months of hell he'd arrived in Melbourne. By all accounts he'd made his way as fast as he could to get to the nearby goldfields. However, after a while he'd fallen in love with the local landscape and decided to try and make a go on the land instead of chasing gold.

Angus worked hard, scratching out a living from the earth with a handful of chickens and a few sheep. But his life turned around when he met Bridie O'Hare. According to his journal, he'd quickly fallen in love with the beautiful black-haired Irish lass with her pretty green eyes and lilting accent. He promised her he'd do his best to build them a happy, comfortable life if only she'd have him.

Bridie accepted and Angus spent the rest of his life honouring his promise. He'd started right here, where this little stream snaked through a gully and green gums towered overhead, building this little two-room stone cottage with his bare hands and rocks that he had hewn from the ground.

Mac crossed his arms and leant against what was left of the garden wall, still gazing at the cottage, a thoughtful expression on his face. He, Jason and Dan had spent many happy days here as kids pretending it was their house. They'd even found an old bible one day in what would have been the ceiling. The roof had deteriorated even more since then and part of the north wall had recently collapsed, but it seemed a shame to let the whole cottage crumple to the ground. Maybe he should try and save it? He'd always enjoyed coming out to this spot. Perhaps it was just family nostalgia but there was a welcoming feeling to the place, despite how rundown it was. Somehow, bizarrely really, it always made him feel hopeful when he came here.

Mac shook his head and frowned. It was crazy, but if things went well with the shearing and the weather, he decided he'd save Angus and Bridie's cottage. After all, without them there would never have been a McKellan's Run or a homestead.

Mac made a mental note to ring Johnno and talk about the feasibility of restoring the old place when he had some time. Johnno might say it was a ridiculous idea but if anyone could help him turn it into something liveable, Johnno could. Meanwhile he better bring that mob of sheep in and get them penned so they were ready for shearing in the morning. Mac checked his battered watch. It was almost half past nine. Damn, where had that last hour gone?

Whistling Razor over, he revved his motorbike, giving the cottage one more glance before he rode off towards the main house. Despite all the stuff he still needed to do, he decided to take the scenic route back—well, that was what he liked to called it anyway. If he took the track to the left, it followed the creek all the way up to the far paddock. It had been a couple of days since he'd ridden that way and it would give him the chance to make sure the fences there were all okay.

Mac stopped his bike at the crest of the incline for a minute just to take in the view. Below, a fast flowing creek wound its way through another gully. Mac never tired of the wildness and rugged beauty of this land.

Following the main track, which veered away from the creek, he rode past the couple of acres he'd planted with oats. By the looks of things the crop was coming along nicely. Soon he'd be able to harvest it for hay. Most of it he'd keep to feed his sheep over winter but, weather permitting, there'd be a little bit left over to sell.

The track swept parallel with the far paddock's fence, which all seemed to be intact. As Mac rode along, a couple of kangaroos bounded up the hill heading towards a small clump of gums. A smile touched Mac's lips as he watched them hop away.

Chapter 8

Mac let out a sharp whistle. 'Razor, get around the back and get them in,' he called, as he and three of the farmhands he'd hired used their motorbikes to encourage the flock of sheep towards the shearing shed.

With a bark, Razor swung in an arc and herded the sheep towards the sheep pen.

'That's it, Razor. Get around, good boy!'

The air was filled with the sound of bleating as the sheep scampered and jumped into the pen. Mac jumped off the bike and then in three quick strides walked to the gate. Pushing off the ground with one foot, he held on as the gate swung shut. The large metal latch clanked closed and Mac stood for a moment and looked at the sheep.

Relief flooded through him as the sun warmed his back. Managing McKellan's Run was hard work but every now and again there were moments when he got to see just what he'd achieved. This was one of those times. The majority of sheep had been rounded up and penned over the past three days, the fleece on their backs was of good quality and wool prices were up for the first time in several years. Now all he had to do was find the few stragglers that had escaped the initial round-up. Whistling for Razor, he headed down to the small billabong at the base of the north paddock.

'What now, boss?' Ben asked as he came and stood by Mac's side.

'Now, we grab a drink and a quick break before we go and pick up the last few that got away,' said Mac, scratching Razor between the ears. 'Good job, Razor, good boy.'

'Sounds like a plan,' said Ben. 'I'll tell the others and meet you at the house.'

'Sure,' said Mac with a nod, staring back at the sheep before running his gaze over the land—his land. He smiled. The sun was shining, the farm was doing well and Violet Beckett had come back into his life—he reckoned he had a lot to smile about.

* * *

Okay, thought Violet, so she had to admit the day was shaping up to be much better than she'd expected. There hadn't been any delays during her drive, she'd managed to pick up all the supplies she needed and a parking spot had miraculously appeared outside the café where she was meeting Lily for lunch.

'What happened to you?' said Lily as Violet reached down and gave her a hug.

'I tangled with the front steps and lost. I'm fine though. Both Holly and I miss you so much,' said Violet, before sitting down.

She stared at Lily for a second. Anyone could tell they were sisters, there was a similarity to their features and the way they carried themselves. They both had hair that was a deep walnut-brown—though Lily had just had hers cut—and they both had the same dark-brown eyes that were said to have been inherited from their maternal grandmother. But unlike Violet, Lily had delectable curves and could pull off the girly look—even sexy—when she put her mind to it.

'I've missed you both too,' said Lily. 'It's just not the same here without you guys.'

'Hey, I like what you've done with your hair,' said Violet, aware that Lily was tearing up. 'It gives you a bit of an edge.'

'Do you think so?' asked Lily.

'Absolutely.'

'I like it, but Pietro prefers it when it's longer.'

'Then Pietro is a fool because it looks fantastic.'

Lily smiled as she looked towards the girl behind the counter. 'Can we have a couple of cappuccinos? Thanks.' She turned back to Violet, running her hand through her short brown hair. 'So tell me everything. How's Holly?'

'Good, she's settled into school really well and has some nice little friends,' said Violet, fumbling in her bag before taking out two bright paintings. 'She sent you these—this one's Princess Lily in her carriage and this is Princess Violet and my prince standing in front of our castle.'

Lily sat in silence for a few minutes as she studied the paintings, looking like she was ready to really burst into tears.

'Thanks,' Violet said to the waitress as the coffees arrived. 'Hey Lily, are you alright?'

'Yeah, I just really do miss you both,' said Lily. 'And seeing you now just makes me realise how lonely I've felt without you.'

'Next time I come I'll make sure it's a weekend and bring Holly with me,' said Violet as she stirred in a teaspoon of sugar into her cappuccino. 'And I'll try to get Skype set up soon. It's just been so busy and I've been battling to stay afloat. My car decided to implode a while ago and I'm still paying off the repairs.'

'I know what you mean,' said Lily. 'Fashion's so badly paid, even when you're at my level, and inner-city rents seem to get more exorbitant by the day.'

'That reminds me, have you had any time to think about what you're going to do with the shop at home?' said Violet.

'Not really. We've been working around the clock on the latest collection. I've hardly had time to breathe, let alone think about the shop. And I have to admit I've got a bit of a mental block about it too. I know you've moved on from how Grandad treated us, but I still can't forgive him for what he put you through.'

'It probably makes a difference having Holly. You become more of a pragmatist about stuff. And him leaving me the house has turned my life around. Makes me wonder what he was thinking in those last years before he died— whether he regretted what he did. Anyway, it seems a shame just to let it sit there and do nothing. I mean it could be earning you some money,' Violet said.

'I suppose. I have to admit I have thought about selling it,' started Lily, taking a deep breath before continuing.

'I know it might sound silly but it's the last link we have to Dad and it seems wrong to sell it.'

'Why not rent it out and give yourself a bit of time before you make any decision one way or the other?' said Violet.

'Yeah, I guess so. It sounds a bit romantic but I'd like to hand it down to another generation of Becketts.'

'Careful, you're beginning to sound like Grandad,' said Violet, laughing.

'God, I hope not,' Lily said, smiling at her sister.

'No, I understand and you're right. Violet Falls *is* the last link we have with Dad. And despite it being tainted by the way Grandad carried on, there's a pull there somehow and I don't want to break it by selling the house either.'

Lily nodded and was silent for a minute. When she looked up at Violet her eyes were overbright. 'I still miss Mum and Dad after all these years. I know I was so young I hardly have any real memories, but even they're fading and every now and then I get hit with this wave of sadness and longing. What frightens me the most is that sometimes I find it hard to remember Mum and Dad's faces in crisp detail. It's as if the pictures in my head are blurring.'

Violet reached over the table and took her hand. 'I know, sweetie. But they'd be so proud of you and what you're accomplishing, just like I am.'

Lily wiped her eyes. 'Sorry.'

'Nothing to be sorry about. I miss them too. So, what's your plan?' asked Violet.

'I'll come up as soon as I can to see you and Holly and we can go and have a look at the shop. I know you've been flat out so on the rare occasions I've given it any thought I haven't wanted to bother you with checking out what needs doing to it if I did decide to rent it out.'

'You know I'd have been glad to do it. But anyway, I'm happy to come with you when you check it out.'

'Thanks,' said Lily, her face brightening.

'So how's work?' asked Violet. 'And how's Pietro? Is he still Melbourne's very own up-and-coming fashion photographer?'

'We're fine, everything is the same as ever. He's always working, he's even been doing some overseas shoots lately, and I've been designing like mad. Oh, Violet, you should see this sample I made. It's in a rich burnished coppery colour. And it's silk; dark, subtle. I swear it's the best dress I've ever made. I showed it to Sam, and she said it was good, really good and she's going to show it to Edwina!'

Violet smiled. Lily had only recently been promoted from junior designer to designer for Edwina Partell, one of Australia's leading fashion houses, and Sam was her boss. This was a big deal for Lily—a big deal that could push her career ahead.

'That's fantastic, Lily. I'm so happy for you.'

'Yeah, I just can't believe it. What about you?'

'Well, I have a new event to plan.'

'That's great. Is it for anyone I know?' asked Lily, finishing up her coffee.

Violet hesitated briefly before deciding not to say anything about Jason's wedding. It'd only worry Lily. 'Nah, there's a lot of new people in Violet Falls these days,' she said.

Violet pulled to a halt in front of Mac's house and switched off the engine. Sarah had wanted to see some of the finishing touches she'd chosen in Melbourne, so she'd agreed to meet her here. It had been a long day and her ankle was throbbing but she had to admit to a frisson of excitement about the possibility of seeing Mac.

'Holly, why don't you go ahead and knock. I'll be right behind you. I just have to get the box,' she said, easing herself out of the car seat.

'Sure, Mummy,' said Holly as she got out and started running towards the house.

Violet smiled, thinking that the kittens were likely to be paid a visit. Opening the boot, she took out the box filled with dark cream silk ribbons, vintage glass pearls and her other antique finds, and followed her daughter down the path. She was too far away to make out the words but she heard a deep rumble of a voice and Holly's animated response. Mac appeared on the path with a frown.

'Violet, are you alright? Holly said you hurt your leg,' he asked, striding up to her and taking the box she was carrying.

'Oh, you don't need to, thanks,' she said with a smile. 'I'm fine, I just fell over this morning. No big deal. Where's Holly?'

'I sent her into the kitchen. Mum is in there waiting for you.'

Violet took a few steps forward but Mac reached out and placed his hand on her arm.

'You're limping.'

'I know,' she said with a nod. 'I fell down the front steps and it hurt like hell. Hey, what are you doing?'

In one fluid movement Mac had put down the box and picked up Violet. 'Carrying you inside to see what the damage is.'

'That so isn't necessary,' Violet protested, blushing. 'You can put me down.'

'Humour me,' said Mac, holding her tight to his chest as he carried her inside, down the corridor and past the great room to the downstairs bathroom. There was little Violet could do but hang on as he flipped on the light switch with his elbow before carrying her over to a large marble-tiled bench.

He perched her on the cold tiles and began rolling up her trouser leg.

'Let's see what the damage is.'

'Really Mac, you don't have to.'

'Shhh,' he said, gently undoing Violet's bandage, a frown creasing his brow as he surveyed the mess that was her shin.

Violet looked down at her leg, it was badly grazed, cut about and a bit weepy in places. It still hurt like hell but there was no way she was going to tell Mac that. 'It looks worse than it is, really,' she said.

'Are you telling me or trying to convince me? Wait here while I get the first aid box,' said Mac.

Violet lay back, thinking how different Mac was to any man she'd ever gone out with.

'You did a good job,' said Mac as he knelt in front of her and started cleaning the wound.

'Well, if you're going to throw yourself down the stairs, I always think you should commit,' she replied, biting back a smile. Soon afterwards she had to suck in a breath as the cloth brushed against something.

'Sorry,' said Mac, going quiet for a moment as he studied her leg. 'There's still a splinter of wood in there. I'll have to get it out.'

'It's going to hurt, isn't it?

'Yeah, it is. Are you ready?' Mac's eyes locked onto hers.

'Okay,' said Violet and held on to the edge of the bench as Mac probed her leg. She dug her fingers into the tiles and tried to think of something pleasant.

'All done. Sorry, if it hurt.'

'It's fine,' Violet replied, lying through her teeth. But the sting receded and Violet was left with the sensation of Mac's fingers touching her skin. Her insides contracted and tingled with each contact. She reached for the fresh bandage. 'Thanks, I can finish up now.'

'It's alright, I've got this.'

Violet savoured Mac's tender ministrations as he wrapped her leg. He was slow at the task and Violet wondered if it was through diligence or wicked enjoyment. Did he know about the effect he had on her?

'There, it's done,' he said, holding her gently as he helped her down.

'Thank you so much,' said Violet as she stepped away from his embrace before he had a chance to stop her. 'Holly and your mum are waiting—I think we'd better get in there, don't you?'

Mac held her gaze and Violet found it hard to look away. She held her breath as he reached out and tucked a stray lock of hair behind her ear. The air seemed charged around them as they stood facing each other.

'Violet . . .'

She gave him a brief smile. 'They'll be wondering what's happened to us,' she said as she forced herself to walk towards the door. His footsteps sounded behind her as she heard him blow out a long breath.

'Yeah—of course,' Mac said. 'Whatever you think.'

Chapter 9

The next morning Violet frowned as she looked out her office window. A couple of work vehicles were heading down her short drive.

'What the hell?' she thought, standing up and heading for the front door. Mac was just sliding out of his ute as she stepped out onto the verandah.

'Hey Violet,' he said with a nod and a smile. 'How's the leg?'

'Fine, thanks. Mac, what's going on?'

Mac ambled over to a verandah post and leaned against it. Looking up, he gave her a wink.

Violet smiled back at him, unable to speak as a wonderful sensation washed through her body.

'I called Johnno and his boys to check out your steps,' said Mac as he gestured to three burly men who were getting out of a truck. 'You remember Johnno from school, don't you?'

Violet tried not to stare at the muscled bloke who was walking over from a truck with the words 'Johnson's Construction' written on the side. Darren Johnson had somehow transformed from the reed-thin boy she remembered, to a well-built guy with long sandy-coloured hair and a three-day growth.

'Of course I do,' Violet answered. 'Hi Darren, it's lovely to see you again.'

Johnno gave her a grin. 'Hey Violet, good to have you back. The town didn't seem right without a Beckett here. Don't worry about anything, we'll have this replaced in no time,' he said, poking at her dilapidated front stairs.

'Um, thanks Darren,' said Violet, smiling at him before bending down and whispering to Mac. 'Can I talk to you for a second?'

'Sure thing,' said Mac, pulling himself up onto the verandah and following Violet inside the house.

'I appreciate you doing this for me, Mac, I really do,' said Violet after shutting the door.

'There's a "but" hanging in the air isn't there?' said Mac.

'When I had a moment I was going to ring around for some quotes to find the best deal.'

'Johnno and his crew are the best. They did some work on my place last year and they've been working out at the Grange for Flynn. Johnno's so good I'm even going to see if he can help me fix up the old cottage.'

'That's fine for you, but . . .'

Mac stepped forward and gently placed his hands on her shoulders. 'I've got this Violet.'

'No Mac, I can't let you do that. I pay my own way. I always have. I refuse to rely on anyone.'

'Let's just call it a welcome home present from one friend to another then.'

'I don't think that's such a good idea.'

'Violet, the steps have to be replaced. It's bad enough you got hurt but what if it had been Holly? Let me do this. Just this once say "Thanks Mac" and let it go.' His hazel-green eyes locked onto hers. 'Please.'

Violet stood there, staring up into his eyes. He was so damned kind it made her want to cry. And she was falling for him big-time, she admitted to herself. For one insane moment she wondered what he'd do if she wrapped her arms around his slim hips and tugged him closer. Why did he have to be a McKellan?

'Alright Mac, just this once. Thank you for helping me out,' said Violet. 'I really appreciate it.'

'See, that wasn't hard, was it?' he said, bending down to kiss her forehead. 'Listen, I've got to get back to work, so I'll see you later.'

'Okay and thanks again. I really do appreciate you doing this,' Violet said. 'Bye.'

Mac paused for a second as if he was going to say something but then he thought better of it and just smiled and turned away. She watched him go, drinking in the heft of his body, his broad shoulders and large work-hardened hands.

'Damn, I really have to get out more,' she whispered under her breath as she turned away into her office. The front door banged shut but Mac's voice carried through the open window.

'It's all good, you can go ahead with the job. Hey Johnno, after you've replaced the steps can you check out the rest of the verandah and the back porch as well? Fix whatever needs to be done.'

'Sure, Mac. No worries,' Johnno said. 'Invoice to you?'

'Yep, and make sure you do it properly. I want to make sure the girls are safe and sound. Oh, while you're at it you might as well have a look at the roof. Better to be safe than sorry and all that.'

'Whatever you say, mate. I'll get the boys on it straight-away. See ya round, Mac.'

Violet smiled. Mac was impossible. Give him an inch and he'd take a mile.

* * *

A hard rap on the door startled Violet out of her work and she walked down the corridor to answer it. She swung open the door to find Mac standing there with his hands in the pockets of his low slung jeans.

'Hey,' he said with that maddeningly gorgeous smile of his.

Violet's stomach did the now-familiar fluttering thing. She couldn't deny it anymore; Mac really had a major effect on her.

'Oh hey, Mac,' she said, trying to sound cool and unaffected. As if.

'I was just passing. I thought I'd stop by and see how the front steps turned out.'

Violet bit her bottom lip to stop herself from smiling. 'They're great. Thank you so, so much. Johnno did a fantastic job. See for yourself,' she said, following him down the steps.

'Yeah, they look good,' said Mac. 'I told you Johnno would make sure the boys did a good job.'

They fell into silence for an awkward second.

'Um sorry, did you want to come in?' said Violet gesturing for him to go up the stairs.

'Sure, did Johnno say if there were any other problems with the house?'

'Only the roof on the back porch. There's a small section that needs replacing but other than that it's all good.' Violet made her way back down the hall towards the kitchen. She could hear Mac's footsteps echo behind her on the wooden floor.

'Look who's here, Holly,' said Violet.

Holly was sitting at a small round table eating a sandwich. She looked up and grinned. 'Hi Mac, I'm a fairy today.'

'I can see that,' Mac said with a widening grin.

'How?'

'Oh, I don't know but maybe it's got something to do with you wearing those pretty fairy wings.'

'They are pretty, aren't they?' said Holly her face alight as she swung around to show him the glittery pink and mauve wings that were attached to her back. 'Aunty Lily made them for me.'

'Well, she did a very good job,' said Mac. 'They're the prettiest fairy wings I've seen in a while.'

Violet turned on the kettle and smiled. She liked the way he leant against the kitchen island and the way he seemed to fill the room. There was something comforting about it—about him.

'Coffee?'

'Thanks, that would be great,' he said as he slid onto one of the kitchen chairs.

'Mummy, I need to get that thing from my room.'

Violet glanced up. 'What thing, sweetie?'

Holly gave her a pointed look. 'You know Mummy, the *thing* I showed you before.'

'Oh, yes of course, *the thing*. Go on then.'

Holly ducked out from the table, then skipped out of the kitchen and down the hall.

'She's great, Violet. You must be very proud of her,' Mac said as he crossed his arms and leant on the bench.

'I am,' said Violet, putting his coffee down in front of him, his hand brushed against hers as he reached for it.

There was a silence as he took her hand in his and moved his fingers across her skin. Their eyes locked for an instant but Violet moved her hand and looked away. She could feel his stare on her back as she poured her drink.

'This is for you,' said Holly, coming back into the kitchen and handing Mac a painting. 'It's your house. There's the shed, and there's Mud and her kittens.'

Violet picked up her coffee and went and sat on the chair next to Mac.

Mac took his time studying the bright picture. And for some unknown reason Violet held her breath.

'Do you like it?' Holly's blue eyes held an equal mix of expectancy and trepidation.

'Why Holly, I think it's one of the most beautiful pictures I've ever seen. Thank you,' said Mac ruffling her hair and giving her a big warm smile. 'I can't wait to put it up on my fridge.'

Violet let out her breath. Why had she been worried? This was Mac and he'd never hurt Holly.

'That's great. I'm going to go and make you another one,' said Holly happily, before skipping from the room.

'I think you might have a fan there,' said Violet. 'Holly's quite taken with you in a way she's only ever really been with Lily.'

'She's a clever girl, she knows just how awesome I am,' he said with a wink.

'Hmmm, maybe. Or perhaps it's because you and your mother are bribing her with kittens, sugar biscuits, horses and the promise of lambs.'

'Ow, that's harsh, Violet. I'm crushed and so would Mum be.'

'I'm sure you'll both bounce back.'

Mac leant in close, and kissed her ear.

'Mac . . .' said Violet, desire gushing through her.

'Aw, come on Violet. Take a chance and kiss me.'

Their mouths were so close; there was barely a breath between them. Anticipation quivered through her as Violet stretched up and closed the distance between them. Mac's hand slid up her neck and gently cradled the back of her head, as if to hold her in place as she fell deeper into his kiss.

The kiss was long and deep and made Violet's heart beat faster. She grasped onto his shoulders as if she needed to tether herself onto something solid. She felt the warmth of his body through his cotton shirt. His tongue swept inside her mouth. A flash of long-buried want seared through her and she pulled him closer. She'd forgotten what it was like to be held by someone. She'd forgotten how overpowering the feeling of connecting with someone was. She clung on to Mac and pressed closer, no longer able to resist her attraction for him.

Without breaking the kiss, Mac wrapped his strong arms around her, encasing her in his tenderness and essence.

She was consumed and for an instant the carefully constructed walls that protected her, tumbled to the ground. Violet wanted Mac more than she'd ever wanted anyone and the only fragmented visions in her head were of her bed and how she could manoeuvre him there.

But any ideas she may have had disappeared in a puff of smoke as the sound of little footsteps echoed down the hallway. Violet pulled back from Mac and tried to catch her breath. Their eyes locked and Holly's voice floated back down the hallway.

'Mummy! Look at this new drawing. I haven't finished it yet,' Holly called out. 'It's going to be of me and the kittens.'

Chapter 10

The sky had a late afternoon golden tinge to it as Violet and Lily got out of the car and walked towards the Victorian terrace that had been in their family for more than a century. Violet had organised a play date for Holly with Amber Laragy to give them enough time to check out the old store, but they'd nearly used up all the time catching up properly on what had been happening in each other's lives.

Stopping outside the shop, Violet watched Lily in silence as she studied the old building in front of them. It was almost identical to the other shops on this part of the street—two storeys with a wide verandah reaching out over the footpath.

'It looks more rundown than I remember,' said Lily.

'Yeah, I thought you might think that,' said Violet. 'Apparently Mrs Halsford kept it in pretty good shape until she retired and gave up the lease,' she continued. 'But since then, well . . . Maybe Grandad just didn't feel up to doing anything about it.'

'It could be better on the inside,' Lily said hopefully.

'Sorry, I should have come and had a decent look at

it months ago,' said Violet. 'It feels like I haven't stopped sprinting since I moved back.'

'It's kind of nice to be checking it out for the first time together, anyway,' said Lily, pulling out a bunch of ancient-looking keys and jangling them in her hand.

The green paint on the front door had bubbled and peeled from age and hot summer days. Lily finally found the right key and jiggled it into the door's old lock.

'So how long since Mrs Halsford left?'

'Almost five years,' said Violet. 'Although if we go by the dates on newspapers on the windows, I'd say it was a bit longer than that.'

Lily pushed open the door and a cloud of musty, dusty air greeted them.

Violet found it odd standing in what used to be Mrs Halsford's Fashion and Intimate Apparel. Even back then 'fashion' had been a very loose description. When she'd been growing up, there had been several dress shops in Violet Falls but Mrs Halsford's was the original, and so was her stock. Everything always looked safe, boring and really, really old.

'Oh God, I half expect to look up and see Mrs Halsford with her chignon and navy cardigan draped over her skinny shoulders,' said Lily, walking over to the glass counter. 'Do you remember, she always had a pair of evening gloves sitting just there?' she added, pointing at the dusty glass with her finger.

Violet smiled. 'Yes, I remember, there being such a high demand for evening gloves in Violet Falls.'

Lily laughed as she looked around the room. 'Look, the walls are the same faded duck-egg blue. Everything in here always seemed to be white, beige or faded blue. And the clothes were just horrible.'

'Is that the fashion designer talking?'

'No, it's any sane woman under one hundred and twenty years old talking. Remember how bland everything was and how it was always about thirty years out of date?'

'I remember. It might not be a bad space if you can dispel the ghost of fashion past. Do you want to get in touch with Darren Johnson? Perhaps he could check the place out and give you a quote.'

Lily nodded. 'Why not, it's a good idea. It's got great bones and I think if it was fixed up a bit and painted, it could be really something. Let's check out the rest.'

Violet and Lily spent the next twenty minutes wandering through the shop. They'd never seen the rest of the building as Mrs Halsford had guarded it as if she was Cerberus at the gates of the Underworld. Behind the main room there was what must have been the stockroom and behind that a small kitchenette and tiny bathroom. Upstairs were two rooms, the largest with French doors leading out to the balcony overlooking the main street. But it was in the little back room that the girls found a mystery. In the corner was a narrow door with a very old padlock on it.

'I wonder what's in there,' said Violet.

'I don't know, but we're about to find out,' Lily replied, reaching into the pocket of her jeans and pulling out the bunch of keys. After a couple of false starts, Lily

96

turned the key and was rewarded with a soft click. Slowly opening the door, she said, 'There's a skinny flight of steps. I suppose it must lead up to the attic?'

'Do you want me to go first?' asked Violet.

Lily turned and gave Violet a hard look. 'I'm not your little baby sister anymore. Just don't mention anything about a psychotic ghost.'

Violet let out a laugh. 'Psychotic ghost, really?'

Lily started up the stairs. 'I told you not to mention that!'

'What can you see? What's up there?' Violet said as she hurried up the creaking wooden stairs behind her sister.

'Something from a horror movie set. God, it's creepy.'

'Nah, it's just old and forgotten.' Violet peered through the turned posts of the staircase. The room was long and dimly lit with a pointed ceiling. The only light coming in was from a small round window which was set just below the junction of the wooden ceiling. A thick layer of dust seemed to cover every inch of the attic. There was a stack of old trunks in one corner and several pieces of furniture scattered about.

Lily paused at the top of the stairs. 'Please tell me there's not a dead person under that dust sheet.'

Violet glanced in the direction Lily was pointing. 'Sure it is. Come on, let's have a look "little baby sister".'

'You know this is how most horror movies start, don't you? Two nubile young women in a creepy-arse house. It will all end in tears and buckets of blood,' said Lily.

'No more horror movies for you,' said Violet, laughing. 'From now on, you should stick with romances and comedies.'

Lily laughed and walked over to the edge of the dust sheet. In a quick movement, she pulled it off to reveal a very old dressmaker's dummy.

'Are you *really* getting freaked out?' said Violet.

'No. Well, maybe just a little bit. You know, Violet, this is pretty cool,' said Lily, taking a step closer. 'This looks really old. Do you think some of this stuff could be from when the Becketts ran the store?'

Violet looked around. 'It's possible. It certainly doesn't look as if anyone has been up here in decades.'

Lily walked over to a dust encrusted old desk. After wiping it with the bottom of her sleeve, they saw that it was made of a dark wood, probably mahogany or cedar. She opened one of the drawers, inside there was still a stack of papers. 'I think I might go through all this stuff. It could be interesting. Maybe I'll find some Beckett family secrets.'

'Well, you never know,' said Violet lifting up the lid of one of the chests stacked haphazardly in the corner. 'Hey, look, there's old bits of lace in here. Maybe you could find something useful for your designs?'

Lily hurried over and gently picked up one of the pieces on top. 'Oooh, it's pretty, and look at this,' she said as she scooped up a bundle of embroidered braid. 'It looks as if it's from the 1930s. This stuff is fantastic! I wonder if there's more of it in the other chests,' she added.

'Maybe you've found yourself a bit of a treasure trove,' said Violet. 'Should we go through them all?'

Lily looked at her watch. 'Shit, didn't you say you needed to pick up Holly now?'

Violet checked the time on her mobile. 'Yep, we better get out of here.'

'I'll have to organise for a builder to come and do a structural report on the place,' said Lily gathering up her bag. 'The floor in the kitchenette looked like it needed replacing and you saw the water damage by the back door. Did you say your new *friend* Mac knew a good builder?'

Violet rolled her eyes. 'I knew I should never have told you about the kiss.'

'Well you did, though I suspect it might have been a bit more intense than you made it sound,' said Lily, laughter in her voice.

'It was only a kiss, Lily. It didn't mean anything.'

'Sure it didn't because, hey, you have so many of them. I think it was a whole lot more than *only a kiss*, otherwise you wouldn't be so cagey about it,' Lily said as she wiped her hands on her jeans. 'It's mind-blowing that you've found yourself another McKellan. Grandad must be rolling in his grave.'

'We better get going,' said Violet, keen to change the subject.

Lily picked up the first little chest she'd looked through and tucked it under her arm. 'This little treasure is coming with me. It looks as if you and Holly are going to have to put up with me coming up for some more flying visits once work settles down a bit.'

'We'd both love that. Lily will be over the moon. I'll get Johnno's number for you and you can give him a call.'

'Thanks, that'd be great. But I'll wait until you've finished the McKellan wedding and we've got the next season's collection sorted out at work.'

* * *

Lily was just locking the front door when Violet caught sight of Flynn ambling along the footpath towards them.

'Hey Violet, good to see you,' said Flynn, stopping in front of her.

'Hi Flynn,' said Violet smiling at him. 'Oh, you remember my sister, Lily don't you?'

Flynn's eyes widened in surprise. 'Lily, wow, I mean I haven't seen you since you were a kid.'

'Hello Flynn, it's good to see you again.'

'And you,' he said, grinning madly. 'What I mean is that the town just didn't feel right without either of you here. I'm glad you're back.'

'Oh, I'm just visiting,' said Lily. 'I had to check up on my sister and niece, and we were just seeing if my inheritance still has any life in it,' she added, gesturing towards the door she'd just locked.

'Yeah, I heard your grandfather had left it to you,' said Flynn, crossing his arms and leaning on one hip.

Flynn had always had such an ease about him, thought Violet. Even when they were kids. It was as if he was perfectly comfortable in his own skin.

'It certainly was a surprise,' said Lily, brightly.

'I hope it entices you to move back to Violet Falls,' said Flynn, with that adorable lopsided grin of his.

Violet frowned. Surely he wouldn't try anything on her little sister, would he? She stared at Lily and Flynn. Was it just her over-fertile imagination or had they moved closer together?

Damn it, thought Violet, Flynn just couldn't help himself. Well, she sure as hell wasn't going to stand idly by while he seduced Lily. Better nip this in the bud before anything came of it. The man was too handsome for his own good and still had the dating habits of an alley cat.

'It's good to see you Flynn, but Lily and I have to get going. We're already late to pick up Holly,' said Violet, making her way to the car. 'We'll see you around.'

'Can't wait,' said Flynn aiming that devastating smile of his at Lily. 'I remember you as a kid, you know. You had long plaits, scraped knees and freckles across your nose.'

Lily wandered over to the car but her eyes never left his. 'Well, I'm not a kid anymore.'

'No, you're not.'

'But I still have some freckles,' said Lily, smiling and tilting her head to the side flirtatiously.

Oh my God, thought Violet, giving Lily that special sisterly look which said, *What the HELL do you think you're doing?*

'I'm so glad you and your freckles came back home, even if it's only for a visit. I'll see you around, Lily Beckett,' said Flynn before saying goodbye to the two of them and sauntering away.

'I didn't think it was possible but he's improved with age,' said Lily, standing by the open car door and watching

101

Flynn disappear down the street. 'Did you ever see such sexy perfection?'

'Oh, get in the damn car,' said Violet. 'He may be Mac's best friend but Flynn is a dangerous flirt who doesn't have a constant bone in his body. He's broken nearly every female heart in town apparently, not to mention the entire Central Goldfields area.'

'Come on, even you can't deny that Flynn's gorgeous. Besides I was just looking, and there's no harm in that,' said Lily as she slid into the car seat and put the little chest on the floor by her feet. 'No big deal. Just chill, Violet. It's not like he seduced me in the middle of the street. Hmmm, though there's an idea,' Lily added with a gleam in her eyes.

'Lily!'

Lily burst out laughing and it took what seemed like ages to get herself under control. 'That was just too easy,' she said when she finally stopped laughing. 'You should have seen your face. Oh, don't get into a flap, I'm just teasing you.'

'I told you, the man is an incorrigible wolf.'

'Yeah, but you have to admit he's a really tempting one.'

'Are you sure you don't want to stay the whole weekend?' said Violet leaning against the open door of her car.

'I'd love to but I can't,' said Lily, her face serious. 'As I said, things are really heating up at work and Pietro is busier and busier with his shoots. We have to grab some time together otherwise it's like we're sharing a flat rather than a relationship.'

'I understand,' said Violet as she got into the car.

* * *

The next morning Lily held Holly in her arms, her expression full of love. 'I've missed you so much baby girl, but I promise I'll be back as soon as I can.'

'Promise?' said Holly, drinking the milkshake between taking bites of the huge biscuit her aunt had bought her.

'Yes, I promise and next time I'll bring you a new dress, just like this beautiful one you've drawn for me,' she said, gesturing towards the drawing on the café table.

'You mean you're going to make it for me? And put some of the pretty lace you found around the neck?'

'Yep, I sure am,' said Lily giving Holly a squeeze. 'You be good for Mummy and I'll see you soon.'

Violet took Holly's hand and led her away to the car. She needed to drop her off at yet another friend's place before she headed out to McKellan's Run, and she was starting to feel nervous about meeting Celine.

'Hey, call me so I know you got home okay,' said Violet.

'God, I'll never stop being your little baby sister. I'll be fine but I'll ring anyway, alright?'

'Thanks,' said Violet.

'I wish Aunty Lily still lived with us,' Holly said with a sigh as Lily drove away. 'I miss her already.'

'I know, sweetie but think about what fun we'll have next time she comes up,' said Violet, taking Holly's hand. 'Come on let's get you over to Kylie's place and once I get back from Mac's place we can cook dinner together. What do you say?'

'Can't I come to Mac's too,' said Holly, looking up at her mother. 'I haven't seen him or Sarah or the kittens for ages.'

'Not today, but maybe I'll pick up some ice cream for after dinner.'

'Yay!' said Holly, doing her favourite 'we're having ice cream' dance in the back of the car.

Chapter 11

'Oh come on, Celine, you have to help your old man out,' said Laurie Thornton, cutting an elegant figure in a beautifully tailored suit.

Celine stood up and wandered over to the window looking out over her father's formal garden bathed in the early morning light.

'Dad, I'm doing everything I can. I've already *given* you all my savings and surely Jason's loan has shored up the business for at least the short term.'

'I truly appreciate how generous you've been, darling, but Jason's loan has only given me a tiny amount of breathing space.'

'Look, I know he's my fiancé but you can't keep hitting him up for money,' said Celine, avoiding her father's imploring expression as she wondered why, after all these years, she was *still* trying to please her father—and yet he *still* made her feel like nothing was ever quite good enough.

'Why not? He can afford it!' snapped Laurie.

'That's not the point. Don't forget he covers all of the mortgage in the house he and I live in—he's never asked me for a cent. And *he's* paying for the wedding, despite him telling his family that you're covering it,' said Celine.

'Which is why you're getting married in some god-forsaken place in the bush. Really, Celine, this wasn't how I pictured your wedding.'

'Listen, you've always encouraged my relationship with Jason. It was you who first talked about the idea of me marrying him,' said Celine.

'Well, the boy is brilliant. Everyone says he's the up-and-coming bright star in corporate law. Youngest partner at Tollingsworth's, someone at the club told me. Mind you, I always hoped you'd marry into old Toorak money.'

'Hey, Jason and I can have a really successful marriage if we put our minds to it,' said Celine. 'We both like the same things and have similar goals. Please don't let your old boy snobbery get in the way. I'm marrying Jason for myself as well as to help you.'

'Yes, yes. I know, my darling girl, and don't ever think I'm not grateful that you're thinking of me. And it's true, I've always said Jason McKellan is a good man and maybe I did encourage you to move things along, though it wasn't as if you needed much of a push.'

'Have you managed to sell any of the apartments at Noosa yet?' asked Celine.

'Some, although it's not going as quickly as I'd like. If I sell everything, including this place, I should be able to hold onto the business, but it's going to be touch and go.'

'Well, I hope you insist on a proper pre-nup next time you fall in love,' said Celine, though she felt bad saying it. Her father had been married three times since leaving Celine's mother, Susan. Celine's psychiatrist had once asked

106

if it was her fear of being cast off like all the other women in her father's life that made her so anxious to please him.

'I don't mind selling the places in Noosa. What I was hoping for was to save the business *and* this house, and the yacht, and the apartments in London and LA.'

Celine flinched at the bitterness in his voice. 'Well Dad, it's not my fault.'

Laurie paused for a moment in an attempt to regain his control. 'No, darling, it's not your fault. There were a lot of factors involved—from the divorce to the GFC to bad advice and over-extending myself. But we have to stick together on this. Haven't I always looked after you?'

'Yes, Dad.'

'And now it's time for you to help me. We can't stand by and let a business that's been in this family for generations slip through our fingers.'

'No, Dad.'

'Good, I'm glad you agree. Now, how are your wedding plans coming along?'

Celine shrugged. 'Jason's mother is overseeing it and she's hired a local wedding planner who wouldn't have the pizzazz to put a six-years-old's birthday party together.'

'Then get rid of her.'

'I can't. As I said, Mrs McKellan agreed to organise it and this woman—Violet something—is a friend of the family. Jason's stepbrother, Mac—the one I was telling you about—even rang and told me I needed to just "chill" and pick one of Violet's "awesome" designs, especially since we'd "sprung everything on them so suddenly".'

'The cheek,' said Laurie.

'I needed to keep Mac on side and since Jason's paying I didn't feel like I could push things too hard. Still, I'll be being having a word with the wedding planner when I head up there with Jase,' she said, looking at her watch.

'That's my girl.'

'Apparently she's close to the family because she and Jason were involved when they were younger. It isn't a dark secret, Mrs McKellan was very up front about it and asked me if I'd feel uncomfortable having this woman help out.'

'Darling, why on earth would you agree to such a thing?'

'Do you really think I'd feel threatened by some small-town girl? She's no one, Dad. Jason said it was just a teenage romance that ended as soon as he finished his law degree.'

'Still, I'd be careful if I was you. You don't want anything to jeopardise this wedding.'

'Jason wouldn't—'

'I'm not talking about Jason. This girl could be trouble, she could see this as an opportunity to get to Jason and his bank balance.'

'Not everyone thinks like you, Dad,' said Celine.

'I mean it. Shut her down, don't let her get the upper hand on anything. And don't leave her alone with Jason. Old feelings can flare up when people are thrown together. Just be careful and clever about this.'

'Dad,' Celine started, then paused until the silence became almost awkward. She was trying to find the right words— ones that wouldn't send her father into a rage. 'Jason has already given you a fair bit of money, even though you think it could have been more. And even though he's earning a lot, the senior partners are all required to reinvest in the business. Plus he's still got a large mortgage, so I'm not sure he'd be able—or willing —to give you much more.'

'He has to, Celine,' said Laurie. 'The entire business faces ruin if he's not able to help us out. Please make sure things work out.'

'Why can't you ask Uncle Andrew and some of your friends to help you out? I'm sure they would give you some financial assistance if you asked them.'

Laurie shook his head. 'I can't Celine, I'd be too embarrassed. I'm the one they've been coming to for answers and guidance about their business matters for the past twenty years. How would it look if they discovered I was about to lose it all.'

'But still, Uncle Andrew would . . .'

'No, Celine, I can't lose face like that—I won't. We'll keep trying to sell off more of our assets and you need to work on Jason to shell out more money.'

Celine's phone rang and she hurried over to her handbag and checked the screen. 'It's Jason,' she mouthed to her father.

'Hi, darling. Yes, I'm almost ready. Ah huh . . . Sure, I'll be waiting outside,' said Celine, then listened to his response with a genuine smile on her face. 'Bye.'

Her father gave her a questioning look.

'He's picking me up in about ten minutes and we're driving straight to McKellan's Run to catch up with his mother and brothers and meet with the wedding planner.

Apparently we're staying at his cottage tonight. I'll be back tomorrow evening.'

'Okay, well just keep in mind what I said.'

Celine walked around the desk and kissed her father on the cheek. Then, as she headed out the door, she paused and turned around. 'Don't worry, Dad. I know how much the business means to you, and I'll do whatever I can to help you.'

* * *

'You're not serious, are you?' said Celine, who was leaning against the picket fence and staring at the little white weatherboard house.

'Of course I am,' Jason said. 'There's nothing wrong with the cottage.'

'Well, I think the correct question would be—what's right with it?'

'Listen, babe, I'm not asking you to live here permanently. It's just for tonight and a few days before the wedding. I'm sure you can cope with that.'

'But it's so quiet here. It's as if we're in the middle of nowhere—what if something happens?'

'Nothing is going to happen. We've got about half an hour before we're due to meet Mac, which will give us enough time to settle in,' said Jason with a smile. 'Okay, I admit we're both used to a bit more luxury, but think of it as an adventure.'

Celine grimaced.

'Oh come on, Celine, it does have running water and a flushing loo,' said Jason as he opened the gate, took her by the hand and tugged her along the path towards the front door. 'I'll finish fixing it one day. It's just with work and everything, I've never gotten around to it.'

'I don't understand why you would bother,' said Celine.

Jason paused on the steps and looked back over the old garden, which was filled with fruit trees, shrubs and flowers. The sound of the nearby creek floated on the air along with the last swarm of bees hovering from one daisy to another.

'Because I love it. I forget just how much it means to me until I get here,' he said, unlocking the door and holding it open for Celine. 'Mum got the place ready for us, so the bed will be made and the fridge will be stocked,' he added as he followed her inside.

On the left-hand side of the one big room they entered was an open fireplace with a battered old leather couch facing it. On the right, a narrow flight of stairs led up into a loft and at the far end of the room was a kitchen. A large old-fashioned sink sat next to a wood burning stove.

Celine looked unimpressed. 'But Jason it's so . . . rustic.'

'Yeah, I suppose it is but it has everything we need.'

'Where's the rest of the house?'

Jason started to laugh but stopped when he saw the look on her face. 'The bedroom is upstairs.'

'And the bathroom?'

'It's through that door and along the back verandah to the left.'

'Do you mean we have to go outside to go to the bathroom?'

'Um, yeah.'

Celine shook her head and started to back out the door. 'I'm sorry Jason but I can't stay here.'

Jason pulled her back into a hug so she couldn't escape. 'Oh go on, Celine, give it a try, just for tonight. You never know, you just might like it.'

* * *

Violet arrived at Mac's at eleven o'clock on the dot. She squared her shoulders and made herself stand a little taller before brushing a speck of fluff off the lapel of her dark-grey suit jacket. Since she'd returned home her wardrobe had become more casual as most of the parties she planned were less formal. But today was different. Today she was seeing Jason McKellan for the first time in nearly eight years and meeting his fiancée Celine—so she wanted everything to be perfect. Today she was Violet Beckett, accomplished party planner and independent professional woman. So there she stood in her grey jacket and a pencil skirt that skimmed her knees, a crisp white shirt and her hair in a half messy up-do.

'Be calm, together and professional,' she murmured under her breath as she knocked on the door.

Mac opened the door and gave her a smile. 'Hey, you look great.'

'Thanks,' said Violet, straightening her jacket yet again. Mac moved in to kiss her but at the last instant she turned her face and he ended up kissing her on the cheek. 'Are they here yet?'

Mac frowned and stepped back. 'Nope, you'll just have to make do with my company.'

Violet felt some of the tension ease out of her shoulders. 'I'm sure I can manage that,' she said, smiling nervously.

'Well, are you going to stand out there all day or what?'

'Oh, right,' said Violet and stepped inside.

'Come on through and I'll make you a coffee,' he said as he followed her. 'No need to be nervous, sweetheart, we've got home court advantage.'

'Oh Mac, it's just . . .'

'That you haven't seen Jason since he broke it off?'

'Yep, pretty much.'

Mac didn't say anything, he just started fiddling with the coffee machine. Funny, all of a sudden there seemed to be an invisible barrier between them.

'And besides that I still have to meet Celine,' said Violet stopping herself from adding a string of colourful terms to Celine's name. 'Have you had a lot to do with her?'

Mac shook his head. 'No, I've only met her a couple of times. Not my type, that's for sure.'

'Mac, promise me you'll step in, if things get tense. I don't want to upset anyone, especially the bride but . . .'

'You get the feeling you're not going to be BFFs,' he said as he handed her a coffee.

'Thanks. Yeah, something like that.'

'I'll do my best. Anyway, it looks as if they've arrived,' said Mac looking through the window. 'Just breathe, Violet, and you'll be fine.'

Violet sat at the kitchen table and sipped her coffee while she waited for Jason and Celine to appear. After several ridiculously long minutes, she heard the front door open, muffled voices and the click of heels across the wooden floors.

When Celine walked into the kitchen she was everything Violet had imagined she'd be—shiny, polished, blonde perfection. Violet put a bright smile on her face and stood up. She was going to be nice, polite and start the meeting off on the right foot. She was the professional and Celine was her client.

'Hello Celine, I'm Violet the events planner. It's lovely to meet you,' she said, smiling and extending her hand towards Celine.

'Oh, hello, Violet,' said Celine coolly.

'Violet?'

She glanced up at the familiar voice. Jason stood in the doorway, looking almost exactly the same as the last time she'd seen him. Golden hair, golden skin and blue eyes that had once been able to see inside her.

'Hello, Jason,' she said as he walked forward and gave her a polite kiss on the cheek. For a second she allowed herself to remember how many nights she'd laid awake in bed wishing Jason was there with her, making everything alright again. Violet pushed away the memories, which were best forgotten, and stood stiff and awkward, waiting for what came next.

Jason stepped back, his smile slipping a little as he looked at her. 'It's good to see you again, Violet. You look great.'

'Thanks,' was about all she could manage. An awkward silence filled the room. Violet moved over to the table to pick up her coffee, only to realise she'd finished it. 'Um, Mac, I don't suppose I could I get a refill?'

Their eyes locked across the room. He was there, holding her up and supporting her. She gave him a smile.

'Sure thing,' said Mac and wandered over to the kitchen bench. 'Anyone else?'

Chapter 12

The only way Violet could describe the first part of her visit to McKellan's Run was frustrating. Celine had been okay until Jason had set off to catch up with old friends, and Mac left saying he needed to check on some stock. After they disappeared Celine had basically questioned nearly every one of her decisions. Violet had tried hard to be accommodating, explaining that the short time-frame had made pulling the wedding together harder than normal, though she'd managed to source nearly everything Celine had requested. But whatever she said seemed to fall on deaf ears. Her fuse had got shorter by the minute.

'Well, I don't see why I can't have the entire outside area and the great room filled with latte-coloured roses?'

'Because there's not enough time to order that number of flowers. And what you asked for when I suggested white camellias was "lots of cream roses".'

'I didn't want *cream* roses I wanted latte-coloured ones.'

When Violet fired up her tablet and pulled up the email exchange between them where Celine had asked for cream roses, Celine had just brushed her off. 'I have to say, Violet, I'm more than disappointed. Sarah assured me you could handle this but I'm wondering if you might be in a bit over your head,' she said.

Stunned at Celine's rudeness, Violet opened her mouth to say something, but had difficulty formulating something intelligible. Gathering herself, she'd laid out the reasoning behind some of the on-the-spot decisions she'd had to make in Melbourne, but again Celine questioned all the choices she'd made. It was while she was doing this that Mac appeared in the kitchen and sat down next to Violet, laying his hand on her leg beneath the table and giving it a reassuring squeeze.

The next time Celine started patronising Violet, Mac said, 'That's enough, Celine. Violet was gracious enough to agree to help Mum out with the wedding. You gave her so little time—just over four weeks. And I didn't know it back then but I've since learnt that most weddings take a hell of a lot longer than you gave Mum to plan. We've all pulled in favours to arrange this because you and Jason wanted to be married here at McKellan's Run. Violet is organising everything from the seating and music to the decorations, and all the designs she's shown me in response to your feedback have looked amazing. Dan's taking care of the food as a gift. As far as I can see, the only thing you have to do is pick out your dress.'

'Oh Mac, don't be cross. Every girl wants their day to be perfect,' said Celine, smiling at him coquettishly.

'Sure, well if you think you can do better than Violet maybe you should take everything over,' he said with stony politeness.

'I'm sorry, Mac,' said Celine looking contrite. 'I guess I got a bit carried away.'

After the conversation resumed with Mac there, Celine dropped her outright rudeness to Violet, replacing it with a more passive-aggressive approach. She'd apologised to Mac when he called her on some of the things she said, but she barely acknowledged it when Violet explained a choice she'd made. She also tried the whole *I'm-too-pretty-and-special-for-you-to-be-angry-at-me* routine with Mac, which Violet found sickening. Did other men really fall for this sort of shit, Violet wondered. Surely not?

Mac caught Violet's eye at a particularly tense moment when she felt like she was just about to lose it with Celine and gave her leg another squeeze. Her skin warmed under the heat of his hand.

When Jason finally returned, Mac had stared at him with barely concealed anger and said, 'What I don't understand is why you're having to do everything in such a rush.'

Before Jason could answer, Celine cut in, 'We're in love, Mac. We just don't want to wait. Surely you understand? It was love at first sight and we can't get enough of each other. Jason is my total soul mate,' she gushed, reaching over and covering Jason's hand with hers.

For the first time since meeting her, Violet sat back and really considered Celine dispassionately. Everything she'd just said about her relationship with Jason didn't really ring true. It was as if underneath Celine's cool exterior there was an eagerness to impress Jason that didn't speak of any type of soul mate relationship. There even seemed to be a nervousness in the way she looked at him.

Violet's thoughts about this were cut short by the arrival of Sarah, who breezed into the kitchen and headed straight for Jason giving him a warm hug and a kiss.

'I've missed you,' she said with a broad smile as she mussed his hair just like she had when he was a little boy.

'Easy there, Mum,' said Jason, grinning as he picked her up and gave her a twirl.

Sarah let out a yelp of surprise before dissolving into laughter. 'Ah, put me down!' she said before going over to Celine and giving her a peck on the cheek. 'Hello dear, you look lovely—as always.'

'Thank you, Mrs McKellan,' said Celine with a tight smile. Again, Violet sensed a nervousness in Celine that she didn't really understand.

Sarah rounded the table, bent down and gave Mac a hug from behind.

'You're in a good mood,' Mac said with a grin.

'Of course I am, I have two of my handsome sons in the one room,' she replied, releasing Mac and wrapping her arm around Violet. 'Everything under control, sweetie?'

Violet nodded. 'Sure is.'

'Good,' said Sarah.

Just then Dan walked in to the kitchen, saying, 'I think you meant three handsome sons, Mum.'

Violet smiled to see Dan after so many years. He was a shade shorter than Mac, with brown hair and the same greenish-hazel eyes as his big brother.

'Hey, long time no see,' he said to Jason before he nodded to Celine. 'Nice to see you, Celine.'

'Hi Dan, it's great to see you too. Thanks so much for agreeing to do the food for us. We really appreciate it,' she gushed. 'I don't suppose you brought the menus with you?' she asked. 'I can't wait to see them.'

'I did bring them with me and we can go over them in a minute,' he said before wandering over and giving Violet a kiss. 'Hey Violet. We've all missed you. I'm so glad that you and your daughter have moved back.'

Violet found herself almost tearing up when he said that. All the McKellans, even Jason, had made her feel as if she belonged today, which was incredibly nice and comforting.

'Thanks Dan, it's good to be back,' Violet replied. And despite how horrible it had been with Celine thus far, Violet realised she really meant it. Thanks to Mac and Holly's friends and their mums and teachers, she felt like she was totally in the right place to be bringing up Holly and continuing on in her life.

Violet went to turn back to Mac but as her eyes swept across the room she caught Jason staring at her intently. He had a strange expression on his face, almost as if he was seeing her for the first time. It made her uncomfortable and wary. She could feel her heart beating as she quickly looked away.

* * *

The arrival of Dan and his mum had completely changed the atmosphere, thought Mac. For one thing, Violet looked

120

much calmer. God, she was so damn hot in that suit it took all of his willpower to keep his hands off her. With her hair swept up, the soft skin of her neck peeped out from under her collar. She was soft and beautiful and totally irresistible. Tendrils of hair brushed against her shoulders and it was all he could do to stop himself from kissing her. His mouth went dry and his cock hardened just at the sight of her. Hell, he had it bad.

When Jason and Celine had arrived Mac had purposely stayed outside talking with them just to give himself a few minutes to recover. He'd caught the surprise on Jason's face when he saw Violet in the kitchen.

And though Violet had seemed fine with Jason—which was a huge relief to Mac—she'd looked so damned vulnerable when Celine started talking about the wedding with her. Still, even he was shocked when he came back and eavesdropped on the two of them. Every time Violet opened her mouth Celine had shot her down.

Maybe Celine was making Violet pay for ever going out with Jason. It was the only explanation he could come up with—Celine was just a totally mean-spirited bitch. He'd never really taken to her but the couple of times he'd met her she'd been pleasant enough. But she was clearly trying to upset Violet and finally Mac had had enough and walked back into the kitchen.

The good thing was that Violet had held her own against Celine, pointing out the difficulties and expense of sourcing some of Celine's suggestions at such late notice.

But the best thing of all for Mac was seeing Violet look so genuine when she'd told Dan it was good to be back.

She was just so beautiful and strong, he thought. He loved the way she doted on Holly and encouraged her in all her passions. In fact he loved the way she dealt with people full stop. She was warm and curious and had integrity and courage. And she was also sexy as hell.

Basically, Violet Beckett was going to be the death of him if they didn't get together this time.

Chapter 13

'I mean it. Thanks for what you said in there,' said Violet, sliding into the driver's seat.

Mac leaned in smiling, his arms draped over the top of the door. 'It was nothing,' he said with a shrug. 'As I said, Celine can be a handful and I suspect she's a bit jealous of you.'

'Me! God Mac, what's there to be jealous of?' said Violet, laughing at the idea. 'She's the one wearing designer clothes, not me. Did you see those shoes she was wearing?'

'Don't sell yourself short, Violet,' said Mac.

'Yeah, because I'm just *sooo* intimidating.' Violet gave him her best fierce look.

'Now you just look crazy,' he said, laughing and shaking his head. 'You know what I'm saying.'

'Yes, I do. I can understand she'd be wary of me because of Jase, but he and I were over a long time ago.'

'I know.'

'It's just that she can be so brutal.'

'Yeah, she can be a total bitch.'

'Well, I wasn't going to say it but yes she can,' Violet said with a grin. 'Anyway, I better go. I've got to pick up Holly. Bye.'

'Okay, drive safely. See you later,' said Mac, stepping back and shutting the door.

After giving Mac a final wave, Violet drove off. She had plenty of time to get to Holly, she just wanted to get the hell out of there. A headache was beginning to build and all she wanted to do was sit quietly by herself for a few minutes. She needed to think. Mac had stood up and defended her today. She wasn't used to that. It made her feel . . . What? Warm, protected, vulnerable.

Violet bit her bottom lip. Man, she was definitely in trouble.

Mac watched Violet's car disappear into the distance. He was glad she'd come today, and held her own with Celine, even if it had been difficult for her.

As he turned to go back inside the front door banged open and Jason hurried out.

'Hey,' said Mac. 'Are you going somewhere?'

Jason looked down at his keys and jingled them in his hand. 'Um, yeah, I just needed to pick a couple of things up at the store. We were in a hurry when we left this morning and I forgot to grab them. I, um, won't be long.'

'Alright, I'll see you in a bit,' said Mac, though he knew Jason was hiding something because of the way he didn't meet his eyes.

'Yep,' Jason said with a curt nod before he strode towards his silver Merc.

Mac headed back inside, wondering what he was up to.

***

124

Violet was halfway up the new front steps with Holly when a car turned into her driveway. She looked over her shoulder and froze as Jason McKellan pulled up. What the hell was he doing here?

'Who is that, Mummy?' Holly asked.

Wow, how exactly should she answer that? Violet swallowed hard before smiling down at her daughter. 'That's someone I used to know. Actually, he's Mac's brother.'

'Oh, he doesn't look like Mac. He's got blond hair,' said Holly with a frown. 'Why is he here?'

'I don't know, honey.' Violet watched as Jason got out of the car and walked towards them, his eyes fixed on Holly. Violet's stomach tightened in nervous knots. She cleared her throat and winced at the shaky sound of her voice, 'Jason, what are you doing here?'

'I . . . I don't really know. I just felt I had to come. Sorry, I suppose it was wrong,' he answered, still not taking his gaze off Holly. 'But I had to come and see for myself.'

'Jason, this is Holly,' said Violet, suddenly feeling a bit light-headed and leaning back on the handrail for support. 'Holly, this is Jason, Mac's brother.'

'Hello, Holly. It's nice to meet you,' said Jason.

'Hi,' said Holly, clearly sensing an uneasy undercurrent between this man and her mother. 'Mummy, are you okay?' she asked, taking Violet's hand.

Her words made Jason start and immediately his frown disappeared. 'I'm sorry, Holly. I didn't mean to frighten you or your mum,' he said softly.

'Are you cross with Mummy?' asked Holly.

'No,' said Jason, and shook his head.

Violet bent down and whispered, 'Holly, there's nothing to worry about. Everything is fine.'

Holly nodded but her gaze was locked on Jason. 'Mummy, can I go inside now?'

'Sure, why don't you put your bag in your room? Then you could watch some cartoons if you want,' Violet said as she climbed up the final step and unlocked the front door. 'I won't be a moment, Jason.'

Holly disappeared inside and Violet tried to regulate her heartbeat before she turned back to Jason.

'She's beautiful, Violet, she really is,' Jason said quietly.

'Yes, I know.'

An awkward silence fell between them. Jason's face appeared pale and he opened his mouth as if to speak but then closed it again.

'Why are you here, Jason?'

'She looks like you, even down to the hair and the shape of your mouth.'

'Yes, I know.'

'But she has my eyes, doesn't she?'

Violet stared back at him, her face stony. 'You know the answer to that.'

'But I thought you were going to—'

'No, you assumed I would. You have no business being here, Jason. You made your decision a long time ago,' said Violet, crossing her arms. 'So, unless you have a question or request about your wedding, I'd appreciate it if you'd leave.'

'I'm sorry, Violet. You're right. I had no right to come. It's just, um, it doesn't matter. I'd better go.'

'Yes, you should,' said Violet going inside and shutting the door emphatically behind her.

* * *

Violet wasn't sure who was covered with more flour, Holly or herself. Holly had decided they should have cheese pastries for dinner, which had seemed a good idea until she'd accidentally dropped the bag of flour. The result was that both of them now looked like extras from a ghost movie.

Ignoring the mess, Holly was now busy rolling out the pastry on the kitchen table.

'Is that good, Mummy?' she asked.

'Fantastic. Now we just have to fill them,' replied Violet, quickly dividing the pastry into squares before setting a couple of bowls in front of her daughter—one filled with a ricotta and spinach mixture, the other with water.

'Right, now all you have to do is pop a couple of spoonfuls into each square, wet the edges and then fold them into a triangle. See, just like this,' said Violet as she demonstrated what to do. 'Got it?' she asked Holly.

'Yep, I've got it,' replied Holly, reaching for the big bowl.

Violet left Holly to her own devices and went to get the baking trays. What she really needed was a little time to try and make sense of her day. But a few minutes of quiet reflection wasn't going to happen anytime soon, not with a budding chef and a flour-bombed kitchen to deal with. After grabbing the trays she headed back to the table.

'So, how's it going?' she asked.

'Great,' Holly said with a grin. 'I've made two of them.'

'Good job,' said Violet as she started to make a pastry.

Soon each of the little triangles were sitting in two neat rows on the trays. Holly helped her carry one of the trays over to the oven.

'They'll take a little while to cook,' said Violet as she slid them into the oven and then glanced at her flour-covered daughter. 'Why don't you go and get cleaned up?'

'Okay,' Holly said with a nod and wandered off towards the bathroom.

Violet doused a sponge under the tap to clean things up before the flour made its way through the house, her mind on Jason.

She should have known he would visit, whether out of curiosity or something deeper, Jason had wanted to meet his daughter.

Over the years she'd convinced herself he would never want anything to do with Holly. Having rejected his unborn child eight years ago, Violet had just assumed he wouldn't want to be part of her life now. But maybe she'd been wrong, she thought. She'd kept her secret to protect Holly, she hadn't wanted to reveal that her father hadn't wanted her. That sort of rejection could cast a long shadow, one that Holly might have carried all her life, and Violet had been determined not to let it happen.

But now there was a chance that Jason had changed his mind. God, he was always so bloody self-centred. He never cared how his actions affected people, just as long as he got what he wanted. If Jason wanted some sort of relationship with Holly, she shouldn't stand in his way but the implications would be far-reaching.

How do you tell your daughter that the father she didn't even know she had now wanted to see her? And if they forged some sort of relationship, would Jason step up and go the distance? Would he be a presence in her life or would he allow his work to be the number one priority? For a child, being forgotten was almost as bad as not being wanted in the first place.

Violet scrubbed the last traces of sticky flour off the table and washed the sponge out.

And how would Holly react? Would she blame Violet for not telling her the truth? Would their relationship change with Jason's arrival? And what impact would this have on all of them—Holly, Mac, Sarah and Jason?

Violet yanked open the fridge door and took out the makings of a salad. She had the return of a headache with all the questions and scenarios that swirled in her mind. Why did everything have to be so difficult?

And while she was on the subject of difficult, what the hell was up with Celine? There was something about her that didn't add up. She seemed to have an undercurrent of tension or maybe even desperation about her. That, and the obvious fact that she hated Violet's guts.

She'd met people like Celine before, back when she was working in the Red String restaurant. It had been a pretty good place to work, except for one odious manager. He'd had a roving eye when it came to the waitresses and he acted as if they were part of his own personal smorgasbord. Eventually, Violet felt she had to leave because of him. The restaurant, which had been very swanky, had been on Exhibition Street up towards Parliament. Most of her customers there had been really nice but there'd been a small group, a particular type that Violet could pick a mile away.

They were young professionals with high-powered jobs, a trust fund and something to prove. Violet had nothing against rich people, but this lot were self-absorbed, condescending and treated Violet and the other staff as if they were totally beneath them.

Yeah, Violet knew Celine's type well enough. It was disappointing that Jason would want to be with someone like that. Not that Violet wanted him back. There were too many years and hurts between them to ever want to revisit their relationship. Seeing him today had cemented that. But still it was sad to think that he would be part of that shallow, money-driven world when he could have been so much more.

'Hey, Mummy, look, I'm all clean,' Holly called out from the doorway as she held up her hands for inspection.

'Well done you,' said Violet. 'So do you want to help me make the salad?'

'Sure thing,' Holly said and skipped over to the table. 'Can we put pineapple in it?'

'Whatever you want, sweetie,' said Violet. 'Whatever you want.'

***

'You went to Violet's, didn't you?' Mac demanded in an undertone as Jason walked in the kitchen. He didn't want to disturb the others who were all out in the garden looking at the various places where the ceremony could take place.

Jason gave him a dirty look. 'What, are you my mother?'

'Just answer the question. I saw that weird look you gave Violet and then you hustled out of here as soon as she left. It was pretty obvious where you were going.'

'So what? It's none of your business,' snapped Jason. 'What's between Violet and me was never any of your business. So just back off.'

'I knew it. Son of a—'

'Fuck off, Mac. Just leave it.'

'What are you playing at, you bastard?' demanded Mac, putting his arm across the doorway.

'I don't know what you're talking about!' said Jason, trying to push past Mac, who didn't budge. 'Look, this isn't the time to get into this. I've got more important things on my mind than Violet and your jealousy. Work's crazy, money's tight, the wedding's coming up. Jesus.'

'Just tell me. Why did you go to Violet's?'

Jason let out an exasperated sigh. 'I just dropped in to see an old friend for a few minutes. Nothing more.'

'Just leave her the hell alone,' said Mac, anger rising inside of him despite his attempt to rein it in. There was no use creating even more tension for Violet ahead of the wedding.

'Why? What's it to you?' asked Jason.

'Everything.'

'I knew it. I knew you had something for her the moment I walked in the kitchen.'

'Shut up, Jason. I mean it. Stay away from Violet. You've messed with her enough.'

'Or what? If I want to see—'

'You made your choice all those years ago, and now you've got Celine,' said Mac, his arms folded across his chest.

Jason was silent as he turned and stalked away.

Chapter 14

Violet had just sunk into the couch and closed her eyes as her phone rang. With a sigh she dug into her jeans pocket and pulled it out. She checked the screen and saw Mac's name flash up.

'Hi, Mac.'

'Hey, Violet. I just wanted to check that everything was alright.'

'Thanks. All good. I've been sitting here thinking that underneath all that bluster of Celine's there's fear and anxiety,' she said, not wanting to mention Jason's visit.

He was silent for a moment. 'Well, she's got no right to take it out on you, whatever it is she feels.'

Relief flooded through Violet. 'Well, anyway, I feel like the worst is over now.'

'Would you like me to come over?'

Damn, kissing him had made everything more complicated, thought Violet. 'I was planning to have an early night.'

'Okay.'

Even from that single word she sensed his whole tone had changed. She was so confused. One minute she convinced herself that staying away from Mac was the best course of action for her and Holly. But then she couldn't deny the way he made her feel. The way Mac had kissed her made her quiver with long-forgotten passion. It was as if he was waking her up from a long, cold and lonely sleep. Part of her didn't want to let go. Her head told her to be sensible, but her heart was a whole other matter.

'I'm sorry, Mac. I'll see you tomorrow?'

'Yeah, have a good night and get some sleep,' he replied in a lighter tone and Violet smiled in relief. No matter what she decided to do about this growing thing between them, she never wanted to hurt Mac. He was a good friend and she never wanted to jeopardise that.

'Thanks for understanding.'

'No worries. Um, Violet, nothing else happened to upset you today did it?'

'Nothing I couldn't handle.'

'Alright then, I'll see you tomorrow,' said Mac.

'Night, Mac, and thanks for checking up on me.'

Violet flicked off her phone and stared unseeing ahead. She was confused and yes, even scared of the feeling Mac stirred within her. For years after Jason broke it off with her and she had Holly, she'd closed herself off from the whole dating/couple's world and concentrated on being the best mother, sister and party planner there was. It had been simple and uncomplicated. She never let any other man get too close so she'd never had to worry about getting her heart broken and trampled on again.

Was she frightened? You betcha. Terrified was a better word because deep down she was certain she couldn't survive again the sort of heartache she'd experienced with Jason.

Jason had turned her into a hollowed-out shell of the girl she once was. Whereas Mac, well, he was so gentle and kind and gorgeous and the thought of him tantalised her with ideas of love and a shared future; which were things Violet had decided long ago were not for her anymore.

He made her think dangerous thoughts and he made her body burn.

Damn it! This was all her fault. She should never have kissed him!

***

Jason walked up the narrow stairs of the cottage and slipped quietly into the loft. Celine was flipping through a bridal magazine by the window and glanced up as he appeared in the doorway.

'Hey, I've been wondering where you'd got to,' said Celine, smiling. 'Your mum gave me a lift back. We had a cup of tea and a chat, I think we're getting on alright together. Which is just as well as I didn't think she liked me when we first met.'

'Mum's always liked you, Celine. I don't know where you got that other crazy idea from. Um, listen we have to talk,' he said quietly. 'I've discovered something and I think you should know because it affects both of us.'

'God, that sounds ominous!' said Celine, putting the magazine down and staring at Jason. 'Well, go on, what's the problem?'

'I've just found out that Violet's daughter, Holly . . . Well, she's mine.'

'What do you mean?' said Celine, a look of shock and disbelief on her face.

'Just that. It turns out I'm her father,' said Jason, looking down at his hands. 'Violet got pregnant the year after she finished school and I was in my last year at uni. She'd been saving up to come to Melbourne but after I got that clerkship in my final year of law school I just realised it wasn't going to work. I'd been meaning to break it off with her for months when she told me she was pregnant. I asked her to have an abortion and I thought she had. She cut off all contact after that last time we saw each other, and even when I got in touch with her grandfather's solicitor to try and get some money to her—after I'd heard she and her younger sister, Lily, had left home—there was still no response.'

'And what, you're only deciding to tell me this now?'

'Like I said, I've only just found out,' said Jason, crossing the room and taking Celine in his arms.

'Seriously, you expect me to believe that?' she said, brushing his arms away.

'It's the truth, Celine,' said Jason walking away from her and leaning against the window. 'I suppose I should have put it together, I mean . . .'

'*What do* you mean?' demanded Celine. 'So now I bet she's trying to get money out of you. Well, we aren't going to let her get away with that.'

'Oh for fuck's sake, Celine. Violet's not after money. She's not like that,' said Jason, running a hand through his hair and looking at Celine with frustration. 'Some people just aren't that money-hungry.'

'Don't you dare lecture me,' said Celine. 'You know I do everything to support Dad and the family business.'

'Sorry,' said Jason. 'I'm just shocked I guess, though maybe I just subconsciously blocked out the possibility she'd gone ahead with the pregnancy. I was working my butt off trying to get ahead in the firm, you know what it's like. All the young mergers and acquisitions lawyers were doing eighteen-hour days. But still, looking back, I could have looked harder for her if I'd really wanted to.'

Celine sat down on the edge of the bed. 'So if it's not money, what does she want?'

'Nothing. That's it. She doesn't want a damn thing.'

'Right . . .' said Celine, though she sounded like she didn't really believe it.

'She doesn't,' Jason insisted. 'And she doesn't want me to have a relationship with Holly either. She said I made my decision years ago and that's fine, I'm not obligated in any way. She basically said that it was her who chose to continue with the pregnancy and Holly has got nothing to do with me.'

'God, Jase, you're so naive,' said Celine, her voice taut as she thought about what her father had said. 'She's playing you. Of course she wants something! It's either got to be money or you. Why else would she have agreed to get involved with planning our wedding?'

Jason shook his head. 'She genuinely doesn't expect anything from me. I ended it, remember? She told me she was pregnant and I turned her away and asked if she'd have an abortion. No, Violet wouldn't expect it. She really isn't that kind of person. She must have been as strong as hell to be able to support Lily and Holly when Holly was only a baby.'

'Oh my God! You're still in love with her!' said Celine, sounding panicky.

'Don't be ridiculous, Celine. I haven't thought about Violet in years. It's just now, with hindsight, I can see I should have handled the whole thing better, and at least checked she was okay. If I had, I'd have known about Holly.'

'And you would have married her because it was the honourable thing to do,' Celine bit back.

'No, I wouldn't have. I told you, even before she told me she was pregnant I knew we didn't have a future together. Still, if I'd known she'd gone ahead and had the baby I'd have helped out and at least seen to it that Holly had everything she needed,' said Jason.

For the next hour or so they fell into an uncomfortable silence, both caught up in their own thoughts and fears. Jason finally tried to make peace with Celine, who was jittery about the wedding and uneasy about Violet. He could understand her feelings about Violet, given that the news of her daughter had just been sprung on her.

Unfortunately Celine felt very nervous about spending the night in the cottage. She disliked the idea of going outside to the bathroom and had insisted that Jason waited for her near the door with a torch. She screamed when a huntsman spider scuttled its way over the bedroom ceiling and jumped at every sound—from a branch scratching against the kitchen window, to a log popping in the fire, to the possum on the roof. The upshot was that Celine hardly slept at all and neither did he. So when she pleaded that they not stay in the cabin before the wedding he'd reluctantly agreed and promised to ring Mac and ask if they could stay at the main house.

* * *

Violet and Sarah sat in the corner booth of the Hummingbird Café. The busy lunchtime crowd had come and gone. Violet had noticed that her presence there with Sarah had drawn a few curious looks, but she was used to people's curiosity by now.

If gossip was an Olympic sport, she was sure several residents of Violet Falls would take the gold and silver. Hell, probably the bronze as well. No doubt by the end of the day there would be some interesting stories about her circulating the town.

'Okay, so now we've had a nice lunch and most of the logistics of the wedding are out of the way,' said Sarah, 'what do you really think of Celine?'

'She's exactly the right type of girl for Jason,' Violet said carefully.

'That's what I always liked about you, darling. You were always so sweet.'

'I'm not sweet. I can be as nasty and mean-spirited as the next person,' said Violet, adding, 'Celine is materialistic, difficult, demanding and blunt.'

Sarah sank back against the chair. 'Unfortunately, you're right. I've tried to get to know her but it's as if there's a brick wall in the way. I used to think it was my fault, but I've really tried to make her welcome.'

'Don't blame yourself. Maybe Celine just needs some more time before she fits in.'

'Hmmm, perhaps. I'm sorry she's been so difficult with you.'

'Ah well, weddings can send some brides a little crazy.'

'Yes, but Celine has been *very* demanding.'

'She has great taste in shoes, you have to give her that,' said Violet, sipping from her coffee.

'I suppose she does,' said Sarah.

'And I suppose what really matters is that Jason is happy.'

'Yes, but that's just it, Violet. Maybe I'm going to turn into the mother-in-law from hell, but I can't shake the feeling there's something not quite right.'

'Like what?'

'I'm not sure but there doesn't seem to be a spark between them. They're meant to be happy and in love but it all seems a bit forced, or at least on Jason's part anyway. I don't know. Maybe I'm imagining it. I know he's always busy at work, and he has all the pressure of being a partner and keeping the big clients coming in. And even though he earns such crazy money, I know his mortgage is enormous. But still, he just doesn't act like someone who's desperately in love and totally mad about his fiancée,' said Sarah.

'All couples are different,' said Violet.

'Maybe,' Sarah said with a shrug. 'All I know is that from the time I met Mac's father, we couldn't keep our hands off each other. I just hope Jason isn't making a mistake.'

Chapter 15

Violet was tempted to let her imagination wander. It was all too easy for her to imagine what a life with Mac could be like. It was silly and she knew she shouldn't do it. To give into daydreaming was carving out a chink in the defences she'd created around her. Some say that to dream is to aspire to how you want your life to be. For Violet, it was setting yourself up to be disappointed and fail.

She hadn't allowed herself to daydream about loving another man in years, not since Holly was born.

She needed to keep her mind from tripping away and heading down the forbidden path which was paved with all her hidden hopes and dreams. How good it felt when Mac had held her, kissed her. How her heart lifted like a balloon when she saw Holly and Mac laughing together. Thinking about what it would be like to wake up next to Mac every morning for the rest of her life.

It was just stupid to let herself be carried away. It was time to face the realities. Like how exactly would Mac respond when he found out Holly was actually Jason's daughter? How could they move past that? Surely, Holly would be a constant reminder to Mac that Violet had once been in love with his brother. Wouldn't it hurt him? Wouldn't that be a blow to his pride?

Yet something deep inside her knew she was selling Mac short. Hadn't he proved to her he was dependable—someone she could count on, if only she allowed herself to do so? If Mac made up his mind to pursue or promise something, he'd follow through. It was in his DNA, it was just who he was. But still, raising your niece as your daughter, wouldn't that be too much to ask?

Violet frowned and ran her hand through her hair.

Of course there was another side to this whole damn thing and one that could be even more problematic. Holly was already attached to Mac. Violet hoped that one day she, Mac and Holly could have a life together. But what happened if it all went pear-shaped? What would happen if even after giving it their best shot, they couldn't make a go of it? There was a very real chance that not only could Violet get her heart broken again but that her daughter would be affected, and that terrified her most of all.

She needed to sit down with him and have a talk. She needed to know exactly how he felt about her, and what he'd think about Holly being in his life. At the moment they appeared to get on well but Violet needed to be sure.

She walked over to the window and looked out at the garden. The sun was beginning to set and cast a pinkish glow over the trees and shrubs. She knew Mac was finding her responses difficult to read. She'd pulled him close and then backed off and that wasn't fair to him. She had to make up her mind. If there was any chance of building a solid relationship with him, she had to get this stuff all sorted out.

* * *

The problem about being back in town was Violet had to deal with the ghosts. Some of the memories were pleasant but some just snuck up and bowled her over with their viciousness. Ever since she'd stepped foot through the front door of her new, old house she'd been having to deal with a score of memories she'd rather forget. Most of them centred round her grandfather.

Her thoughts danced away from her, she tried to rein them in but they twirled down a road she never wanted to walk down again.

Her grandfather had been a disappointed, sad and bitter man. The sadness Violet could understand because she felt the same hard immovable lump of hurt and pain deep inside her, having lost her parents in a car crash that also robbed her grandparents of their only child—Lily and Violet's father.

Until that time Lily and Violet had enjoyed a wonderfully happy life in Melbourne. After their parents' death, Violet had tried to be strong for Lily's sake, when they were moved to live with their grandparents in Violet Falls. Grandma Stella had been the buffer between the girls and Silas and for the first couple of years, life was bearable. However, after their grandmother's health started to fade, their grandfather went into his rants more often.

'We used to own this whole valley, did you know that?' he'd say, time after time. 'The Becketts were the most successful farmers in the area and Sunrise Reach was the richest spread.

'It all started when a young Robert Beckett arrived from England. He came from a small village right up near the Scottish border . . .'

It was pointless for Violet to protest as he droned on.

'But our fortune changed when your great-great-grandmother, Violet Beckett, was drowned in the falls. She was swept away and all the family luck went with her.'

'They never found her body. Might she have just run away?'

'No, she perished in the fast-moving waters. There had been a lot of rain and the river was swollen, she wouldn't have had a chance,' he said, before adding, 'it was all the McKellans' fault. Bit by bit they stole, bought and tricked us out of our land until there was nothing left. They have brought ruin onto us and one day they will pay.'

Violet remained silent. It was useless to point out it had actually been a Beckett ancestor who had lost almost half the land in an ill-fated poker game. Or that her great-great-grandfather was more interested in the bottle and had a knack of investing in dodgy get-rich-quick schemes that had taken the rest.

'I swear to you, Violet, the McKellans will never take anything else of ours again. They may own the town but it will be a cold day in hell before any of them step foot in this house. I know those McKellan kids go to your school but you're to stay away from them! Do you hear me?'

It had come as a surprise when Violet actually met the McKellan boys. From all the stories her grandfather had told her she'd expected they'd be monsters. Instead they were two of the most sigh-worthy boys she'd ever seen.

'Did you hear me, Violet? Promise me you'll stay away from those boys.'

'Yes, Grandad. I promise.'

Violet got up and walked over to the window, rolling her shoulders to try and ease their tightness as she tried to break free of the emotions the memories evoked. She felt just a little bit guilty. Perhaps deep down she really was a bad person after all. She'd always tried to meet her obligations and keep her word, but she'd defied the promise her grandfather had extracted from her when she was sixteen at the kitchen table.

She'd never been able to stay away from the McKellan boys—not then and not now.

* * *

The sky was only beginning to lighten as Mac walked into the courtyard with a mug of coffee in hand. He suppressed a shiver as the chilled air still held a touch of frost. The cold pinpricked his face and made its way under his shirt collar and around the back of his neck. He rearranged his jacket and pulled it a little closer before taking a gulp of the

146

hot coffee to ward it off. In the distance the first chorus of birdsong began to fill the surrounding hills.

Mac had been reliving kissing Violet over and over again in his brain. It was an image he couldn't let go of. He closed his eyes for a second and recalled the feel of her soft body as she pressed against him. For an instant he almost caught her flowery scent and not only how she'd returned his kiss but how she'd plundered his mouth.

She'd wanted him just as badly as he wanted her.

His first instinct was to go and sweep her off her feet and carry her to the nearest church or registry office and marry her. Oh, he wanted her, and wanted her to be his wife. But he didn't want to spook her. As much as he wanted to stampede ahead, with all that had happened in the last month he knew Violet needed some time.

And then there was Holly.

Mac knew now that Holly was Jason's child but he hadn't broached the subject with Violet yet. He was hoping she'd tell him what exactly had gone on all those years ago but so far, she'd remained silent.

He wandered through to the small wrought-iron gate that led to the rose garden. The first rays of sun were falling from the pink-tinged sky, lighting up the flowers. A smile tugged at the corners of Mac's mouth as he saw the beauty around him. He could almost imagine Holly running between the rose bushes wearing her colourful fairy wings.

When it all came down to it, Jason had turned his back on Violet, and Mac wanted her and Holly more than anything. He wanted to love them, protect them and make a family.

147

As far as he was concerned as soon as he could get Violet to agree to be his wife, from that moment on Holly would be his daughter.

He didn't know how Jason would feel about it but then he didn't really care. Jason had already had his chance and he'd screwed it up big time.

Besides, for Mac it was more than just putting an old wrong to right. He needed Violet and Holly to make him feel whole.

Chapter 16

Violet walked into the great room, pulling her tablet and tape measure out of her bag. She didn't have much time but she wanted to check her measurements to make sure all the tables would fit into her floor plan. She walked over to a small table partially hidden by a large ornamental screen and had just dumped her handbag on it when a voice drifted through the house.

'Hi, Dad . . . Yes, Dad . . . Yes, we're still at McKellan's Run . . . I know, Dad, I said I know how important it is,' she heard Celine say.

Celine was back and staying at the Run until the wedding. After only one night she had refused to ever stay again at Jason's cabin. Apparently between the wildlife, the rustic conditions and the possibility of her and Jason being murdered by some psychotic hillbilly (Mac's words) she had begged to stay somewhere more civilized.

Violet stepped closer to the embroidered silk screen, not knowing what to do. Should she make her presence known or just hide until Celine had left?

'Don't worry; I think I've come across a way to get the funds you need.'

Violet frowned.

Celine's heels clicked across the floor closer to the entrance. Violet hunkered down behind the screen.

'I have to think of the best way to spin it and use it to our advantage,' Celine said as she opened the door and walked out into the courtyard. 'I've had this information drop into my lap. I'm sure I could at least get a little leverage out of it . . . Um . . . Yes . . . It's sound. So, have you managed to sell the Noosa flats? Oh . . . okay, well keep me posted.'

Violet waited until Celine's voice became fainter as she walked outside into the garden before she stepped out from behind the screen.

What the hell was that all about? Celine was obviously up to something but what could it be?

***

Violet placed a bowl of cereal in front of Holly and dropped a quick kiss on the top of her head.

'There you go.'

'Thanks, Mummy.'

Violet checked her watch. 'We're going to have to hurry, love.'

'Mummy . . .'

Violet rounded the kitchen bench and grabbed her coffee. 'Yes, sweetheart?'

'Can Mac be my daddy?'

Violet spluttered her mouthful of coffee. Where the hell

had that come from? Picking up the nearest tea towel she dabbed at her indigo blue cardigan.

'Why would you say that, Holly?'

Holly shrugged her shoulders and stared into her cereal bowl. 'I don't know. It's just, well, he really, really likes you, I can tell . . .'

Violet walked over to the table and sat down. She'd have preferred not to have a conversation like this at 8.15 a.m. just before she had to head out to McKellan's Run.

'Come on, Holly. Tell me.' she said, smiling.

'Amber and Kylie were talking about their daddies. And they asked me about mine.'

'And what did you say?'

Holly picked up her juice and had a sip. 'I said that I didn't have one.'

'Ah.'

'Amber and Kylie said I should get one. And I thought Mac would be good because he's nice and I like him, and he's funny,' said Holly as she scooped up a spoonful of cornflakes.

'Anything else?' asked Violet.

'Well, he does have kittens,' Holly answered with a grin.

***

Mac came through the front door as soon as Violet pulled up at the house and walked over to see them. Holly immediately asked if she could go and see the kittens and led them both towards the shed, skipping along the path and doing a twirl by the open door. 'Come on, Mummy!' she called.

'Alright, we're coming as fast as we can, Holly,' Violet said with a laugh.

As they walked into the old shed, Mac's hand lay on the small of Violet's back. It was comforting and yet disturbing at the same time. His simple touch made Violet jittery but in a good way.

Thin shafts of sunlight shone through the high windows as Violet's boots echoed across the old wooden floor and the air smelt of dust and straw.

'You don't use this much?'

'No, I mostly use the new shed down there,' he said as he pointed out the door. 'This used to be the original shed. It's mainly used for storage now.'

Holly's eyes lit up when she saw the kittens.

'This could be trouble,' Violet whispered to Mac as they walked forward.

'Nah, I already thought Holly would want one.'

'You planned this?' said Violet, leaning against the wall and watching her daughter play with them. Two of them were dark tabby like their mother, whereas the third was tortoiseshell. They'd lost some of their wobbliness and become bold. The tortoiseshell kitten sniffed Holly's hand. Holly giggled and looked over her shoulder at Violet, grinning.

'Aw, come on Violet every kid needs at least one pet,' said Mac softly.

Violet shook her head and stared at him. 'Oh my God, you really did plan this.'

'Well, what could I do? Holly asked if I was going to keep them all to myself or, hang on let me get her exact words right, *"Do you think . . .? Is it alright . . . for me to have one?"* I mean, it would just be plain selfish if I kept them all for myself.'

Holly was now waving a piece of straw in front of the tortoiseshell kitten and it was readying itself to pounce. It wiggled its butt before it launched itself at the straw.

'Mummy look. Isn't it cute?' said Holly, laughing.

'Yes, it is,' said Violet, sighing. Adorably cute, drat it, she thought. She'd been set up well and truly here and she knew it.

Violet looked at Mac and saw amusement in his eyes. 'You knew this would happen, didn't you?'

Mac shrugged his wide shoulders. 'Kind of. So it's okay?'

'Have they got names yet Mac?' Holly called out as she picked up the tortoiseshell kitten and gave it a cuddle.

'Not really, I hadn't thought about it. I suppose we could call them Stripy, Blotchy and Grey. What do you think?'

Violet leant towards him and whispered, 'I don't think you should be allowed to choose names.'

'Why not, I'm great at it.'

'Seriously? Stripy, Blotchy, Grey, Mud and Razor. I rest my case.'

Mac edged towards her and Violet could feel the heat from his body as he leant down and whispered in her ear. 'Okay, if that's how you feel. I promise you can name our children.'

Her stomach seemed to flip and contract at the same time. Heat flooded into her cheeks until they burnt.

'The things you say, Mac McKellan. You shouldn't joke around like that. You know how people gossip in this town.'

'Me, joking?' His warm breath fanned her ear and a tingle ran through her. 'Why, Ms Beckett—I think you're blushing.'

'Mac?' called Holly, and Mac instantly pulled away from Violet.

'Yes, Miss Fairy?'

Holly giggled again. 'I'm not a fairy today. I'm not wearing my wings.'

'You always look like a fairy to me.'

'Mac, can we name them something else?' Holly shook her head. 'I don't think your names are pretty enough.'

Mac gave a sigh to match Violet's earlier one. 'Everyone's a critic around here. Name them whatever you like, Holly. I don't mind.'

'*Truly? I* can name them?' she asked, her expression incredulous.

'Yeah and while you're doing that you'd better decide which one you'd like to keep,' said Mac, squatting down and adding in a not-so-quiet whisper. 'I think I've almost convinced your mum to agree.'

Holly's eyes widened as she looked first at Mac and then at Violet. 'Can I, Mummy? Can I really keep one?'

Violet smiled. Somehow she'd known Holly getting a kitten was a fait accompli before they'd even walked into the shed.

'Yes, sweetie, you can have a kitten. As long as you remember it's a lot of responsibility. *You* have to look after it.'

'I will. Promise! I'm going to have this one, I think he already likes me,' said Holly as she held the tortoiseshell kitten to her chest. 'Can he come home with us now?'

'Not quite yet, fairy,' said Mac, smiling. 'They have to stay with their mummy a bit longer.'

'Okay, Mac, but I promise to take good care of him. I really will.'

'I know you will, sweetheart,' he said as he leant over and ruffled her hair.

* * *

Violet frowned and checked her watch after a knock sounded on her front door. It was a little after nine-thirty in the evening. She put down her book and pushed herself off the bed. Things had been so busy lately she'd promised herself a lazy evening of reading in bed with a cup of tea and some chocolate. She tightened her dressing gown around her and walked down the hall hoping to God there was nothing wrong with Lily.

Flicking on the outside light, she peered through the peep hole. Her heart thudded. Mac was standing on her porch. Quickly she unlocked and opened the door.

'Hi.'

Mac looked a little sheepish as he produced a bunch of roses from behind his back. 'I could lie and say I just

155

happened to be driving past and accidentally found these on the way but somehow I don't think you'd believe me.'

'No, maybe not,' said Violet, suppressing a smile as she leaned against the doorway.

'They're from the garden. Don't tell Mum,' he said, handing her the bouquet.

'Thank you, they're beautiful,' said Violet. 'Did you want to come in?'

Mac shook his head. 'No, I just wanted to give you the flowers.'

'Well, thanks—' said Violet before Mac suddenly stepped forward and swept her into his arms, pulling her close. Dipping his head, his lips sought out hers. Feeling Mac's taut body against hers, Violet let go of the bouquet, which thudded onto the bare boards of the verandah. She put her arms around his shoulders and clung on. He made her quiver and that long-forgotten heat took hold and began to burn within her.

She gave a gasp of disappointment as Mac pulled away from her.

'Night, Violet, I'll see you tomorrow,' he said with a grin.

'You're *going*?' said Violet.

'Yep. Have a good night, sweetheart,' he said as he walked down the stairs to his car.

'But . . .' stuttered Violet.

'See ya,' Mac called out as he slid into his ute and, without so much as looking back at her, turned on the engine and backed down the drive.

Violet stooped down and picked up the flowers. She held

them up to her face and breathed in their scent as she watched Mac's headlights disappear down the road. Walking back inside, she closed the door and wandered down the corridor and into the kitchen in search of a vase. After riffling through the bottom cupboard, Violet found an old cut-glass vase that had once belonged to her grandmother. She filled it with water and started the task of arranging the blooms.

Mac's kiss had left her unsettled and she suddenly felt wound up and disconcerted. She could still feel his lips against hers and the warmth from where his hand had held her back.

Why had he taken off like that, wondered Violet as she placed the stems, one by one, in the vase. What man arrives on your doorstep, gives you flowers, kisses you and then disappears into the night with hardly a word?

Charlie McKellan, that's who.

Violet jumped.

'Ouch,' she muttered as a thorn snagged her finger. A bright bead of blood formed on its tip. 'Damn it.'

Violet plunged the rest of the roses into the vase and set it on the kitchen table, before heading back to her bedroom and flopping down on the bed. Taking a deep breath she picked up her discarded book and started to read. Her eyes slid over four paragraphs before she realised she wasn't taking in anything. She was seeing the words on the page but they weren't getting into her brain because it was filled with Mac and his damn sexy lips and wide shoulders.

She tossed the book aside in disgust.

Chapter 17

Violet dropped Holly off at school before she hurried over to McKellan's Run. The next lot of deliveries were arriving today; including the wrought-iron rostrum she'd hired for the ceremony. She could only hope and pray her measurements, which she'd double-checked a dozen times, were right and the rostrum would fit into Mac's courtyard without the need to cut into the flowerbed.

Other than that, the eight oversized urns for the floral displays were arriving, along with several free-standing candelabras. The table, chairs and tableware would turn up closer to the actual wedding day.

The days and hours were slipping by at what seemed a breathtaking rate and Violet knew that her time was down to the wire.

The morning disappeared under a hoard of deliveries, trying to solve the mystery of a missing urn and three phone calls from Celine. It occurred to Violet that she was no longer counting the days to the wedding but rather to the day when she'd never have to see, speak, or listen to Celine ever again.

At first, when Sarah had roped her into helping with the wedding she'd thought her biggest problem would be seeing

Jason again. She'd been completely and utterly wrong about that—the problem was Celine.

Mac's house was a hive of activity. Sarah greeted her at the door with a wide smile.

'Thank goodness you're here. I was beginning to panic,' she said with a nervous laugh.

'You must never panic,' said Violet. 'Please leave me to do all the panicking.'

'There's been so many people coming and going, I wasn't sure where everything was meant to go.'

'Wherever you directed them will be fine,' Violet said as she followed Sarah into the house.

Sarah pointed to the large boxes that were sitting in one corner of the great room. 'I just told the men to put those there, the invoice is on the top box. And the rostrum crew are already assembling it in the courtyard.'

Violet looked through the French doors. Four men were busy putting the structure together and it wasn't going to impinge on the flowerbed, thank goodness.

'It's going to look great! Now, let's take a breath and put the kettle on,' said Violet, putting her arms around Sarah. 'Come on, relax. Everything is going to be fine.'

* * *

Mac arrived back at the house after one o'clock and took a quick look at the chaos which had enveloped his normally tranquil home, grabbed Violet's hand and pulled her out the back door.

'Mac, I have a hundred things to do,' said Violet in mock protest, since she was quite pleased with how the day was going.

Mac turned and saw the laughter in her eyes. The afternoon sun caught her hair which shone deep-brown with hints of red. She was wearing it up again today, the dark tendrils snaking around the elegant curve of her neck and brushing her collarbone. Mac bit his lip to stop himself bending down and kissing the smooth skin of her throat.

She looked so pretty in her tight blue cardigan and jeans which clung to her curves. She raised her head and smiled and his heart seemed to expand. God, she was beautiful.

He tugged at her hand and led her away from the house.

'Mac, where are we going?' she asked. 'I really do have heaps of things to do before the afternoon's out.'

'Just down here,' said Mac, pointing to a large gum tree standing near the paddock fence. 'I just want you alone for a few minutes. It's so busy at the house, I can't hear myself think.'

'Alright, but I can't be gone too long,' said Violet letting him lead her along. 'The rostrum is up but I have to double-check the RSVPs again. The cut-off date is past but they keep dribbling in and I'm the one who'll have to tell Dan he has to feed more people than he thought.'

'I'm sure he can handle it,' said Mac. 'He had to feed hundreds of people at some of the restaurants he worked at before he came home. What's a couple more?'

'Maybe, but he didn't look too pleased yesterday when I confessed there were another six attending.'

'Hey, it's not your fault. Jason and Celine should have given you more time.'

'I know, but I'm the one getting it in the neck—mostly from the blushing bride.'

Mac grinned—he just couldn't help it.

'What? Why are you grinning at me?' said Violet.

Mac gave a shrug before he pulled her into his arms. 'I don't know. Maybe I just like how you stand your ground with Celine.'

He leant his back against the tree and held her close. Staring out across McKellan's Run while holding Violet Beckett in his arms—life couldn't get much better than this.

'I'm not a nice person, Mac.'

'Sure you are,' said Mac.

Violet shook her head and held up her finger and thumb to demonstrate. 'No, over the last couple of weeks I've been this close to telling Celine what exactly I think of her and where she could put her wedding.'

'And what stopped you?'

'A range of things—like I need the money and I didn't want to disappoint your mum since she was depending on me.'

'Yep, you're really a horrible hard-arse.'

Violet gave him a nudge. 'Oh shut up.'

Mac chuckled and kissed the top of her head. 'This may not be the right time to ask but I have a few questions,' he said, his expression more serious.

Violet stiffened in his arms. 'Like what?'

He had to ask, he told himself. This wasn't the right time but he couldn't wait any longer.

'Is Holly Jason's daughter?'

Violet stepped away from his embrace, turned and walked towards the house without looking back.

Mac winced as he felt an impenetrable wall slam down between them. It had been such a happy and relaxed moment and he'd gone and ruined it all. But he needed an answer so he . . . *they* could move on and build a relationship.

He wanted Violet more than anything but if they were going to have a future together he needed to know the truth from Violet. Deep down he already knew the answer but he needed to hear it from her lips. Mac quickly caught up to Violet.

* * *

'Tell me the truth, Violet. Is Holly my niece?' Mac asked as he took a step forward and stood directly in front of her.

Violet swallowed hard. She wouldn't lie to him, he deserved better than that. 'Yes, you'd already worked that out, hadn't you?'

'Pretty much, but I needed you to tell me.'

She raised her head and looked at him. His expression was serious but she saw both softness and love for her in his eyes. 'I wouldn't trade Holly for anything. She's made my life better than I could ever have imagined.'

'I know that. You're an amazing mother and she's a wonderful kid,' said Mac as he bridged the gap between them. He reached out and placed his large hands on her shoulders. They were warm and comforting. 'Why didn't you tell me earlier?'

162

Violet tried to pull away but Mac wouldn't let her. 'It doesn't really matter, does it? It was years ago. It's all forgotten, in fact I've rarely thought about Jason. I just got on with looking after Lily and bringing Holly up. Of course I couldn't avoid reliving it all when I moved back home but I'd had so much time to move on. And then it wasn't until your mother badgered me into helping her with the wedding that I really had to confront it all again.'

Mac dipped his head and whispered in her ear, 'Please Violet, just this once tell me what happened.'

The warmth of his breath made her tingle. 'Grandad kicked me out of his house once I told him I was pregnant. Lily said she wouldn't stay here in Violet Falls without me, no matter what I said. She's stood by me through thick and thin; and believe me, there was a lot of thin,' Violet added with a smile. 'Anyway, we packed up my little car and headed to Melbourne. I drove straight to Jason's new share house. I thought . . . God, I was an idiot back then. I thought Jason might be happy about the baby now that he had a job and all.'

'But he wasn't . . . right?'

'That would be an understatement. It was as if three years together had counted for nothing. He said he'd been wanting to end the relationship for a while. That the part of his life with me was over and we were both far too young to be having a child. He said he needed to concentrate on his job and I should have an abortion. Anyway the upshot was that I was pregnant with no prospect of him being around. I know a lot of people would have had an abortion and I respect that but I just couldn't, so I found an apartment and used the money I'd earnt over the previous year to tide us over until I got a job.'

Mac held her against his chest not saying anything.

'As I said, it was a long time ago and he did try to get in contact with me through Mr Taylor a while later. Your parents did too, even though they couldn't have known I was pregnant. You have to understand, Mac, I never once regretted having Holly. Whatever I had to go through in the past, she was worth it.'

There was a sense of relief for Violet as she looked up into Mac's eyes. Her mind had played over this scene a hundred times, not knowing how it would affect Mac's feelings for her. But Mac wasn't Jason. He was dependable and strong and made her feel safe.

'Anyway, everything worked out—Holly, Lily and me. We were, we *are*, just fine.'

'You amaze me, Violet,' Mac said softly.

'Why?' said Violet. 'I just did what I needed to do.'

'Because you were so young and everything you did must have taken a lot of courage and hard work,' said Mac, drawing her even tighter.

Violet felt so protected in his arms. She was caught in his essence, his scent, his spell. She couldn't pull away now—not that she wanted to. The stolen kisses he had taken over the past few days had all been leading to this moment.

She wouldn't waste any more time. She wanted Mac McKellan more than she thought possible.

His lips touched hers and she responded, savouring his kisses—which changed from gentle and cosseting to all consuming. Violet wrapped her arms around him and hung on, heat licking through her body, her heart thumping as she pressed against him.

His tongue rubbed against hers and all of a sudden she couldn't seem to get him close enough. She needed to feel his skin next to hers.

Lust, want and need burned through her like a bushfire. She'd denied herself for too long. She'd suppressed this aspect of herself, burying it deep. Violet had spent all of her time trying to be the perfect mother and sister and denying the woman within. Love and passion had changed her life once and she'd shied away from it ever since. Not trusting it or herself. But this was different, Mac was different. This force circled her and pulled her into its depths, overwhelming her utterly.

As Mac pushed against her, she slipped her hands under his shirt and rubbed them across the warm expanse of his back. She wanted Mac McKellan more than she'd ever wanted anything in her life. And he wanted her so he could fix everything.

Where the hell did that idea come from?

But she was right wasn't she?

This was Mac's way of making things right. Cleaning up his brother's little mess. Oh God!

She pulled her hands out from his shirt and tried to take a step back but there was nowhere for her to go.

'I need you, Violet. I love . . .' Mac raised his head. 'What's wrong?'

'I think we got a bit carried away.'

'That's okay. We can slow things down, whatever you want, I'll do it,' Mac said his arms still wound around her.

'I'm not sure if this is such a good idea, Mac, I mean with our history . . .'

'What history? Violet, what the hell are you talking about?'

'Okay fine, the history I have with your family, with your brother.'

'I don't give a damn about the past, Violet. Fuck the history. I just want a future, with you,' he said as he released her.

Violet felt bereft without his touch. Here she was trying to do the right thing, the noble thing and not let him sacrifice himself. Mac deserved so much more.

'You don't mean that, Mac. You're just trying to fix things like you always do. You want to protect me and Holly and I can't tell you how much that means to me. No one has ever wanted to do that before. But I can't let you; it wouldn't be fair.'

'Is that what you think?' he asked. 'After what just happened? You think I'm with you out of some sort of misguided duty?'

'You're a good man but I've said it before, I'm not *your* mistake or *your* problem.'

He pushed away from the fence and walked off without a look or a word.

'Mac! Mac, please don't leave like this. Please don't just walk away.'

He whirled around and faced her, crossing his arms in front of his chest as if he was putting a barrier between them.

'Is that the way you want to play it? Damned if I know if you're stubborn or just plain blind. Either way, I can't talk to you right now.'

'Mac.'

'Just leave it, Violet. Before something is said that can't be taken back,' he said, turning again and walking away, his anger palpable and the air almost crackling with tension. The look in his eyes made it clear she'd hurt him. She'd never meant that to happen.

'Mac!'

He didn't answer or stop, he just kept walking, his back stiff and unyielding.

***

Mac cut across the paddock and stomped his way up the hill towards a small clump of gum trees on the ridge.

Violet was doing his head in. He burned for her; he wanted her so badly he could hardly think straight. And the way she'd just kissed him back. Man, he still felt scorched by it.

Mac leaned against the nearest tree and breathed in the eucalyptus-scented air. He rubbed his hand across the back of his neck and stared out across the grey-green of the distant bush. He inhaled deeply and then blew out, trying to take some of the edge off his anger. It didn't. Mac dropped his gaze and kicked up a bit of the ground with his boot but stopped when he saw a line of bull ants scurrying over the upturned earth and dead gum leaves. Letting out a loud sigh filled with frustration, he slumped against the tree trunk. He tried to calm down but all he could think of and feel was Violet's lips on his.

Shit.

He pushed himself away from the tree and started walking down the other side of the ridge. A couple of kilometres ahead was the ruined cottage of the first McKellans, perhaps by the time he'd made his way there he could come up with some sort of solution. He doubted it but maybe the walk would clear his head.

How was he going to get Violet to see that he loved her for who she was—strong, courageous, amazing and beautiful? Yes, he did want to love her, protect her and make her and Holly his family, but not because of some weird and misguided duty that he needed to fix his brother's mistake.

How could Violet ever be a mistake? How could she even think that?

He walked across the pasture, his work boots crushing the soft green grass as he went.

And how the hell was he going to get her to believe him?

Chapter 18

Mac didn't call Violet that night and he wasn't anywhere to be found when Violet arrived at McKellan's Run the next day. He was avoiding her, and who could blame him?

She'd hurt him and that was something she never meant to do. She thought she'd worked it all out. Mac was a great guy but one who had a need to make everything right. She'd been so sure that was his main reason for their fledgling relationship. But the more she thought about it, the more she began to think she was wrong.

She let out a long sigh as she turned over and plumped up the pillows for the third time. The little clock on the night-stand said 3.24 a.m. and she bit back a groan.

Violet rolled onto her back and stared at the ceiling. She was scared, that was the truth. Deep down inside, she was terrified that if she let Mac in then he'd end up breaking her heart just like Jason had done.

Since her break-up with Jason, Violet had been very careful about seeing anyone. She kept everything light and friendly. Over the years she'd had a couple of flings but nothing that lasted more than a few weeks. She didn't do serious—serious could screw you up. So she never let anyone get too close—it was safer that way.

But Mac McKellan was different. For the first time in years, Violet caught herself picturing a future with him. He was kind, gentle and as sexy as hell. His kisses aroused her more than anything she'd ever experienced. He was that dangerous. She was letting her guard slip and it terrified her.

She'd built a thick wall around herself and she didn't think she'd survive if she was hurt again.

But it wasn't fair; Mac was nothing like his brother. It was just that Mac seemed so sure of what he wanted; her. And that made her uneasy. Could she really trust another McKellan with her heart? Or worse still, with Holly's?

Did she have the right to start something, something that could be amazing and wonderful? Did she even deserve it? But what would happen if it didn't work out? Should she even contemplate exposing Holly to that? Holly was already emotionally attached to Mac; what happened if it all soured, how would her little girl cope with that? How would she?

Violet closed her eyes in an attempt to finally fall asleep. But as soon as her eyelids shut, an image of Mac with his smiling hazel-green eyes swam in her head along with his words: 'Ah, come on Violet, take a chance and kiss me.'

* * *

After a sleepless night Violet knew she needed to fix things with Mac. Somewhere around 5 a.m. she'd come to a decision. She'd spent years avoiding relationships and she finally recognised that she had trust issues. Dragging around that much baggage could be exhausting but no matter how unfair it was—she always knew that nothing would last.

She'd been let down and hurt in the past but it wasn't fair to assume that Mac would do the same. She wanted to believe that but it was so hard. What she needed was a little faith—no man she'd ever met held a candle to Mac. She wasn't giving Mac a chance to prove himself and she knew it.

Well, she was going to do the right thing and trust him or at least try. The key was to take everything slowly. She'd been too quick to fall under his spell. She wanted time to take a step back and try to get her head together. Maybe after a few months they could think about going out.

Violet tried to ignore the burning ache he'd aroused inside her when she was in his arms. If this was going to work, she needed to rein in her lust and try and build a friendship and then if she was lucky, a relationship. She needed this time, and if Mac wanted to be with her, she just hoped she could get him to see that this was the right course of action.

* * *

Violet swung her car into the drive to McKellan's Run. A frown flickered over her face when she reached the house and realised his ute wasn't parked out the front. Maybe he was up at the shearing shed.

She kept driving past the house until she reached the track which led past the big shed. After a few minutes

171

she crested a gentle hill and could see the shearing shed sitting in the middle of the eastern paddock. The sky was blue with a few thin streaky-looking clouds and the pasture in the paddock was a vivid green. The old wooden shearing shed had a bygone charm about it and it was surrounded by several holding pens, one which was full of woolly sheep.

As she drew closer she could see Mac's ute among several cars parked near the shed. Violet stopped the car as she drove up to the long metal gate on the edge of the paddock, jumped out, unlatched the gate and then swung it open.

Violet walked back to her car but paused for a second as a breeze from the far hills blew over her. She brought her hand up and shaded her eyes against the sun as she took a moment to take in the beauty of McKellan's Run. Tipping her head back, Violet watched as an eagle dipped and soared above her. There was a magnificence about this land she'd forgotten. She'd been so caught up with moving back here, trying to start her business and the stress of this wretched wedding she'd forgotten to stop for a moment or two and just allow herself to be in the landscape.

With one more glance at the distant rolling hills, Violet slipped back in her car, drove into the paddock and got out, shutting the gate behind her. She toyed with the idea of leaving the car where it was and walking the rest of the way. Now that she was in the sunshine, she was loathe to leave it but she still had to make peace with Mac, and then get on with the dozens of things she had to do for the wedding before picking up Holly.

Her car bumped along the track to the shearing shed and just as she was pulling up outside, Mac appeared in the doorway. Violet dragged in a breath as she watched him head over to her. Funny, it wasn't until this second that she realised just how nervous she was.

'Violet, what are you doing here?' he asked.

She scrambled out of the car and gave him a nervous smile.

'I know you're busy with shearing but I think we should talk.'

Mac was silent, a frown creasing his brow, his arms folded over his chest.

As each second ticked by everything about this meeting felt more and more awkward. There was a barrier between them, it was as if a great sheet of glass was separating Violet from Mac. It was so tangible, she thought, that if she stretched out her hand an invisible force would repel it.

'We need to clear the air between us,' Violet said.

'Okay,' said Mac, arms still folded.

God, he wasn't going to make this easy.

'I think I was wrong about what I said. I like you, Mac. I really do.'

'*Like*? Jesus, Violet,' he said.

Yeah, this was going really well.

'As I said, I like you Mac,' said Violet, and looked down at the ground. 'I buried myself in my job and raising Holly. I'm not very good at trying to sustain any sort of romantic relationship. I mean, what I'm trying to say and not doing a very good job at it is that I'd like to try.'

Mac remained silent, waiting.

'All I wanted you to know is that I'd like to try for us to be together,' said Violet.

'Glad to hear it,' said Mac.

The barrier started to melt and Violet sent up a silent prayer.

'But I think we need to take it slow; you don't mind do you?'

'Nope, I don't mind at all. I want you in my life, Violet, and I'm willing to wait. That is, if you promise to get that crazy idea out of your head.'

'What idea?'

'The one about you thinking that I want to be with you out of some sort of obligation, because it's not true.'

Violet gave a nod. 'Okay.'

'I mean it. I want you for you and not out of some mis-placed sense of duty. I want you, Violet, and I sure as hell don't want to be just your friend.'

'I understand, Mac.'

'Really?' asked Mac.

'Yes, I do,' she said as she leaned on the car next to him. 'So you don't mind us slowing down? I need to get this wedding out of the way and my business established as well as easing Holly into the idea of introducing someone else into our little world. I was thinking that after I've done all that then we could start spending more time together.'

'But why do we need to wait?' asked Mac.

'Mac, it's just with the business, moving back here, trying to plan this wedding, I think it would be best if we didn't see each other for a while.'

'I don't care about rumours. In this town there's always gossip. This is about you, me and Holly. Everyone else can take a long walk off a short pier as far as I'm concerned.'

'I, yes, I know but still—'

'I said I'd wait but not having any contact for a while is a bit hard to swallow. What are you *thinking*?'

'That I need time to sort myself out.'

'But for how long—weeks, months? I'll do it, I'll wait, but is this about sorting yourself out or about the fact that you can't bring yourself to trust me?'

'No, that's not it.'

'Then why? Come on, Violet, why would you want me to walk away?'

'Because of all the reasons I mentioned. Because I need time to come to terms with . . .'

'I'm not Jason!'

'I never said you were.'

'But that's what you think deep down, isn't it? That maybe you can't trust me with your heart or with Holly because one day I'll hurt you, just like my brother did.'

'That's not fair, Mac.'

'Isn't it? That's what's at the bottom of this whole thing. You can't bring yourself to trust me. I said I'd wait and be patient but will you ever be ready to take the next step? Will I have to wait another eight years?'

'This was a mistake,' Violet said as she spun away and jerked open the car door.

'Violet, don't walk away.'

She slid into the car seat. 'Why not, Mac—isn't that what I do best?' Violet turned on the ignition and without another glance, she drove away.

Chapter 19

Mac watched Violet drive off, her little car bumping along the track, tearing up dirt and turf as she went. He walked past the full holding pens in an attempt to get his head together, the sheep bleating as he passed.

He headed towards a copse of trees on the far side of the paddock. He needed a few minutes to calm down and work out what the hell just happened.

Mac leant against the nearest tree and stared unseeing off into the distance.

He had the right to ask Violet how long he was expected to wait, didn't he? It wasn't an unreasonable request, was it? But deep down he knew what was rankling him and it wasn't to do with the waiting but rather the lack of trust. He couldn't spend the rest of his life knowing that every time he put a foot wrong, Violet would instantly jump to the worst-case scenario and compare him with Jason.

He had to admit he hadn't handled the situation very well. He knew he should have backed off and tried to approach the subject in a calmer manner but the words had kept tumbling out of his mouth.

Mac blew out a long breath. The whole thing was a complete and utter screw-up.

He spent the rest of the day at the shearing shed, working alongside the sheep handlers, tossing the freshly shorn fleece on the wool table and then skirting it, which was pulling the dirty wool from certain sections of the fleece.

The shed was filled with sheep handlers, or rousties as they were called, four shearers and a wool classer. The work was quick and back-breaking. Normally, Mac would hire his crew and just check in every now and then to help out when needed. But this time it was different, he needed to immerse himself in work to take his mind off Violet.

The buzz of the electric shears filled the shed, along with the bleating of the sheep. The scent of lanolin hung in the air and it was good to feel the wool, *his wool*, between his fingers. But it didn't seem to matter how fast he worked, he just couldn't get Violet out of his mind.

Mac rolled his shoulders as the shed wound down for the day.

'If you're alright, I'm going to head off now.'

'No worries, Mac,' one of the shearers called out. 'Hey, you make a pretty good roustabout. If you ever want to give up McKellan's Run, I just might hire you.'

Mac shook his head and grinned as the shed filled with laughter.

'Thanks, Jack, I'll keep that in mind.'

'You do that.'

Mac made his way to the door. 'Thanks everyone for your hard work today. I'll see you tomorrow.'

He gave a brief wave to the chorus of goodbyes and let out a whistle as he walked over to his ute. 'Come on Razor, let's go and see what Flynn's up to,' he said as he opened the car door and waited for the dog to jump in. 'Maybe if I drink enough I can get her out of my head, just for tonight anyway.'

**

The sun filtered through the peppercorn tree as the cool breeze blew in from the south. Violet sat in her sheltered garden and looked down the winding path towards the peach trees at the back. She smiled as she remembered picking the peaches with her grandmother and Lily. She'd always been so impatient, waiting for the fruit to ripen and then biting into the soft white flesh, the sweet juice running down her fingers. Each mouthful tasting of summer.

She missed those days and she missed her grandmother. Today, the garden didn't seem complete without her. Life had been gentler when Stella Beckett had been alive. She'd tempered her husband's strict and overpowering nature and given desperately needed love to her two granddaughters. Things had changed after her death. Their grandfather had become harder and more embittered.

The warbling song of a magpie caught Violet's attention, dragging her out from the shadows of the past. She took a sip of her coffee. It was time to let the past go, not just for her own sake but also for Holly's. Holly was her future and so was Mac, if she let him.

Violet frowned. She hadn't realised how much she'd come to look forward to seeing Mac every day. Like a drug, her dependency had grown; she told herself she was in control but that was a lie. It had been three days since she'd seen him; three days since they'd fought and he'd turned away. Her body hurt, there was a deep ache inside as if she'd lost a piece of herself.

The more she thought about it, the more she started to believe she'd been wrong. He'd said he cared for her and wanted a future with her and Holly. The look in his eyes told her this was more than just a man doing the honourable thing. He wanted her for herself, not because his brother had thrown her away. She'd seen it and yet she'd pushed him away. Why?

Because she was scared. Terrified to open herself up and let Mac's love in. She didn't want to admit it, but the break-up with Jason had shattered her to the core. And what scared her to death was the thought that history would repeat itself. But that wasn't fair to Mac, as he was twice the man his brother was.

Taking a chance and opening herself up again was proving harder than she thought. In the back of her mind was the taunting voice reminding her it wasn't going to work and Mac would let her down just like Jason. Violet sighed, as she placed her cup back on the small metal table.

Not that it mattered, as there was a good chance Mac would never want to see her again.

Hell, how had she managed to screw everything up?

180

She needed to make it right and the only way to do that was to find him and make him listen to what she had to say.

* * *

Mac dropped back a gear as he drove up the winding track that led to the Grange. This was the third evening he'd headed over to Flynn's house after a hard day's shearing and each time he'd got drunk enough to stay the night. He needed to get himself together. He stopped and looked up at the Grange, trying to calm himself. The house sat on a hill that overlooked a mix of bush and green pastures. The land at the back of the house fell away into a deep gully with the rushing Landoc's Creek snaking its way through the centre.

The Grange was a two-storey stone house that dated back to the 1880s but it had fallen into disrepair until only the shell had remained. When Flynn inherited the land, he had spent a heap of money and most of his free time restoring the old building. The effect was breathtaking, the Grange was now a fusion of Victorian and modern architecture and stood as a testament to Flynn's sheer determination.

As Mac pulled up he saw a little red sports car parked beneath the peppercorn tree on the far side of the house. Flynn clearly had company tonight.

Mac sat back in his seat and pondered for a moment as the ute idled.

'You know, Razor, we should go, 'cos it looks as if Flynn is otherwise occupied.'

The little dog tilted his head and looked at Mac adoringly.

'But where's the fun in that?'

Razor's tail thumped against the seat.

'You like that idea?' he asked as he gave the dog a pat. 'Me too.'

Mac switched off the engine, got out and held the door open. 'Come on boy, let's go and ruin Flynn's evening.' He grabbed the beer from the back of the ute and sauntered his way to the door at the back of the house.

'So what's up?' Flynn asked, pulling a t-shirt over his head just as Mac walked into the kitchen.

'Nothing, I just thought we could have a few beers again tonight,' said Mac holding up the half-dozen stubbies.

'Sure, but you're going to have to give me a minute,' Flynn said as he turned and started to walk into the lounge room.

'Listen, if I've caught you in the middle of something . . .'

Flynn turned around and gave him a grin. 'Let's just say you almost caught me in the middle of something. But that's okay, grab a seat and I'll be back.'

Mac dropped onto the old leather couch and watched as Flynn disappeared through the far door. He turned back and stared out to the eucalypts on the far side of the gully. Three sides of the Grange were the original Victorian walls but the entire back of the house was made of steel and glass, which brought the outside in and filled the rooms with an abundance of light.

Somewhere above him Mac could hear the under-current of an annoyed female voice, which he recognised as belonging to Charlotte Somerville. Charlotte was the self-proclaimed princess of Violet Falls, as her father was the current mayor. The family were rich blow-ins who'd only settled here about fifteen years ago. There was no denying Charlotte was attractive, from her pretty face to her long legs. But Mac had always thought she was spoilt and would be high maintenance and too much trouble to bother pursuing. Obviously, Flynn didn't feel the same.

The sound of high heels clicking down the stairs filled the silence of the house. Mac heard Charlotte make her way across the slate floor of the foyer. The front door creaked open and was then slammed shut, the force reverberating through the building. Charlotte wasn't happy.

A few seconds later Flynn reappeared. 'Sorry about that,' he said with a sheepish grin.

'I saw her car. I shouldn't have come in,' Mac admitted.

Flynn shrugged. 'No big deal. Charlotte and I have an understanding.'

'What? Are you together?'

Flynn let out a laugh. 'Fuck no! We're convenient; when neither of us has anything else going on we tend to gravitate towards each other. We have a drink, and a laugh and some fun. No strings.'

'You've never been in love, have you?' said Mac, his expression suddenly serious.

Flynn snagged a beer and sank down into the couch next to him. 'No,' he said, laughter in his voice. 'God, why would I? I mean things are just fine as they are.'

'You have a good time.'

'Abso-fucking-lutely. Why try and change something that's already perfect?'

Mac took another swig of beer. 'I suppose not. It's just . . .'

'What, not as deep and meaningful as what you feel about Violet? I know you're in a bad way,' said Flynn as he leant over and rapped Mac on the head. 'She messes with that. I've never seen you drink so much as in these past few days.'

'Shut up.' Mac pulled back.

'Admit it, Violet has you whipped.'

'Maybe I like it that way. Besides she's the only one I ever think of . . . or want.'

'Then what the hell are you doing here?'

'It's complicated. I just think we're moving forward and then she slams on the brakes.'

'Is she scared of something?'

'Perhaps.'

'Then you'd better figure out what it is or move on.'

'No, moving on isn't an option. I love her.'

Flynn tipped back the stubby and took another drink before turning to Mac and grinning. 'Just like I said, whipped.'

Chapter 20

Something was shaking his shoulder. Mac groaned and tried to open his eyes.

'Come on Mac, it's almost six.'

Mac pushed himself into a sitting position. He'd ended up on Flynn's couch yet again.

He raised his head and stared blearily at Flynn who was grinning stupidly at him. 'How can you be so fucking cheerful?'

'Well, you're a grumpy bum aren't you?' Flynn's grin somehow got wider.

'Grumpy bum, seriously? You're an idiot.'

'I have a natural sunny disposition,' Flynn called over his shoulder as he headed towards the kitchen but he paused in the doorway to pat Mac's dog on the head. 'There's food and coffee, if you want it. Razor and I have already had our breakfast, haven't we, boy?'

Razor thumped his tail on the polished wooden floor. Mac flinched and Flynn roared laughing.

'Oh shut up.' Mac sent him a dirty look.

'That'll teach you for trying to drown your sorrows. I told you before that you have to sort this thing out with Violet; she messes with your head.'

'I know.'

'Hey, aren't you meant to be backlining the sheep today?'

Mac rubbed his hand over his face in a vain attempt to wake up and think clearly. 'Yeah, I am. What did you say the time was?'

'Almost six.'

'Right, I'm on it,' Mac said as he stood up and followed Flynn into the kitchen.

'Yeah, course you are.' Flynn nodded as he handed Mac a mug of coffee. 'I think you better drink this before you hightail it out of here.'

'Thanks,' said Mac.

'No worries. Did I mention I ran into Lily Beckett the other day? It was a surprise seeing her again.'

'Why?' Mac was half-listening as he sipped his coffee.

'Because I haven't seen her since she was a kid. And there she was standing in the middle of the main street with her cute freckles and her curvy lusciousness. She was so breath-taking I almost collapsed on the spot.'

Mac started to chuckle but then the thought of his best mate turning his attentions to Violet's baby sister sent a wave of panic through him.

'Flynn, I don't think you should be messing with Lily.'

'Why not?'

'Well, don't take this the wrong way but you don't exactly have a great track record when it comes to women and commitment.'

'I'm always up front with my intentions or lack of them. Girls know where they stand with me. Besides I just said

I *saw* Lily, I didn't say I wanted to marry her. I was only commenting that she looks a whole lot different from the scrawny little kid I remember.'

'Hmmm.' Mac wasn't convinced. 'Anyway as far as I know Lily is living with a guy. Some sort of photographer, I think.'

'Lucky bloke then,' said Flynn, turning away and rinsing his mug in the sink before dumping it on the drying rack.

Mac drained his mug and walked over to the sink.

'I'd better get going. Thanks for the coffee,' he said as he ran the mug under the tap. 'And for the company and the pizzas these last three nights and for last night's movie with the exploding heads.'

Flynn shrugged. 'Anytime. Well, you know it's not true male bonding unless there's beer and action movies with car chases and exploding heads.'

'What are you up to today?'

'Moving the mob down from the top paddock. The shearers are arriving tomorrow,' said Flynn.

'Do you need a hand with anything?'

'Nah, I've got it covered but if something comes up I'll give you a call.'

'Do that. I'll catch you later,' Mac said.

'Yeah, you will. Bit by bit I'm getting roped into this bloody wedding,' Flynn said with a smile.

'Welcome to the club. Besides, it's all hands on deck—the family is expected to help out,' Mac grinned as he opened the door.

'You see, normally that would make me feel good but that Celine does my head in.'

'As I said, welcome to the club. Come on Razor, let's go.'

'See ya.'

* * *

Mac adjusted the straps of the harness, the container of pour-on lice treatment strapped to his back. They were about to begin backlining the sheep.

'You see, Ben, you have to spray it from between their ears, right down the middle of their back to the tail,' he said as he demonstrated.

'Like this?' Ben sprayed the sheep's back. It was a bit blotchy. Mac looked at the applicator and twiddled with the nozzle.

'Here, try it now.'

This time Ben managed to paint a line down the sheep.

'How's that?' he asked with a frown.

'Yeah, almost but you're a bit off centre. Just remember you have to get it right down the middle. Gravity helps the product move down the body, so if you start in the middle the whole animal will be protected. Give it another go.'

Mac had taken on Ben Jamison a few months ago. He'd just turned eighteen and was a bit rough around the edges but he worked hard and always tried to prove himself. Life hadn't been rosy for young Ben. Mac knew that the kid had a few problems at home which were bad enough for him to kit out one of the rooms above the old stables for when Ben needed somewhere to crash. Rumour had it that Trevor Jamison, Ben's father, was a drinker and had terrorized his family for years, the bastard.

As far as he knew, Ben was making use of the room more and more frequently.

Ben tried again, this time administering a perfect dose of purple liquid from between the sheep's ears and all the way to its tail.

'Perfect, now you just have to do the rest of them,' Mac said with a wink.

Ben looked over at the full holding pens. 'I think we're going to be here a while.'

'Are you good?'

Ben nodded. 'Yep.'

'Then let's get this done,' Mac said as he started to spray the next ewe's back.

Mac tried to concentrate on the business at hand, back-lining sheep after sheep after sheep. But Violet kept invading his mind and the fact he'd do nearly anything to have this bloody hangover go away. It was his own damn fault but it still didn't make it any easier.

***

Another day had passed, another day of Mac steering clear of her. Violet couldn't get him out of her mind and she was beginning to realise her heart was more than involved as well. He'd been avoiding her and she didn't blame him.

He'd been nothing but honest and upfront when it came to his feelings. It was Violet who was hiding—hiding from herself.

Violet glanced at the clock on the wall. She still had a couple of hours before she had to pick up Holly from school. Grabbing her bag, she headed out the front door and banged it shut.

It was time she made Mac see just how much she wanted him. Did she love him?

Violet's hand stilled on the car door. No, it was too soon to even start using that word, wasn't it?

But do I love him?

Violet opened the door and slid into the driver's seat. No. Yes. Maybe I do.

Violet pulled out onto the road and headed towards McKellan's Run. The problem was, no matter how she felt about him, she wondered if he was still in love with the idea of the girl she used to be. Before they could have a future, she needed to know if Mac was in love with the girl that was or the woman she is now.

* * *

Celine dug around her handbag looking for her mobile. It had rung twice before she managed to pick it up. A slight frown marred her face when she saw it was another call from her father.

'Celine, have you spoken to Jason yet about the money?'

'I don't think I can get you any more, Dad. He said he'd

already loaned you enough to get some of your creditors off your back until you sold off some more assets.'

There was silence for a moment. 'I see.'

'What about the flats, have they sold yet?'

'There's been an offer but it's nowhere in the region I wanted. That fool estate agent said that there's a housing slump at the moment. Personally I think he's just hopeless at his job.'

'Then go with another firm.'

'There isn't time. If I want the money fast, I'll have to sell them at a loss. It will help but it still won't be enough to get us out of this mess. Can't you convince Jason to give me a little more money?'

'I'm sorry, Dad, but—'

'You're clever, I *know* you can get Jason to give you the funds. Just try, Celine, *please*. You said you'd help me, look after me—just like I've always protected you.'

'But—'

'I'm sure you can come up with something. Please Celine, I'm counting on you to do it for me.'

'I'll try again, but I can't promise anything,' Celine replied.

Chapter 21

Violet took a breath and tried to ignore her stomach clenching into hard knots as she pulled up behind his ute. As she walked up to the homestead she saw that he was standing, staring out the office window.

'Mac, we need to talk.'

'I don't know what else I can say, Violet. It's like every time I open my mouth, you push me further and further away.'

'That's not true.'

'Isn't it?'

'Please, I'm standing here, hoping you'll agree to give us a chance.' Violet uncrossed her arms and took a hesitant step forwards. Mac's profile was lit by the light from the window. His jaw was set and he didn't look around. His silence frightened her and Violet prayed she hadn't lost something precious before it truly had begun.

'Mac, please. Look, I'm sorry I pushed you away. It was just that you were getting so close, so quickly, that I panicked.'

He turned his head and stared at her. 'Panicked?'

'Yes. I don't do this well.' Violet waved her hand between

them making an invisible link in the air. 'The truth is, I don't do this . . . ever.'

'Are you telling me you haven't had a relationship since Jason?'

Violet felt a burst of heat flush in her cheeks and dropped her gaze to the floor. 'No. Well . . . yeah, I've never had anything serious since then. I didn't have time to look for love. I was too busy trying to survive and bring up Holly.'

Mac remained silent.

'Look,' said Violet. 'I really want this to work but we're only at the very beginning. We have to get to really know each other and take it from there.'

'For God's sake, Violet, we've known each other since school. I know who you are. I love—'

'Don't!' Violet snapped. 'Don't say it.'

Mac planted his feet and crossed his arms. 'Why?' He said as he stared her down. 'Why the hell can't I say it?'

'Because it's not true—at least not yet.'

He ran his hand through his hair. 'You're driving me crazy. What the hell are you talking about?'

'Please don't tell me you love me,' said Violet.

'I do love you, Violet.' Mac closed the distance between them. 'Why shouldn't I say it if it's the truth?'

'How can you love me; it's only been a few weeks?' Violet took his hand and squeezed it. 'I want you, Mac, I care about you and I hope that whatever this thing we have between us will build into something more.'

'Violet, I know it was hard—'

Violet let out a laugh and stepped away from him. She needed the distance, a barrier between them.

'Hard? I barely slept for two years, although I suppose it's the same for most new parents. I worked two jobs before Holly was born. I bullied Lily into study whenever she argued she should leave school and get a job so we would have enough money to survive. I wouldn't let her. She was only fifteen and had left everything here in Violet Falls to come with me. I wasn't about to let her give up her education as well.'

'You looked after her.'

'Once Holly came things got worse. I had to give up my day-time job. I couldn't afford reliable childcare and pay the rent. So Lily and I would work as a tag team. I'd stay home while she went to school and then she'd mind Holly while I did the evening shift at whatever restaurant or bar I was working in at the time.'

She glanced at Mac but he said nothing, giving her the space to tell her story.

'Things went bad when one night a manager from the Red String tried to kiss me. I knew what he was like and up to that point I had managed to stay under his radar. I quit the same night; I had rejected him and I knew he would make it impossible for me to stay. The problem was that we were living hand-to-mouth and without that waitressing job, things got difficult really quickly. I tried to find another job, anything to tide us over, but that can take time. All I knew was I didn't have a job and the rent was due. The restaurant owed me some wages but without working the full week there was no way I'd have enough money. I didn't have anyone I could turn to. I could find another job but even if I started it the next day, I still couldn't make the rent, let alone have enough to feed us until the new pay cheque kicked in.'

'Did you call your grandfather?'

'Hell no, although I was so desperate I did toy with the idea of sending Lily and Holly to him just for a week or so. I didn't think he hated Lily quite as much as me. But anyway, Lily wouldn't go. To tell the truth, I glossed over the details and made out the situation wasn't quite as bad as it was. But Lily doesn't know what I'm about to tell you. Promise you'll never say a word.'

'I promise. Your secrets are always safe with me, Violet.'

'You asked me once how I became an events planner and I said I fell into it. Well, that isn't exactly true. I don't know if I met Angela Swiftford through luck or divine intervention. All I can say is that she found me on the worst night of my life. You have to understand I was desperate, I needed money for the bills, there was no food in the house and I hadn't eaten in almost two days. Holly and Lily depended on me, I had to find a way somehow . . . I didn't want to, I never wanted to . . . But what else could I do?' Violet choked back a sob.

The room seemed to almost fade away and she could feel the sleet, it was icy and she was frozen to the bone. She was walking along the street, the sound of her heels echoing on the wet footpath. It was late and dark with the only light coming from the widely interspaced streetlamps. The cold wind blew against her bare legs, she'd pulled her trench coat tightly around her but the thin material did little to keep out the chill. Terrified, she'd never felt so alone in her life. Several cars slowed as they drew alongside her but she kept her head down and kept walking. She knew she had to do it, but she wasn't ready—not yet.

A movement caught her eye and she looked up. She was standing back in his office staring at Mac. He'd taken a step towards her but she held up her hand.

'No, wait. Let me finish it,' she said as she shook her head and tried to steady herself. 'I was at rock bottom; I was going to sell myself to get the money I needed to save my family. I knew I had to do it as it was my only option. But every time a car slowed, I just couldn't do it. I kept walking and up ahead there was a building, I don't know, it was a sort of hall. The lights were on and there were a couple of cars and a van outside. I thought, maybe if I sat down in the light for a moment, I'd be able to gather myself and do what I had to do.'

Violet glanced up at Mac. His mouth was still in a grim line and his face was inscrutable. Swallowing hard, she continued.

'But when I sat down on the step, a woman who was about sixty with a shot of bright red hair came up to me. She asked me what I was doing, I tried to be cool and aloof. I told her I wasn't any of her concern; that I was fine and she didn't have to worry about me. But Angela was persistent and wouldn't go away. She put her arm around me and just sat there in silence, waiting for me to spill my guts. The next thing I knew I was crying like a little kid in her arms and telling her everything—and I mean everything—including what I was about to do. She told me she was a wedding planner and she and her team were just dismantling and packing up their latest triumph. Angela is one of the kindest people I have ever met. She offered me a job then and there. Within twenty minutes my life had changed and I was being introduced to other staff members and taking down swathes of cream satin from the bridal table. She gave me a solid job, an advance and not only saved me, but Holly and Lily as well. She took a chance on me and I will always be more grateful than she'll ever know.'

She looked up and saw the only thing she never wanted to see in his eyes.

'I don't want pity, Mac. I didn't tell you this for that reason. I just wanted you to know that the woman who stands before you is very different from the girl you remember. If you can love me for who I am, that's amazing. If not, then I think for both our sakes we should walk away now.'

Mac strode across the floor and took her in his arms. He crushed her against his chest and held her tight.

'Baby, I'm not going anywhere.'

Violet trembled and tightened her hold on Mac.

'I promise I will try and slow down but I'm not going to lie to you either. I want you and I want us but I'm willing to wait until you are ready.' Mac held her close. 'Everything is going to be alright.'

Chapter 22

'It's a beautiful view,' said Violet as she carried in a large crystal vase filled with colourful blooms and placed it on the sideboard.

Celine glanced over her shoulder. 'Yes, I suppose it is. I've been so stressed out about the wedding and everything during this visit I've hardly even noticed it.'

Violet nodded before turning her attention back to the flowers.

Celine walked over and joined her. 'I know we've barely spoken, Violet, but I just wanted to say thanks for all your hard work with the wedding.'

'You're welcome. I hope it turns out to be everything you wanted,' said Violet, a bit taken aback by the change in Celine.

'Thanks, I know I can be difficult. It's just that I want everything to be perfect,' said Celine, smiling.

'I'll do everything in my power to make sure it is,' said Violet as she rearranged a couple of the roses.

'Are you still in love with Jason?'

The question came out of left field and took Violet by surprise. Her hand stilled midway on the vase. 'No, Celine, I'm not.'

'I just wondered because I saw him looking at you,' said Celine. 'I mean—'

'I was once,' said Violet, looking at Celine. She wouldn't lie to her. 'But we were just kids, and it finished a lifetime ago.'

'What happened?'

Violet leant against the sideboard. 'There's not much to tell. We met when I was sixteen, he was two years ahead of me. We started hanging out together and slowly it turned into something more. Things changed when he went off to uni. We kept it going while I finished high school and worked here in Violet Falls but after he finished law school and got his first job, it all fell apart.'

'And that's it?'

'Yep, that's it. Until Sarah asked me to help with the wedding, I hadn't seen Jason for eight years.'

'Thank you,' said Celine with what seemed like an embarrassed smile. 'I don't know where my head is lately. I keep coming up with crazy ideas.'

'Nothing to worry about. Weddings can do that to you.'

'I just want to get the wedding over and done with so we can head back to the city,' said Celine as she walked back to the window.

'You don't like it here?'

'No, rural life isn't really for me. Perhaps I should talk Jason into selling this place. I doubt we'll ever visit.'

Violet paused, a frown on her face. 'But McKellan's Run belongs to Mac, not Jason, so it's not Jason's to sell,' she said.

'But this is Jason's family home! This is where he grew up! And he's the eldest of the brothers, isn't he?'

'Yeah it was, but when John McKellan died Mac inherited the bulk of McKellan's Run. John did manage to get approval to break off two small twenty-acre lots for Jason and Dan; and they were given trust funds, but the farm was left to Mac.'

'That's not fair,' Celine said, her cheeks flushed pink. 'It must be worth a fortune!'

'It may be, but then you have to factor in all the hard work,' said Violet.

'But why did Mac inherit it all?' asked Celine.

'Because McKellan's Run has to be kept pretty much intact for future generations and Mac was the best choice. The place is in his blood and he's always been the one who was most interested in it. He's absolutely slogged his guts out from dawn till dusk to keep it as a going concern. He'd rather cut off his arm than sell an inch of it. Also, neither Jason nor Dan ever showed much of an interest in farming. They might still love the land but they never wanted the responsibility of McKellan's Run. Jason also knew he wanted to be a corporate lawyer when I met him. And Dan did a chef's apprenticeship in Melbourne as soon as he left school and went off to Europe to get experience.'

'But I thought . . .' Celine started, then stopped.

Violet shook her head. 'Nope, McKellan's Run is all Mac's.'

Celine had gone white and started to look genuinely distressed while Violet was explaining things and now she turned on her heel and raced out of the room, pulling out her mobile as she did.

Violet stood still there for a while, wondering what the hell was going on. Then, shrugging, she got back to work. She needed to check on the number of plates and cutlery and all manner of paraphernalia.

* * *

Violet was just brushing some dust off her black skirt when she looked up to see Mac walking through the French doors. He made his way around the numerous stacks of chairs and boxes until he stood in front of her. He reached down, grabbed her hand and tugged her towards him. Thrown off balance by the unexpected move, Violet found herself plastered across Mac's chest.

'Hey, what do you—?'

He cut off her words with a kiss.

Violet kissed him back, she enjoyed the moment and the way his lips danced across her mouth. She softened into him and for a few precious seconds the wedding preparations faded away, leaving Mac to fill the void. But before the kiss deepened Mac pulled away.

'Come on, we're leaving,' he said as pulled her by the hand towards the French doors.

'Mac, there's a million and one things to do. I can't just drop everything.'

'Yes, you can. I'm only asking for half an hour, Violet. You can give me that, can't you?'

There was a gleam in his eyes and a smile on his lips. Violet focused on his mouth. Lord, he was tempting.

'Oh alright, but just for a little while.'

'Trust me.'

He led her through the courtyard and around the back of the house towards the shed.

'Mac, where exactly are we going?'

'You'll see,' he said as headed over to his motorbike. He picked up a helmet and handed it her. 'So when was the last time you rode one of these?'

Violet's eyes narrowed as she stared at the helmet.

'Seriously? This is what you wanted me for?'

'Yep, the house is full of noise, people and voices—especially Celine's. She came in a while ago looking daggers at Jason. They've gone off somewhere. Anyway, we could both do with a little peace, even if it's only for half an hour. So will you come?'

Violet put the helmet on and clipped it beneath her chin.

'Okay, sure. Why not?'

'Good, get on.' Mac put on a helmet and straddled the motorbike.

Violet settled on the seat behind Mac and wrapped her arms around his waist. She felt the warmth of his body through his shirt.

'Are you ready?

'Yep.'

'Hold on then, here we go.'

They took off down the dirt track and away from the house. Violet held on to Mac as the sun filtered through eucalypts. A little way up the road he turned left and drove towards an old metal gate. He slowed the bike as they approached.

'I'll get it,' Violet said as the bike came to a halt. She jumped off and unhitched the gate before swinging it open. Violet waited until Mac rode past her and she shut the gate again then got back on the bike and held on. She always felt so protected when she was with Mac.

'You right?' Mac asked.

'Sure.'

Without another word Mac rode over the green grass of the paddock and towards a ridge. As soon as he reached the top, Mac turned the bike to the right and continued along the ridge to its highest point. A lone ghost gum sat at the very top. Family legend was that the first McKellan, Angus, had planted it there but perhaps that was just a tale thought Violet.

Mac cut the engine as they drew under the shade of the tree. Violet got off the bike and took off the helmet. The air was cool and the sun was warm on her body. As she looked across the gullies, hills, pastures and bush she thought again about how beautiful this land was.

Up here, Violet listened to the near silence as the breeze blew gently against her face, the melodious song of a magpie coming from somewhere overhead. By her feet, the grass was sprinkled with bright yellow dandelions. Everything was perfect.

Mac walked over and stood by her.

'It's breathtaking, Mac. I'd forgotten just how beautiful it was.'

'Yeah, sometimes I just need to come up here and think.'

'Is that what you do?'

Mac nodded his head as he wound his arms around her and drew her in close.

'Do you see that gully snaking through the middle of the paddock to the base of the far hill?'

Violet nodded her head. 'Yes.'

'That was part of your family's land.'

'It's lovely. But should you be telling a Beckett where their land used to be? I mean, your ancestor did steal it from mine. Better be careful or I might try and steal it back,' Violet said with a laugh.

'Well, according to our family legend, your ancestor was drunk and bet the whole parcel of land away on the turn of a card.'

'I've heard the story. But according to Grandad your ancestor was a moustache-twirling rogue.'

'He would have said that wouldn't he? He hated every single last one of us—living or dead.'

'He was a bitter person. He used his hatred to hide behind,' said Violet with a shrug. 'I understand that now, but his hatred was hard to take when I was growing up. He was always dissatisfied with his life, especially after my grandmother died; which is why the family history meant so much to him. It was easier for him to blame the McKellans than his own failings.'

'It was a sad way to live.'

'I know, but it was his choice.'

They stood on the ridge, holding each other and let the silence wash over them. Violet liked the way it felt and lay her head on Mac's chest. He was solid and dependable—just like the land.

'I think about us when I come up here—you and me.'

'Do you?'

'Yes, we're bound up in this place. Bound by blood, family and history. And I wouldn't have it any other way. I want you, Violet, I always have. I want a future with you here at McKellan's Run. I won't push you into marriage, and I'll wait as long as it takes. I just want you to know that I don't feel right unless you're standing by my side.'

'The things you say!' said Violet

'It's a promise, Violet. Whenever you're ready, I'm here,' Mac said before leaning over and kissing her.

Her arms tightened around him as his lips covered hers. A jolt of desire passed through her body as his tongue rubbed against hers. Mac's kiss was warm, encompassing and made her heart skip a beat. Her hands skimmed over the hard planes of his chest, she loved the feel of his body against hers. Perhaps she couldn't make a firm decision about her entire future but there was something that she instinctively knew—she wanted Mac. She needed to feel his strength and love around her.

She pulled back from their kiss and looked up at him.

'I can't promise everything, Mac—I still need a bit of time. It's just that my life seems in flux at the moment. Look, I realise that my timing is probably right off but I . . .'

'I said that I'd wait and I—'

Violet reached up and placed her finger against his mouth and smiled.

'You didn't let me finish. I want you, Mac.'

'Violet, sweetheart—what are you saying?'

'I want you, no, that's not right. I need you, Mac.'

She saw his eyes widen in surprise before cradling her gently next to him. She breathed in his scent as his warmth and masculine presence washed over her.

'Are you sure?'

'Yes.'

'Would you like to wait until we can go somewhere a little more comfortable?' He asked as he rested his head against hers.

Violet shook her head. 'No Mac, I wouldn't.'

'Then hang on a sec,' Mac said as he let her go. He walked over to the bike and opened up the small tool kit; inside was a packet of condoms.

Violet let out a chuckle. 'Thank God, you're such a boy scout.'

Mac walked back to her. 'Well, it pays to be prepared,' he said with a quick smile. 'Now come here.'

He snagged her around the waist and pulled her close. She felt the solidness of his body press against her as she tilted her head to capture his mouth.

Mac ran his hands down her back before they cupped her bottom and drew her in closer. She felt his hard cock push against her.

A surge of excitement spiked through her as she deepened their kiss. They fanned each other's need with touch, kiss and taste. Violet unbuttoned Mac's shirt and ran her hands over his hot skin. He tugged up her top and pulled it over her head before trailing a series of tantalizing kisses along her neck. He used his hands and then his lips to brush against her

206

breasts, causing her nipples to bead with desire. The breath caught in her throat as Mac slipped the bra strap off her shoulder and took the rosy peak in his mouth. Violet's head fell back as the tingling feeling spread throughout her.

His hands slid under her skirt, his fingertips skimming across her smooth skin. He hooked his thumbs over the sides of her lacy knickers and eased them down.

'You can't imagine how much I want you,' he whispered.

'Then take me.'

Without any hesitation Mac undid his jeans and unwrapped the condom packet. A moment later she was back in his arms. As he lifted her up, Violet spiked her fingers through his hair as she kissed him. An urgency filled her, she needed to touch him and feel his skin next to hers. She wrapped her legs around his hips, opening herself up to him.

Their eyes locked as he entered her. Violet bit her bottom lip as the delicious sensation built within her as Mac started to move.

'Ah Violet, there should have been flowers, music and at least a bed,' Mac whispered. 'I wanted our first time to be perfect.'

She held on tight. He was the only thing anchoring her as she started to be swept away. 'It is, Mac. It is.'

* * *

He hadn't wanted to let her go. Mac had wanted to keep Violet by his side, hell, he wanted to tuck her up in his bed and forget about everything. After they had made love on the ridge, a kind of peace settled over him. Mac couldn't really explain it but it was there. Violet had looked so beautiful, her hair was all mussed up, there was a faint flush to her cheeks and her lips were red from his kisses. She had taken his breath away. Back at the house it had taken them a good fifteen minutes and another dozen kisses before Mac managed to control himself enough to help her into her car. In that moment he was soaring as high as the eagles over the ridge.

Mac walked into the house after seeing Violet off, just in time to hear the sound of shattering glass coming from the floor above. He ran as fast as he could, a hundred different explanations running through his head. But his footsteps slowed as he heard the sound of raised voices coming from the guest room where Jason and Celine were staying.

'Fuck it, Celine, what the hell do you think you're doing?' Jason barked through the closed door. 'That vase was my grandmother's.'

'How could you let me think all this was yours?'

'What are you talking about?'

'McKellan's Run, of course. You said we were going to be married at your home.'

'It is my home. I grew up here.'

'But you don't own it.'

'I never said I did. I told you about the cottage by the river's bend.'

'But I thought that was just a quaint little getaway. I thought you owned McKellan's Run along with your brothers. You're the eldest for God's sake.'

'I never said I'd inherited it. It belongs to Mac. I don't see . . .' Jason's voice trailed off. 'Oh yes I do. You've been brewing some little scheme in that head of yours.'

'Don't be ridiculous. I never—'

'Yeah, right,' snapped Jason. 'McKellan's Run belongs to Mac and that's all there is to it.'

There was a bitterness in Jason's voice that Mac had never heard before, which caught him off guard. His hand reached for the doorknob but he stopped himself. This was wrong. He shouldn't be eavesdropping. He turned to leave just as Celine screeched, 'Why didn't you tell me the truth?'

'I did,' came Jason's voice, sounding softer. 'There's still enough money for you to keep up your current life-style. But please don't ever think you'll ever get an inch of McKellan soil.'

'What do you care about this place anyway? Your heart's in the city not in this grubby little town in the bush. Besides, John McKellan wasn't even your real father.'

Mac winced at Celine's harsh words. She sure didn't pull her punches. He couldn't understand what Jason saw in Celine and why he wanted to marry her. There was a long silence and Mac knew he should creep away, but he needed to know what was going on.

'Yes, Celine, he was. John McKellan was my father in every way that counted. He loved me and I loved him.' There was a crack in Jason's voice.

'If he loved you so much, why didn't he split the land between all three of you?'

'Because Mac wanted it and I didn't. I never had any interest in staying here and farming. I love what I do, no matter how crazy the hours are and how stressful it can be. But even if I did own it there's no way I'd stand by and let anyone come along and try to sell my father's legacy.'

Mac backtracked as silently as he could and walked back down the stairs, a lead weight in his stomach. He needed to get to the bottom of this and work out what exactly was going on. Because as far as he could see, his brother was making the biggest mistake of his life.

Chapter 23

It was time to lay the ghosts to rest. Violet walked over to her desk and picked up her grandfather's letter. She needed to let go of the past so she could have a future with Mac. If she closed her eyes she could almost feel his arms around her, his mouth kissing her. A wave of warmth rippled through her. She'd be damned if she would allow the past to steal away her happiness.

She ripped open the top of the envelope and, after a moment's hesitation, pulled out the pages inside. She saw that one was for Lily, so she set it aside. Her hands trembled as she started reading the letter addressed to her.

Dear Violet,

I'm sorry.

I pray you will find it in your heart to forgive a stupid old man, though I know it's more than I deserve.

I allowed my hatred of the McKellans to cloud my judgement and for the second time in my life let them take away the people I held most dear.

The McKellans were instrumental in the decline of our family's fortunes. However, you were right when you once said that my grandfather drank and gambled away our wealth.

I've had years to think about how I alienated you and Lily. It's always easier to blame someone else, some outside force rather than your own flesh and blood. But the Becketts of the past must be held accountable for not only losing the family's money but the land as well.

I lectured you and Lily more times than either of you want to remember about how the McKellans took everything from our family. Well, the truth is they took everything from me.

Long before I married your grandmother there was a girl called Isabella Cartwright. She had hair as dark as the night sky and sparkling blue eyes. Isabella was the most beautiful girl in Violet Falls. I loved her so much and for one perfect summer, I thought I was the luckiest man alive. I thought she loved me too but I was wrong.

Things changed the minute Lucas McKellan arrived back in Violet Falls to take over the farm. He wooed her with flowers, pretty words and promises and before too long she'd all but forgotten about me. They were married on the first day of spring in the rose garden at McKellan's Run.

I want to say she chose Lucas because of his fine house and healthy bank balance but that would be a lie. You only had to see them together to know what they meant to each other. And that knowledge hurt like a sharp thorn in my side, which rubbed and pricked through my entire life.

I can almost hear your accusation, Violet. 'But what about my grandmother?' you ask.

All I can tell you was that she was a good and fine woman who loved you and your sister. I cared for her and that's the truth but I could never let Isabella go. I tried to be a good husband but deep down I was wracked with guilt because I just didn't love her the way I should have.

I hope you can forgive me. When you told me about the pregnancy, my hatred for the McKellans overwhelmed me. It was another example of them destroying our family.

I should have supported you and, to my never-ending shame, I didn't. My pride, hate and guilt were all-consuming and destructive. I should have turned from it but I didn't.

I blamed the McKellans for destroying my family but I've had years to reflect and come to the realisation that it was all my own doing.

I should never have chased you or your sister away.

I can understand if you don't want to but I hope you keep the house.

There's always a Beckett in Violet Falls, and that Beckett should be you.

Yours, Grandad

Violet sat down on her desk with a bump and re-read the letter before folding it up again and putting it back in the envelope. After slipping it into the top drawer of her desk, she felt lighter and years of a tension she hadn't even realised she was carrying, seemed to melt away.

She sat still for a few minutes, the soft tick of the wall clock marking off the seconds.

'You cheated yourself out of a family. It was your loss, but I'm sorry for it,' Violet said softly as she stood up and walked towards the door. 'I forgive you.'

***

Violet's eyes widened with surprise when she opened the door later that day. She'd taken a break from the wedding to catch up on emails and organise the logistics of a fortieth wedding anniversary at the Botanic Gardens. She couldn't wait till Jason's wedding was over and she could turn her attention to other events.

'Jason, what are you doing here?'

'Can I come in please,' he said, looking uneasy. 'I need to speak to you for a minute. I promise it won't take very long.'

Violet's stomach lurched, wondering if Celine had said anything to him since their conversation. Something was very wrong, she could sense it.

'Well, if it's important I guess you better come this way,' said Violet, gesturing for him to follow her into the office.

'I like what you've done with the place, Violet. It looks good—welcoming.'

'Thanks, it was definitely time for a re-do. Nothing had been done to it in, like, sixty years,' said Violet, sitting down at her desk and pointing to the opposite chair. 'Please, sit down.'

She watched as he sat down, his hands fidgeting. He was clearly nervous.

'So, what's up, Jason?'

'Um, Holly isn't here is she?'

Violet shook her head. 'No, she's at school. Why?'

'Oh, just wondering.' His hands stilled as he placed them on his lap. 'I've been thinking since the other day. You know, about you and me and Holly.'

A cold, prickling sensation ran between Violet's shoulder blades and down her back.

'I see . . .'

'No, I don't think you do, Violet. I was wrong all those years ago and I know I acted like a jerk. And . . .'

'What?'

'I want to be part of Holly's life. I know I told you to have an abortion but since seeing her, knowing she's mine—well hell, I don't know,' said Jason, fidgeting again. 'I guess what I'm saying is I want to see her and get to know her.'

Violet sat stunned for a minute as she tried to wrap her head around what he was saying.

'So, let me get this straight,' said Violet, after taking a deep breath. 'You want me to let you see Holly after you told me to get rid of my pregnancy. You didn't want me, Jason, and you sure as hell didn't want a baby. And now, after eight years, you think it's okay to play daddy?'

'Come on Violet, it's not like—'

'Yes it is,' said Violet, interrupting him. 'You're not thinking about anyone except yourself. What a surprise.'

'Violet, I have a right.'

'Didn't you waive that when you told me to have an abortion. As far as you were concerned I dealt with the problem. Wasn't that what you called it?'

'I admit I was wrong. Fuck, I was young and stupid and selfish. But things are different now.'

'Are they? You weren't there when I was working two jobs to try and support her, you didn't nurse her through her first fever or pick her up each time she fell. You could have, I gave you that opportunity but you didn't want it. Why should I let you now?'

'That's not fair. If I'd known—'

Violet stood up and walked over to the door. This meeting was over.

'Marry Celine and just forget about me and my daughter. You two are perfect for each other and you can have your own kids.'

Jason stood up to leave. 'Look, Violet, I do have some rights. I'm Holly's father—I could ask for visitation rights, and maybe even part-custody.'

'Custody?' said Violet. 'Do you know how disruptive it'd be for Holly to move to Melbourne again?'

'Well, if not custody then visitation rights,' said Jason, before walking out the front door.

Violet slammed the door shut and stood leaning against it, her forehead pressing against the hard wood. Her body shook and a wave of fear threatened to engulf her. Just when she and Holly were happy and settled and could envision a future in Violet Falls, Jason McKellan had come along talking about visitation rights.

* * *

'Look, I've had a lot on my mind over the past few weeks,' Jason said as he stared out the kitchen window.

'All I'm saying is, if there's a problem or if there's anything you want to talk about, I'm here,' said Mac leaning back in his chair.

'Why would you even care?' said Jason.

'Because we're McKellans and brothers and I've got your back.'

Jason let out a bitter-sounding laugh. 'Yeah, since when?'

'Since always.'

'Nup, you're playing at something. I haven't got time for this. My head is spinning with work and the wedding and Celine's stressed out of her brain,' said Jason.

'Well if you want to talk any time, just ask.'

Their eyes locked for a moment before Jason looked away, turmoil etched on his face. 'No, I'm on a set path. I'll marry Celine and go back to the city and get back to work,' he said, before hesitating on his way to the door.

'Actually I would like to know what's going on between you and Violet.'

'What?' said Mac, frowning.

'Are you and Violet together and is it serious?'

'Well, I really want us to be together, and I know she cares for me, but there's nothing fixed as yet. I've been busy with McKellan's Run, she's busy with work and Holly,' said Mac, sensing there was something bad coming his way.

'Then you should know I want to be part of Holly's life. You might want to encourage Violet to let this happen. Holly is my daughter and though I did act like a jerk when Violet told me she was pregnant, now that I've met my daughter I want to be able to see her and have some sort of father-daughter relationship. I've told Violet this too,' said Jason.

'Jesus, did you threaten her?'

'Of course not. It's just that Holly is my daughter, no matter what happened between me and Violet, and I have a right to see her. There's nothing wrong with that.'

'How do you manage that with you in Melbourne and Violet here. And what if Violet refuses?'

'Then I'll have to resort to petitioning the courts.'

Mac uncrossed his arms and clenched them by his side. 'Fuck it, Jason, you hurt her badly once and she's never trusted a bloke since. And she's done an amazing job bringing up Holly. Please just move on with your life and let everyone else move on with theirs.'

'I can't.'

'Why not? You've got your career and Celine. Just leave Violet and Holly alone.'

Jason shook his head. 'I hear what you're saying but the thought of you having Violet and raising my daughter is too much. Holly's mine, Mac, and I want to be the one she sees as her father,' said Jason before leaving the room.

Mac stood open-mouthed and stared at the doorway. Anger surged through him and all he wanted to do was wring Jason's bloody neck.

Chapter 24

Violet fell into Mac's arms as soon as she opened the door.

'It's alright Violet, I'm not going to let anyone hurt you or Holly,' said Mac, holding her close and feeling her trembling against him.

'He says if I don't tell Holly he's her father and let him see her, he's going to . . . He's going to take us to court for visitation rights, or maybe even custody.'

'It won't come to that, I promise. Jason has always devoted all his attention to his career, and Celine is a handful. And I doubt she'll want a stepdaughter sprung on her right after getting married. Give him a bit of time and everything will sort itself out,' said Mac, rubbing her back.

'He can't take her away from me, Mac. I don't know what I'd do if—'

'He won't, Violet. No one is taking Holly from you, okay?'

She peered up at him through tear-misted eyes and sniffed. 'Okay.'

'Come on, let's get you calmed down. What time do you have to pick up Holly?'

Violet dashed a couple of tears away with the back of her

hand. 'In about half an hour. Which probably gives me just enough time to fix my mascara.'

'Yeah, well I wasn't going to say anything but I don't think emo chick or gothic bride is really your look.'

'Says you,' said Violet, smiling through her tears.

'Yeah, says me. Come on, go get ready and we can pick up Holly together. Why don't I treat you both to pizza and ice cream tonight? The last thing you need is to have to cook.'

'But there's still so much to do. I mean, I should go through the—'

'Not tonight, you don't. Tonight it's all about you, me and Holly. McKellan's Run and the blasted wedding can wait.'

Violet squeezed him a bit tighter. 'Thank you, Mac. You always know how to fix everything.'

* * *

It was almost midnight by the time Mac got back to McKellan's Run, feeling sort of buzzed. He grinned as he pulled out his keys. He'd spent the evening with Violet and Holly and a warmth and a gentleness wrapped around his heart because tonight he'd felt like he was part of a family in a way he hadn't since his Dad died and Sarah had moved into town. They'd eaten pizza and sat on Violet's couch and watched Holly's favourite movie. Holly made him smile as she sang along with all the songs while Violet held his hand on the couch all night. After Holly had gone to bed, he and Violet had watched an old movie. Halfway through the movie, Mac had thought, this is all I've ever wanted for so many years.

He turned the key in the front door and wandered into his dark house. For the first time ever, it felt cold and lonely. Mac headed into the kitchen to grab a drink before going to bed. He pulled open the refrigerator door and stood there checking out his options.

'You're late.'

Mac turned around to find Celine leaning against the doorway.

'Yeah, just off to bed. Where's Jason?'

'He said he was taking off to his cottage for a while,' Celine replied with a shrug.

'You didn't want to go with him?'

'He said he wanted some time alone. Apparently he needed some time to think—about what, I have no idea. We're meant to be focusing on our wedding and he's running off to commune with nature.'

'Ah,' said Mac.

'I suppose you've spent the evening with Violet?'

Mac grabbed a bottle of water and slammed the fridge door closed. 'Yeah, I have. Now, if you'll excuse me, I've got a busy day tomorrow.'

'Oh, I know how hard you work, Mac. You're really dedicated—I admire that,' said Celine.

Mac opened the bottle of water and looked away.

'Oh well, someone has to keep the old place running.'

'I suppose they do. You're so dependable, aren't you, Mac?'

'Hmmm, well not sure about that. Besides there isn't anyone else to run it,' said Mac before chugging down some water. He wasn't sure where the hell this conversation was going but he was beginning to feel uncomfortable.

'Guys like you are pretty rare but I know your type. Family comes first and you'll sacrifice everything for the ones you love,' said Celine.

'Well, that's what it means to be a family . . . now if you'd excuse me.'

'Oh, I understand. You see my dad is in bad financial trouble. He's in the process of selling all his assets to try and save the family business—and even then there's still a chance he'll lose everything. I'd do anything to help him out.'

'I'm sorry to hear that, Celine. I didn't know,' said Mac.

'As you say, you have to protect your family,' said Celine.

A chill shimmied down Mac's spine. She was up to something but he wasn't sure what.

'What are you getting at, Celine?' said Mac. He hated games, preferring people to just say what they mean.

'I just wonder how you and Violet would feel if Jason and I sought complete custody of Holly?'

'Given she's a great mother and she's brought her up by herself these past nearly eight years, it's incredibly unlikely you'd get custody.'

'Hmmm, but what would a judge think about her purposely keeping knowledge of the child from him?'

'What the hell?'

'Come on Mac, you have to agree that it's a pretty awful thing to do—keeping a secret like that?'

'You know as well as I do that Jason never wanted Holly.'

'Perhaps. But something like that . . . I mean Jason's best friend is one of Melbourne's most successful family law lawyers.'

Mac felt a spark of anger ignite in the pit of his stomach. 'How in God's name could you take Holly away from Violet?'

She crossed her arms over her chest.

'I want five hundred thousand dollars, otherwise I'll encourage Jason to seek custody.'

Mac stilled and slowly lowered the bottle. 'Excuse me?'

'You heard. Pay up or I'll encourage Jason to go for total custody.'

Mac felt as if he'd just been kicked in the guts.

'As if you could.'

'Oh, don't doubt me, Mac. I'm more than capable.'

'Celine, why would you do such a thing? Violet hasn't done anything to you. How can you hate her that much?'

'My father needs the money, it's as simple as that. I don't hate Violet or Holly but they're a means to an end. Okay, I admit that the woman rubs me the wrong way and I can't stand how everybody falls all over her but that's beside the point. Unless you pay up, Violet and Holly will be, let's say, collateral damage.'

'And if I give you the money?'

'I'll discourage Jason from going for custody.'

'Really, and what happens next time you're strapped for cash?'

223

'This is a one-off. My father needs a quick injection of cash and you have my word.'

Mac let out a hollow laugh. 'Like I would ever trust you!'

'You really don't have a choice. That's the offer and I'll give you a couple of days to think about it. It all comes down to how much you care about Violet and Holly. And if you're willing to pay five hundred thousand dollars to protect her.'

* * *

Mac stomped into his bedroom.

'What a bitch!' he said as he dumped the bottle on the nightstand.

He opened the window and let the night breeze blow over his face. It was cold and clear but it didn't abate his anger. Somewhere in the dark an owl hooted.

'Hope you're having a better night than I am, buddy.'

Mac stared out into the darkness. Five hundred thousand dollars was a hell of a lot of money. His mind raced as he tried to work out how he could come up with such an amount. McKellan's Run was worth a tidy sum but nearly all the money Mac earned was poured back into the farm. There was always something to buy, fix or replace. Last season he'd been forced to buy a new tractor when the old one spectacularly blew up in the middle of slashing. He'd also replaced the roof on the old shed, bought two more water tanks, added a few more ewes to his flock and purchased a prize-winning ram for breeding. So even though the farm was rich in assets, Mac's available funds were always a bit tight, well at least until the next wool cheque came in. And he'd hoped to do something about the old original cottage.

He sucked in a breath. Could Celine really be that conniving?

The only positive thing to come out of the whole ugly conversation was that he was pretty sure that Jason didn't have anything to do with it. They had always had their differences and probably always would but at least Mac could find some comfort in knowing his brother was above blackmail.

He ran his hand through his hair and sighed. He could raise the money and he'd do it for Violet. However before he fronted up at the bank he needed to talk to Jason and probably his mum as well.

How he was going to broach the subject with his brother he had no idea. He could hardly walk up and slap him on the back and say, 'Oh by the way, your fiancée is black-mailing me to the tune of five hundred thousand big ones.'

Hmmm. It wasn't the best way to start a discussion.

He'd do anything to protect Violet and Holly but this whole situation was making him sick. Getting a loan wouldn't be that much of a problem but it still hurt. He could almost imagine generations of McKellans rolling over in their graves. It made him feel that he was going back on his promise to his dad, the one where he vowed to protect McKellan's Run no matter the cost.

He closed his eyes and tried to shut out the image of the overly bright hospital cubicle. His father lying way too still in the narrow bed. It wasn't right, his dad should be out riding across their land with the cold breeze, not lying there—small, pale, a shadow of the man he was.

'I won't let you down, Dad. I promise McKellan's Run will be safe with me until I can hand it down to the next generation,' Mac had said, clasping his father's hand.

For a moment the old man's eyes burned bright. 'I know you will, son. We McKellans draw our life from the land. Look after it and it will look after you.'

'Sure, Dad.' Mac's throat seemed to close up and there was a hot prickling at the back of his eyes.

His father squeezed his hand. 'It's alright, Mac. I've been lucky enough to love two amazing women, who have given me three sons that any man would be proud of; well, four if I count that rascal, Flynn. Just remember to follow your heart, and everything will work out.'

'Dad, I—'

'Go on, take your brothers out of here. I need a few minutes with your mum,' he said, looking past Mac to Dan and Jason, who were standing at the end of the bed. He stared at them for a moment as if he was committing them to memory or etching them on his heart.

The brothers walked silently out of the ward. Mac turned around and caught his Dad watching them go. He gave Mac a smile before he turned to Sarah.

That was the last time Mac had seen his father alive.

* * *

Mac ran his hand over the back of his neck. He'd made that promise to his dad to keep the Run safe. Getting a loan to help Celine and her dodgy father wasn't putting the land first. That amount of money wasn't going to destroy McKellan's Run but it would certainly hurt and make things hard next year. Would his father forgive him or would he expect him to honour it when Violet, Holly and Mac's happiness was at stake?

Mac drew in a shuddering breath. If it came down to a promise, or Violet and Holly, it was a simple enough choice—Violet wins. He loved her and would do anything it took to keep her and Holly safe; even if it meant paying off bloody Celine.

Mac grabbed his keys off the nightstand and headed out.

Chapter 25

It was a clear night and the almost-full moon bathed the countryside in a pale light. Mac drove through the shadowy bush and down long familiar tracks until he took a left turn down a rough dirt road. He wound down the window and rested his arm as the ute bumped along.

Mac slowed down as he caught sight of a roo in the headlights. The animal appeared startled but after a moment's hesitation it bounded back between the trees. As the ute neared the crossroad, Mac changed down gears and took the turn to the right. A fresh breeze blew in the open window, bringing with it the scent of water. Mac nudged the accelerator as he drove up a steep rise and reached the top. Below, a small cottage sat on the high bank of Landoc Creek.

The cottage had been built a hundred years ago or so and was situated on the edge of McKellan's Run. It had always been a beautiful and peaceful spot. When they were kids, Mac, Dan, Jason and Flynn used to fish in the spot where the creek wound past the cabin. It belonged to Jason now and he'd spent a small fortune modernising the plumbing and sewage but other than a paint job on the outside it was still the same as it always had been. The weatherboard cottage was surrounded by an old-fashioned garden filled with apple and pear trees, with Marguerite daisy bushes sitting on either side of the gate and an ancient climbing rose bush, running and twisting its way up and along the verandah. When it bloomed in the late spring you could smell the fragrance from the blood-red roses for miles.

Mac parked the ute outside the picket fence, got out and stood for a moment gazing up at the moon; the night was still and all he could hear was the soft sound of the creek trickling past. Taking a deep breath he unlatched the creaky gate, and made his way over the flagstones to the front door. He knocked on the door and waited a few seconds before he knocked again. From inside came a muffled voice, a crash and a string of profanities. The door jerked open and Jason stood there rubbing his shin.

'Hi, Mac,' he said as he wobbled slightly. Even from where Mac was standing he could smell the alcohol.

'Hey, what happened?' Mac asked as he gestured to Jason's leg.

'I collided with the table. What's up?'

'I need to talk to you.'

'Listen, if this is about what I said to Violet, I'm not backing down. Although I admit, I lost my temper and could have handled it better. I just want a chance to get to know Holly . . . so if you're here to ball me out about that, don't bother.'

Mac shook his head. 'Why are you upsetting Violet like this? She's working flat out on your wedding and the last thing she needs is you giving her a hard time,' he said.

'I understand you were shocked to find out about Holly and I get it. But pushing Violet into a corner and threatening her isn't going to help anyone, especially Holly.'

'If you've come here to give me a lecture—'

'It's not why I'm here.'

Jason looked surprised as he stepped back from the door. 'Come in.'

Mac walked into a large room. The slate-tiled floor and wood gave it a masculine feel. An old well-worn leather couch sat opposite the open fireplace and at the far end was a kitchen and a battered-looking refectory table. A narrow wooden staircase ran up the right wall and it led to a bedroom in the loft.

Jason got a couple of beers out of the stainless steel fridge, which was the only modern piece of furniture in the whole cottage and looked out of place. He tossed one to Mac.

'So, what is it you need to talk to me about?' said Jason taking a swig.

Mac settled himself at the table. 'Before I tell you why I'm here, I've just got to ask—why are you here and Celine is at my place?'

'I needed some time to myself, so I could think,' said Jason, looking a bit bleary-eyed.

'I don't know how to say this, so I'm just gonna say it,' said Mac. 'I don't want you to have the wedding at the homestead and I'd prefer if Celine left today too.'

'What? If this is about Violet—'

'No, well I suppose it is but not in the way you're thinking. Celine is trying to blackmail me.'

'Oh get out of it, as if she—'

Mac broke in, 'Jason, she tried to blackmail me.'

'Seriously?' said Jason, a look of disbelief on his face. 'How could she blackmail *you*?'

'She said if I don't give her five hundred thousand dollars she'll encourage you to seek full custody of Holly.'

'What? That's the last thing she'd want,' said Jason.

'Jase, she seemed absolutely serious about the custody thing.'

'What did she say exactly?'

'Apparently her father has already sold off some assets but he still doesn't have nearly enough money to save his business. What I can't understand is why, if you love her enough to want to marry her, you aren't helping her father out?'

'Because I've already given him a huge amount of money. She's been pressuring me for more help but I refused. Mac, her dad still has real estate he could sell but he can't bear to put it on the market. He's got a beautiful house in South Yarra which he refuses to part with. Don't think for a moment he'll be destitute or starving because that isn't the case. I'm really sorry you've got caught up in this.'

'Even if there's only the slim possibility, I can't let Celine ruin Violet.'

'She won't. I promise that I'll have this all sorted by the morning. Now about the wedding—'

'God, you still want to marry her? Jason, I'm sorry if you love her but Celine's a nightmare. Maybe you should rethink the whole thing because I think you're making a big mistake.'

'I can't explain but I have my reasons.'

Mac put his can on the table next to him. 'Well, it's your future, but I really don't understand how you could marry someone who's prepared to blackmail your brother. If this whole mess isn't sorted by lunchtime, I don't want the wedding at my house. I still don't understand why you even wanted to have it here. I would have thought a Toorak wedding would have been more Celine's style.'

Jason nodded. 'I'll get to the bottom of it.'

'Alright then, I'm off to Violet's for the night. I don't want to be under the same roof with Celine,' Mac said as he walked to the door.

* * *

Jason stomped up the stairs of his brother's house and entered the bedroom Celine was using, slamming the door behind him.

'Would you like to explain why you decided it was a good idea to blackmail my brother?' he demanded.

Celine sat bolt upright in bed and held the covers over her breasts. 'He told you?' she said, a startled look on her face.

'It's even worse than that. I suspect Mum will know by the morning as well.'

'Your mother is going to find out? Can't you stop him from telling her?' said Celine, her voice uncharacteristically small and unsure. 'I didn't expect him to say anything. It just proves he doesn't really love Violet.'

'Of course he bloody well loves Violet. What the hell were you thinking?'

'But Dad's desperate.'

'What made you even think that Mac had that kind of money lying around?'

'This place is worth a fortune. Why wouldn't he have the money?'

'You don't know much about farms do you? Yes, McKellan's Run is worth a lot of money but it's all based on the capital value, there's not lots of cash lying around, that's for sure. And Mac puts his blood, sweat and every spare penny back into it.'

'I was just trying to save my father, you can't fault me for that.'

Jason gave her an incredulous look. 'You tried to blackmail my brother!'

'You don't even like him.'

'God, Celine you sound like a spoilt little princess who'll stop at nothing to get what she wants.'

'I wouldn't have to go to such lengths if you just agreed to help Dad out.'

'I'm marrying you not your father. Of course I'll provide the lifestyle you're accustomed to but that doesn't include shoring up your father's business anymore than I already have. I know he's sold some of his assets, but I'm also aware he's still got more properties and he's going to have to consider selling his house.'

'But why can't you help him, Jason?'

'I already have! I'm not a bottomless pit and you really need to come to terms with that fact.'

'But he's going to have to sell his house which is his pride and joy. It's where I grew up. He's never let it go, even through all his marriages.'

'He won't be homeless, Celine. He can buy a more modest place nearby. Anyway, why should he keep his house at Mac's expense? Enough is enough. Leave Mac, Violet and Holly out of your schemes. Do I make myself clear?'

'And if I don't?'

'Then I don't want to marry you.'

'That would mean Dad and I could no longer provide all those introductions and referrals to you. Without us, you won't maintain that illustrious client list you've worked so hard for.'

'That's a chance I'm willing to take. And without me, or more to the point my bank balance, you'll need to readjust your lifestyle. No more ladies' lunches with your charity boards, no more fundraising dinners. Who knows, Celine, you may have to get a real job.'

'I have a job.'

'Two days at your aunt's boutique hardly qualifies, let's face it. Look, we had fun together and I thought that would be enough but now I'm not so sure.'

'What do you mean by *that*?' demanded Celine.

'I thought because you loved me just as I loved you, I thought we had shared goals about how our lives should be and we could have a happy marriage, but after this stunt of yours—'

Celine crossed the room until she stood in front of Jason. 'I do love you, I really do. As you say, we want the same things and the sex we have is amazing.'

'How can you say you love me if you're prepared to blackmail my brother for God's sake?' shouted Jason.

'Please forgive me darling. I screwed up. Dad's been so desperate. He's always looked after me and I'd do anything to help him out. I'll apologise to Mac and smooth things over.'

Jason was silent but he didn't pull away as Celine's hand trailed lower down.

* * *

Mac had spent the night next to Violet. He hadn't told her the truth about Celine's threats because he hadn't wanted to worry her. Instead he'd said that Celine and Jason were having an argument and he had felt like a stranger in his own house. Violet being Violet had welcomed him into her arms and then into her bed. He had held her close for the remainder of the night and kissed her before he slipped away just as the sky was beginning to lighten.

The sun was just breaking over the hills as Mac got home and headed to the shed. He'd hardly slept after talking to Jason but now it was time to concentrate on work. He packed the brush cutter, shovel and pick onto the quad bike. It was time to tackle those bloody blackberries near the top dam. He'd thought about poisoning them but as they were close to the dam water he'd decided to go old-school—cutting, hacking and digging the bloody things out.

He wasn't looking forward to it but it had to be done. If he didn't get rid of the blackberries they would spread over the whole paddock.

He swung by the house and picked up some supplies before he spent the morning battling the prickly bushes. Even with gloves and protective gear he still managed to get scratches all over him.

Halfway through, he stopped for a minute and took a breather, rolling his aching shoulders and trying to ignore the trickle of sweat down his back.

Why the hell hadn't he hired someone else to do this?

At about nine o'clock, Mac sat down, took his hat off, ran his hand through his hair and closed his eyes as a cool breeze blew over him. Cutting blackberries was hot work and he was glad of a break. He opened up his thermos and poured a coffee but just as he raised the cup to his mouth his mobile rang.

'Hello?'

'Hey Mac, it's Jason. Listen can you come back to the house?'

'I'm in the middle of something.'

'Can you get away? It's important.'

'Alright. I'm on my way.'

About fifteen minutes later Mac walked into the kitchen, wondering what was going on. To his surprise he found Jason, his mother and Celine sitting around the kitchen table. A frown flickered over his face when he saw his mother's pale face.

'Mum, what are you doing here?'

'I called her,' Jason said as she looked up at Mac.

'You called her, but, but I thought—' Celine stammered.

Jason ignored her. 'Celine has something to tell you, don't you?'

'Yes, yes I do,' said Celine looking incredibly nervous.

Celine glanced at Sarah and then Mac. 'I need to apologise to you for last night.'

'You think?' said Mac.

'What I did, I mean what I said was unforgivable. But I hope that you can find it in your heart to forgive me just the same.' Celine dropped her gaze looking repentant.

'There's no excuse,' she continued, 'but I've been so worried about my father, I haven't been able to think straight. I'm sick with anxiety and every time he rings he sounds so defeated. He wanted me to ask Jason to lend him more money, but he's already given him so much, I knew I couldn't ask. I guess last night, after Jason went to the cottage I had one glass of wine too many. I just sort of snapped and came up with this crazy way to save Dad. I'm so sorry, Mac. I really am.'

'Well you might be sorry, Celine, but that doesn't excuse your appalling behaviour,' said Sarah. 'Very soon you're going to become part of this family and instead of embracing it you chose blackmail!'

'I'm sorry, I just don't know what else to say. With all the pressure from the wedding and then Dad's troubles, it was just all too much for me.' Celine's shoulders shuddered and there were tears in her eyes. 'I'm very ashamed.'

Mac wasn't buying it. The only thing Celine was sorry about was that she'd been caught. The woman was diabolical. What was Jason thinking?

Mac looked over at his brother. 'If you still want to get married here, I won't stop you. But if I so much as hear a hint of a rumour or any gossip aimed at Violet all bets are off. Understand?'

'Thanks, Mac,' Jason said with a nod.

'That's very gracious of you, Mac,' said Sarah with a forced smile.

'I think it'd be best if you both stay at the cottage,' said Mac to Celine. 'You and the bridesmaids can use the room upstairs on the day of the wedding but I'd prefer if you spend as much time as possible away from McKellan's Run.'

Chapter 26

Violet's phone started ringing and she hurried over to the table. Typical, someone always rang just as you were in the middle of something. She placed the mixing bowl down and looked around for something to wipe her sticky fingers on. She was out of luck so she wiped some of the chocolate cake mixture on her jeans before she picked up the receiver.

'Hello?'

'Oh hi, Violet, it's Sarah. I've been trying to ring Mac. Is he there, please?'

'Hi, Sarah, actually you've just missed him. He and Holly have just gone into town to grab a few things at the supermarket,' said Violet, frowning. 'I don't know why he wouldn't be answering his phone though,' Violet added, looking around the room and suddenly zeroing in on Mac's mobile. 'Ah, I've found the answer to your question. He's left his phone on the bench.'

'Well, look, could you get him to give me a ring? I can't say we've managed to sort everything out with Jason, but at least we've put a halt to Celine trying to extract money out of Mac.'

'What?'

There was silence on the other end of the line for a moment or two.

'Ah, I see I've let the cat out of the bag. Sorry, it really wasn't my place to say anything. It's just I was so damned mad with Celine.'

'Sarah, I don't understand.'

'Well, uh, I shouldn't say any more.'

'What's happening, Sarah, is Mac in trouble?'

'No, Violet, look I'll tell you but please don't say anything to Mac,' Sarah said.

'Okay, I promise.'

'Celine told Mac that if he didn't pay her she'd make things very difficult for you and Holly.'

'What did Mac say?' asked Violet.

'He was totally prepared to pay the money. You know how much he cares about you. He'd do anything for you,' said Sarah.

Violet's heart seemed to contract and her vision blurred as tears welled.

'He did that?'

'Of course he did. Mac loves you.'

'Yes, he does,' answered Violet as she clutched the phone to her ear.

'I didn't mean to blurt it out. I suppose Mac had his reasons for not telling you. He probably just didn't want you to worry. Oh and you'll be relieved—or maybe not—to know that even though this happened, the wedding is going ahead. Lord only knows what Jason is thinking and why he'd want to marry Celine after a stunt like this, but Celine will be staying at Jason's cottage until the wedding and I think she'll be completely supportive of everything you choose.'

'Oh?' said Violet, wondering why on earth Jason would want to go ahead and marry Celine. She knew, despite everything, that Jason had a core of decency, but she couldn't say the same about Celine.

'Would you get Mac to call me?' asked Sarah.

'Sure, I'll tell him as soon as he gets back.'

'Thanks. Oh and Violet, don't worry. I know things seem complicated now but I'm sure we'll work it all out.'

'Thanks, Sarah, and thanks for telling me about Celine.'

'I couldn't not,' said Sarah, sounding worried nevertheless. 'Talk to you later, Violet. Bye.'

'Bye.'

Violet hung up the phone and retrieved the mixing bowl. About ten minutes later, the front door opened and Mac and Holly came in laughing. Mac carried two bags of groceries while Holly held a large brightly coloured box.

'Mummy, look at the pretty dolly Mac bought me!'

Violet ran her hand over her daughter's hair. 'Let me see. It's beautiful, Holly, I hope you remembered to say thank you?'

'She did,' Mac said, taking the bags through to the kitchen, then opening one and taking out a small bunch of bright pink, yellow and orange gerberas. 'And these are for you,' he said, handing them to her.

'Thank you, they're beautiful,' said Violet.

'You look worried. Is everything alright?'

'Yep, all good,' said Violet taking a vase from the cupboard under the sink.

'So you say, but I think there's something wrong.'

Violet busied herself with the flowers and didn't look him in the eyes. 'There's nothing wrong. Oh, your mum called. You forgot to take your mobile so she wants you to call her back.'

'Did Mum upset you?' Mac asked, as he came and stood behind her. His hands circled around her waist and he held her tight.

Violet could feel his warm body against her back. It was comforting and Violet knew that whenever she was with him, Mac always had the ability to make her feel special, wanted and protected. McKellan's Run was in his blood, it was the family legacy that defined him and yet he'd been willing to give up a substantial amount of money for her and Holly. It was unimaginable and Violet felt humbled at the depth of his love for her. She turned her face against his chest and willed herself not to cry.

'Since when would your Mum ever say anything to upset me? She's the most wonderful woman. How could you even think that?'

'I don't know. Everything was great and you were smiling when we left and now we're back to you looking as if you want to cry.'

'It's nothing, Mac. Really.'

'So there *is* something wrong. I knew it!'

Lord, he was like a dog with a bone. But before Violet could try and persuade him everything was fine, Holly came to the rescue.

'Mummy, Mac, I can't open the box and get the dolly out.'

Mac let Violet go. 'Duty calls,' he whispered in her ear before he turned and grinned at the little girl. 'Okay, I'm on it. Here, Holly, give it to me and we'll see if we can rescue the doll from its prison.'

Holly giggled as she handed him the box. 'You're silly, Mac.'

'Thanks. I try.'

Mac and Holly headed over to the table and started to undo the box. Violet smiled as she watched them. Holly's head was bowed over the box in concentration as Mac attempted to take apart every little tie twist, plastic tab and sealed plastic bubble.

'Hey, I think we have it now,' Mac said as he tried to yank the doll out.

'No Mac, see, her hair is still stuck there, and there's another tie around her tummy,' said Holly.

Mac glanced up at Violet. 'They don't make this easy do they?'

'No they don't, but I think you're doing a good job,' said Violet as she retrieved her mixing bowl. Gosh, it was odd how life could spin and change so quickly. She'd known for a while that Mac loved her, but now she realised just how much.

'Really, then why are you looking at me funny?'

Violet turned away and hid a smile. 'Mac, I really have no idea what you're talking about.'

***

243

Back in the cottage, Jason turned on his side and rested Celine's head in his hands. She looked beautiful.

'Even though that was immensely satisfying, it doesn't mean I've forgotten what you've done.'

Celine wiggled up the bed and lay against the soft pillows.

'I know—' she said with a sigh. 'And I completely understand.'

'So what's the deal? Why are you so bloody mercenary?' Jason sat up and leant back against the bedhead.

'All I can do is apologise again about all that business with Mac. It's Dad, he keeps ringing to see if I can get him some more money. I know you've already lent him a lot but he won't take no for an answer.'

'Celine, I gave him twenty thousand dollars and lent him another hundred and fifty thousand.'

'What? Oh, I didn't know it was so much.'

'Yeah I know.'

'I've tried to reason with him but he has this way of talking me around. I suppose it's partly because since his last divorce there's only been the two of us.'

'He manipulates you, just like he tries to do with everyone else.'

'Yes, I know you're right. It's just that he's been there for me. I try to say no and he makes me feel so damn guilty— like I'm betraying him. I know one day I'm going to have to stand up to him but I've always tried so hard to please him.'

Jason glanced at her. 'It's your life, Celine. You're not a little girl anymore. You risked our relationship trying to please him.'

'I know, I know.'

'Okay, so I get the whole Mac, money and your dad thing but what the hell are you doing with this wedding?'

'What do you mean?'

'Oh, come on, Celine, you've picked holes in everything Violet's done and you've been so difficult to please.'

'It's our wedding, Jason. It's meant to be perfect. I have an idea in my head and I want it to match the reality. I know I've been difficult at times but . . .'

'Difficult! I suppose that's one way of putting it. Let's be honest, you've been appalling to Violet.'

'I just don't think we share the same vision for the wedding, that's all. I'm not being picky. I'm just making sure that I get what I want,' said Celine with a shrug. 'I don't see anything wrong with that.'

'If you say so. I thought you might've been uncomfortable because the family likes her, or something like that.'

'Not at all. I just don't warm to her and I can't understand what all the fuss is about her.'

'What fuss?'

Celine gave him a hard look. 'Oh you know exactly what I'm talking about. Ever since I've arrived it's been, "Violet this, Violet that. Don't upset Violet and isn't she pretty, clever and every damn thing else." Not to mention that she's the mother of a child you didn't even know you had. I'm sick of everyone pandering to her. This is my wedding, not hers.'

Chapter 27

'Hey, Lily,' said Violet when her sister finally answered the phone. 'Sorry to call so late.'

'Not a problem, I wasn't asleep. Is everything alright?'

'No, not even close.'

'What's up? Holly isn't sick or anything?'

'No, Holly's fine. It's just the whole McKellan wedding, its causing more trouble than I ever thought possible.'

'Come on, Violet. You're planning the wedding of Holly's father and your ex-boyfriend; old feelings and memories are bound to be stirred up.'

'It's not just that. Jason worked out he's Holly's father and he's threatening to go to the courts for custody,' said Violet.

'No fucking way.'

'His fiancée tried to blackmail Mac into giving her money. Despite her having no interest in kids she said she'd support Jason in any custody battle.'

'Oh, come on you're just making this up. God, tell me you're making this up!'

'Nup. Celine was trying to convince Mac to give her a large sum of money or she'd do her. And if that wasn't enough, Mac's in love with me and I've fallen headlong in love with him.'

'Violet, my head's spinning. I'm so happy about you and Mac but what the hell are we going to do about Jason and Celine? Shall I come up? If I leave now . . . what's the time?'

Violet glanced at the clock on the wall. 'Almost midnight.'

'Well, I can be back in Violet Falls just before two o'clock.'

'No, stay where you are. I'm fine, and Mac and I will work this out. I don't want you to worry.'

'Yeah, as if.'

Lily was silent for a moment, before saying, 'So you really love Mac?'

'Yeah, I do.'

'That's great about you and Mac. So what's happening with Jason and the wedding?'

Violet leant back against the couch. 'To be honest, I'm sick to death of the whole affair. Celine's been appalling at every single turn and now Jason has decided he wants to play daddy. I wish that I had never agreed to help out.'

'So what are you going to do?'

'I suppose I have to see it through. You know, professional pride and all that. Not to mention that I couldn't bail on Sarah.'

'So how much longer do you have?'

'Three days and then I'll be free of Celine at least.'

'And Jason?'

'He says he wants to be in Holly's life. He says he made a mistake all those years ago and he's not the same person.'

'You have every right to feel the way you do. Jason was a total arsehole. *But* I just wonder as Holly gets older maybe she'd want to be told about Jason. Most people want to know, if it's possible, where they come from.'

'You're right, I hate it but you're right. It's just that I really fear that once he gets to know Holly he'll want to have joint custody,' said Violet.

'You're allowed to feel like that. Just try and keep an open mind. Not for Jason but for Holly. One day she'll want the truth.'

'I know that part of what you're saying is right but Mac adores Holly and she adores him and I'd prefer her to see him as her father.'

'And Jason comes along and starts to screw everything up?'

'Yeah, basically.'

'You can't change the past, Violet. Besides you wouldn't want to. Even though Jason McKellan is an arsehole, without him you wouldn't have Holly.'

'Point taken. Hey, when did you get to be so smart, little sister?'

'Born with it. It's a Beckett trait,' Lily said with a laugh.

* * *

Violet could understand that the bridal party would want a quick run-through of the ceremony. It made perfect sense that everyone needed to know what was going on and where they had to stand. But what she didn't understand was Celine's desire to go over it again and again and again.

Violet stifled a sigh as she leant against the wall of the courtyard while Celine and her bridesmaids walked down the imaginary aisle for the fourth time. The only person who appeared to be enjoying the whole thing was Holly, who was sitting with Sarah looking totally rapt.

Violet looked towards Mac who was standing with his brothers. He looked uneasy, while Dan let out a loud yawn and even Jason's mouth was set in a grim line.

Yep, the groom and his men certainly didn't look happy.

'Really, Dan, is it too much to ask for you to take this seriously?' Celine snapped as she stopped halfway down the aisle.

'I didn't yawn on purpose,' Dan muttered.

'Well, now we're going to have to start again.'

Jason shook his head. 'I don't think so, Celine. This is the fourth time you've walked down the aisle and you're yet to make it to the front.'

'This is important, Jason,' said Celine. 'It's our final wedding rehearsal.'

'Yeah, but you don't have to rehearse walking up and down this many times. I think you've already got that down. Besides, everyone's got places they'd rather be. I've got to ring the office, Mac needs to be doing stuff around the farm and Dan's got a restaurant to run. And I'm sure the brides-maids have things to do too. Let's just get on with this and get it over and done with,' Jason said.

'How can you say that? This is important, it's our *wedding*,' cried Celine, her voice shrill.

'The wedding, yes. The rehearsal, no.'

Mac caught Violet's eye and winked at her.

'You could at least pay attention, Mac,' Celine said as she stomped down the aisle with her bridesmaids hurrying in her wake.

'I am, Celine,' Mac said evenly. 'Anyway, isn't your dad giving you away? Shouldn't he be here as well?'

'I said earlier that he's got an important business meeting he couldn't get out of. He'll be here in time for the wedding. Now, can we please just focus on the rehearsal?'

Violet bit back a giggle and pretended to inspect several large vases that were lying nearby.

'I guess she told him.'

Violet glanced up to see Flynn standing next to her.

'I suppose she did,' said Violet, smiling.

Flynn's gaze shifted towards the bridal party. 'Celine's good-looking, but man, she's a piece of work.'

'You have no idea,' said Violet.

'Ah well,' said Flynn, 'how's everything with you?'

'Fine,' said Violet, 'but I can't wait until this wedding is over.'

'Yeah. I've been meaning to say that I'm really glad you and Holly moved back. It's been really good for Mac.'

'Thanks,' said Violet. 'Holly and I are really happy here—Holly's even enjoying this damned wedding rehearsal. And I'm so happy about Mac.'

'I've never seen Mac like this, Violet,' said Flynn. 'I knew he liked you a lot when we were at school, but you and Jason were so in love there was never going to be any chance for you and Mac. These past years he's never taken any woman very seriously. He's always been caring and everything, but what he feels for you is something different altogether. He really loves you, you know.'

'Yes, I know and I can't tell you just how fortunate I am.' For a second, tears blurred Violet's vision and she wiped them away with the back of her hand. Raising her head she looked straight into Mac's eyes. He gave her a questioning look and Violet smiled back, but her tears must have been obvious because Mac broke from the wedding rehearsals and walked straight up to her.

'Mac, where are you going?' said Celine, turning around.

'Something's come up,' said Mac.

The breath seemed to catch in Violet's throat as he took her in his arms.

'What's wrong?' he asked.

Violet wrapped her arms around his shoulders and hung on. 'Nothing Mac, everything is fine.'

'Violet Beckett you're a lousy liar. You were crying, I saw you,' he said as he rested his head against hers. 'Did Flynn say something to upset you? Because if he did I'll—'

'Flynn didn't upset me. It's just that I finally worked something out.'

'Oh and what's that?'

'That I'm fond of you.'

'Fond of me? Can't you do better than that?'

'Maybe . . . How about I'm *quite* fond of you?' Violet said with a teasing grin.

Mac's arms tightened around Violet as his mouth crushed down on hers. The kiss scorched its way right down to Violet's toes. It was hot, possessing and it consumed her. Her fingers spiked through his hair as she anchored him to her. He kissed her until she forgot where they were and that they weren't alone.

She sucked in a breath as Mac pulled back and broke the kiss. He nuzzled the side of her neck which set off a wave of ricocheting heat through her body.

'I love you,' he whispered against her ear.

'I know you do,' she said as she looked over his shoulder. The entire wedding party were staring at them with slack-jawed surprise. The exceptions were Sarah and Holly, who both had a smile from ear to ear. 'Maybe you should put me down, everyone is looking.'

'Nah, I don't think so. I've only just got you,' Mac said before he kissed her again.'

'Jeez, maybe the two of you should get a room,' Flynn chuckled as he walked away.

Chapter 28

Violet sighed as she watched Celine boss around and micro-manage friends and family alike.

'No, Pam, I want that swag straighter. It just doesn't look right.'

'Like this?' one of Celine's bridesmaids answered as she fiddled with the silk material.

'Nooo! See that bit there, it's all scrunched up,' said Celine, impatiently pointing to the corner of the swag.

'Is that better?'

'No!' Celine snapped as she walked over to the table and readjusted the material. 'Do I have to do everything myself?'

'I swear she's doing my head in.'

Violet smiled as Mac's voice came from behind and he wrapped his arms around her. 'Every bride wants the perfect day.'

'Yeah, but every bride isn't bat-shit crazy. Where's Holly?'

'Your mum's taken her down to the shed to see the kittens before it gets too dark,' she said as she turned around in his arms and faced him. 'You know she can't come to McKellan's Run and not see them.'

'I thought it was all about coming to see me,' said Mac, smiling, and dipping his head to brush his lips against hers.

'Okay, you two, come on there's children about,' said Dan with a laugh as he walked past.

Violet jerked back but Mac wasn't letting her go anywhere.

'Ah, you're just jealous, little brother.'

Dan shrugged and gave them a smile. 'Maybe I am. It seems as if my big brother has managed to snag the prettiest girl in town. About time too. Listen you haven't seen Flynn around, have you? He said he'd give me a hand lugging in a few crates of wine.'

'He was in the courtyard a while ago but he said he was taking off before Celine found him anything more to do,' said Violet.

'Typical,' Dan said with a snort. 'Mac, can you please give me a hand? I'd like to get this all stowed away before our brother scoffs it all.'

'Whatcha mean?' asked Mac.

'You haven't noticed Jason is chucking back the wine? Must be pre-wedding nerves,' said Dan.

'That's not like Jason,' said Mac, frowning as he let Violet go. 'I'll give you a hand. Will you be okay, sweetheart?'

'Of course I will,' Violet said with a smile. 'Go and help Dan. I'm going to grab a coffee and drink it on the verandah.'

Mac leaned closer and whispered in her ear, 'Come on, admit it, you're just trying to get away from Celine's dulcet tones.'

Violet bit back a laugh and gave him a gentle push. 'Maybe I am. Go on, go and help your brother.'

Mac dropped a quick kiss on her lips before he straightened up. 'Won't be long,' he said before he turned and followed Dan outside.

Violet headed into the kitchen and made a coffee. With mug in hand, she peeked around the kitchen door and heard Celine still barking orders at anyone who crossed her path. Well, she'd had enough of it for tonight. She slipped down the little corridor and out the side door, towards the verandah.

Outside, she tipped her head back and stared up at the million stars that blinked in the night sky. It had been a while since she'd stood in the starlight and breathed it in. Sometimes she'd looked up into the heavens when she'd lived in Melbourne but the lights from the city had dulled the sky. At McKellan's Run, everything was so clear and beautiful. Despite everything with Jason and Celine and this blasted wedding she was so glad she'd come back.

The air was crisp as Violet wandered over to the railings and leaned against them. In a nearby clump of trees, Violet could hear the growl of a possum declaring its territory. For such a cute-looking animal, possums certainly made a weird noise she thought, something like a chainsaw winding down.

She took another sip of her coffee as she walked over to a chair and sat down. The stillness settled around her and she closed her eyes and let herself drift into the silence, until the sound of footsteps came and she turned to see Jason.

'I'm sorry for being an idiot and letting you down when you needed me,' Jason said as he sat down next to her. 'I made a mistake, one I'm only now beginning to understand. I'm sorry I threatened to try and get custody. I wasn't thinking straight. All I knew is I wanted to spend time with Holly and get to know her.'

255

Violet put her mug on the nearby table and clasped her hands together.

'It was a long time ago, Jase. We were just kids,' Violet said with a shrug.

He took her hand in his. 'So, you forgive me?'

'I mostly forgave you a long time ago. Melbourne was often hard but after a while I did begin to understand that you were only starting your working life when I got pregnant, and you had all sorts of dreams and ambitions of your own. I just couldn't have an abortion, I really couldn't. And I've never regretted going ahead and having Holly,' said Violet.

'It was a surprise to see her. She has my eyes,' said Jason.

'Yes, she does,' said Violet.

'Meeting her made me feel, I don't know . . . different and I really want to get to know her better and be a father to her.'

'Jason, whatever the legalities of it, the reality is I wanted her, I kept her, I raised her, I love her, and you've had absolutely nothing to do with her. Holly and I don't need you,' she said standing up.

Jason reached out and grabbed her hand so she wouldn't walk away. 'But what if I need you, Violet? What if I've always needed you?'

'What are you playing at, Jase? You're getting married, why are you saying things like that to me?'

'I mean it, Violet. I was wrong about us. Seeing you again and meeting Holly has opened my eyes,' he said as he stood up in front of her.

He was standing too close and Violet tried to take a step back but Jason still had hold of her hand. 'Yeah well, shut them again because it's not going to happen. Do you really think after all this time I'm going to fall into your arms?'

'Maybe. Just think of it, Violet, we could be a family. You could leave this shithole backwater and come with me to the city. Think of all the fun we used to have. You, Holly and I could have just as much fun in the future. We could have the perfect life.'

'I'm making a good life here, Jason,' she said as she snatched her hand away. 'And you say all this out of the blue. You want me to uproot Holly and drop everything: my business, my friends? And Mac,' said Violet, shaking her head, incredulous.

'Yes, I do. I've got more to offer you than Violet Falls and Mac.'

'Oh my God! I've just worked it out. This isn't about you and me or even Holly. This is you trying to get back at Mac,' she said as she waved her hand at him.

'What? Why would it?' said Jason.

'Because you know Mac and I are together and that just kills you. Not because you have any feeling for me but you're so jealous of him that it twists your insides. You don't want me but you don't want him to have me either,' she said starting to walk away.

'Don't be ridiculous, Violet, I loved you.'

'That was when we were kids, Jason. You don't even know me now.'

'I know you've got principles and you're a good person. And I could love Holly and you.'

'No Jason, you won't. And anyway, Holly and I deserve more than that. You don't want me to be with Mac because you're jealous of him.'

'No, I'm not! How could I be, I'm a successful lawyer with a great bank balance and lifestyle. Why would I be jealous of a man who spends his days outside with sheep shit?'

'I don't know, Jason, it's your twisted hang-up. You tell me,' said Violet, swinging around.

'He can't have you.'

'That's not your call. Just leave, Jason. You've had too much to drink and it's clouding your judgement. Get married and go back to Melbourne with Celine so you can enjoy your high-powered career. That's not what I want in life.'

'Mac can't have *my* daughter,' said Jason. 'She can have a much better life in the city, go to decent schools and enjoy the best of everything.'

Violet was so angry she could hardly think. If she didn't get away from Jason she was seriously going to lose it.

'Funnily enough, this isn't about you. It's about what I feel, who I love and what's best for Holly, Mac and me. You don't get to have an opinion or a say. You lost that right a long, long time ago.'

'Violet, I didn't—'

'Just grow up, Jason, or go and get some help. At the end of the day, beneath all the crap, I thought there was a good man inside of you. He's the one I fell in love with all those years ago. I don't know where he's gone but for your own sake, maybe you should think about what you value in life and sort yourself out, Jason. You'll be a whole lot happier if you do.'

'Violet . . .'

She held up her hands as she backed away. 'We have nothing more to say to each other.'

'But we do, I just can't let you and Holly go. I can't imagine anyone else being her father.'

Before she had time to react, he closed the distance between them, wrapped his arms around her and brought his mouth down on hers.

Rage surged through Violet and she placed both hands squarely on his chest and shoved him as hard as she could. Jason staggered back a couple of steps and Violet took that second to drag the back of her hand across her mouth. She could still taste the Scotch on her lips.

'Stay away and don't ever touch me again.'

Jason swayed a little on his feet and gave her a bemused look.

'Aw come on, baby, you don't mean that. What we had all those years ago was good, Violet. You just need to remember,' he said as he took another step towards her.

In that moment the pain, resentment and hurt from the past welled up inside her. Violet pulled back her fist just as Jason dipped his head to try and kiss her again. She let fly with a punch. His head snapped to the side as the blow caught him on the side of the nose.

He reeled back and covered his face with his hand.

'Christ, Violet why did you *do* that?' Jason slurred.

'As I said—stay the hell away from me,' Violet said as she pushed past him and headed back into the house.

* * *

Mac stood in the shadows at the end of the verandah. He'd been looking for Violet when he'd stumbled across Jason talking to her. His first reaction was to go charging over and demand why she was anywhere near Jason. But he stopped himself, instead waited, listened and ground his teeth.

His hands clenched into fists as he watched Jason grab Violet and kiss her. Time seemed to stop and reverse. It spun Mac back to all those years ago when he'd had to endure watching his brother with Violet. There was something too familiar in the way Jason had tried to take her in his arms.

Mac was about to go in and physically rip his brother off her when Violet pushed Jason back and told him where to go.

It wasn't until this very moment that he truly realised Violet's past with Jason didn't matter. He couldn't change the past and Jason was Holly's father, but it didn't matter because Violet didn't want Jason. Violet had chosen him.

The ache disappeared from his chest.

God, he was proud of her. He just wanted to wrap her in his arms and tell her so.

Mac realised he'd been holding his breath, slowly he exhaled and calmed himself, waiting for Violet to leave before he strode forward onto the verandah towards Jason.

'You might want to put a bit of ice on that,' he said, gesturing to his nose.

Jason looked up. 'Oh, shut up, Mac—'

'I don't believe you tried that on Violet!' said Mac. 'Leave her the hell alone, you've already done enough damage.'

'I don't know what you're talking about, I said it was nothing,' said Jason, staggering towards Mac.

'You're drunk.'

'Don't be ridiculous, I'm perfectly fine. I have every right to talk to Violet.'

Jason obviously didn't realise that Mac had heard the entire conversation.

'You're meant to be getting married in two days. What the hell is the matter with you?'

'I'll always be Violet's first love. Women never get over a thing like that. They're sentimental.'

'Trust me, she's over it,' said Mac.

'Doubt it. I'm the one who broke her heart.'

'Yeah, well I'm the one who fixed it,' said Mac. 'I'm warning you Jason, brother or not, don't mess with Violet again. Oh, and try and pull yourself together and sober up,' he said before walking away.

**

Back in the kitchen Violet leant against Mac's chest as his arms wrapped around her. They were warm and comforting. She took a breath and let some of the anger and irritation from her confrontation with Jase slip away.

'Are you okay, sweetheart?

'Yes, I'm fine. I'm glad you found me,' Violet said as she snuggled a little closer. 'I was waiting for you on the verandah.'

'Sorry, I got held up with Mum. Is everything alright?'

'Yeah, I guess. I got into an annoying conversation with Jason but other than that, it's all good.'

'Um, about that . . .'

'Oh my God, what happened, Jason?' Celine shouted from outside.

Violet looked over, just in time to see Jason walking past the window holding a wad of bloody tissues to his nose. She turned around in Mac's arms as the heat started to burn in her cheeks.

'Do you want to talk about it?'

'There's not much to say. Jason wanted to kiss me and I didn't want him to,' Violet said with shrug.

'You amaze me, you really do.' Mac hugged her a little tighter. 'He won't try it again.'

'Well, I should hope not.' Violet watched as Celine ran over to Jason. 'Do you think I broke it?'

'I don't know. Even if you did, he can still breathe through his mouth.'

Violet leant against Mac and sighed. 'I'd better go home,' Violet said as she stood back. 'It's getting late and Holly needs to be in her own bed.'

Mac leant down. 'Hey, the things Jason said and did were out of line. I'm sorry if you were upset.'

'I'm okay, but I need a good night's sleep.'

'Okay, let's get Holly and your stuff and I'll help you to your car,' said Mac. 'And maybe I should stay with you and keep you company,' he added with a grin.

'Tempting as that is, Mr McKellan, and it *is* very tempting, the answer is no. I'm sleeping alone in my bed,' said Violet, running her finger along his jaw then letting it trail down his neck and inside the collar of his shirt. 'Naked.'

Mac made a funny, sexy, growly noise at the back of his throat. 'You're a harsh and cruel woman, Ms Beckett.'

'Thanks Mac,' she answered with a grin. 'Nice of you to say so.'

Chapter 29

The day before the wedding seemed to just fly by. One minute Violet was dropping Holly at school and in what seemed like an hour later she was picking her up again.

'Are we going home, Mummy?'

Violet glanced up into the rearview mirror. 'No sweetheart, we have to go to McKellan's Run. I have to set everything up for the wedding.'

'Great,' said Holly. 'That means I can play with the kittens and Mud.'

'Yes, you can,' said Violet as she drove along the gumtree-lined road, the narrow eucalyptus leaves dancing in the breeze. 'I've packed some books, drawing paper, pencils and a couple of your favourite DVDs, so I think you'll be set.'

'Uh huh. But I'll be playing outside with the kitties.'

'Yes, but remember I don't want you wandering off on your own, okay?'

'Okay,' Holly said with a nod.

'There's lots of people coming and going and I don't want you getting lost.'

'Uh-huh. I won't.'

Violet fell silent as she checked and doubled-checked her mental list of tasks. There was still so much to do. The flowers were being delivered at four-thirty and she was hoping the cake had arrived by now. They'd promised to get it there by one o'clock and it was just after three-thirty. Hopefully, that little detail had slipped by Celine. The last thing Violet needed was another mini-meltdown by the bride.

Violet swung down Mac's driveway. Ahead, she could see several vans and people hurrying about. She sighed with relief when she laid eyes on the bright blue van with the words *A Taste of Perfection* painted on the side. Thank goodness—at least the wedding cake had arrived. If the pictures were anything to go by, the cake was a thing of beauty, with four pearlised tiers covered in delicate icing that looked like old-fashioned lace, with pale pink, cream and latte-coloured sugar roses cascading down its sides.

She parked the car and then turned and smiled at Holly. 'Okay, after you've been to see Mud and the kittens we'll find you somewhere quiet so you can do your drawings and then, after dinner, you're going to hang out with Mrs McKellan and spend the night with her. That'll be fun won't it?'

Holly nodded as she unclipped her seatbelt and started gathering her things. 'Yep, I like her.'

'So do I. I'm afraid there's an awful lot of things to do before the wedding and it's probably going to be a very late night.'

'Nana Sarah said we were going to have chocolate cake, and she was going to read me a story about princesses.'

Violet stilled for a second as she wondered if her hearing

had suddenly become defective. 'Sorry sweetheart, what did you call Mrs McKellan?'

'Nana Sarah. She told me I could call her that.'

Violet seemed to have trouble dragging in the next breath. It was official, Holly had been accepted into the McKellan clan. There would never be any hiding again. Whatever happened between Jason, Mac and herself didn't matter because one way or another Sarah had claimed Holly as her granddaughter.

'When did she say that?'

'The other day,' she said as she opened the door and wriggled out. 'Is everything alright, Mummy? Your face looks funny.'

'I'm fine, sweetie.' Violet got out of the car and smoothed down the skirt of her green wrap dress, shouldered her bag and held out her hand. 'Come on then, my beautiful girl.'

Holly placed her hand in her mother's and started to skip alongside her. 'Mummy?'

'Yes, sweetheart?'

'I don't have to talk to Celine do I?'

'No, not at all. I think Celine is going to be very busy and very . . .'

'Mean?'

'Well, er, I wasn't going to say that but why do you ask?'

'Oh, she reminds me of one of the princesses in my book.' Holly let go of her mother's hand and rummaged in her bag. She pulled out a fairy-tale book and flicked through it. She held the book up to Violet. 'See, Celine looks like her.'

Violet had to admit there was a slight resemblance. The princess was blonde, pretty and looked just as shiny and put together as Celine.

'Um, I guess they do look alike.'

'Yes, Mummy, but you see she really looks like this,' said Holly, flicking through a few more pages until she found what she was looking for.

Violet tried hard not to laugh as she looked at the picture of a wicked witch.

'She says nice things but she doesn't mean them,' continued Holly. 'There's a look in her eyes—a mean look.'

'Yes, I understand what you're saying, sweetheart. You don't have to talk to her. In fact it's probably better if you stay out of her way. We'll find somewhere for you to sit, far away from Celine.'

'Good,' said Holly as she put the book back in her bag.

* * *

Mac walked through the house and headed to his study. Violet had managed to transform the interior of his house into a sparkling space.

Dear God, he'd be happy when this fiasco of a wedding was over and he could reclaim the house. A smile twitched at the corner of his mouth, maybe he should ask Violet to re-decorate some of the rooms; starting with what he hoped would become their bedroom, and then one for Holly.

The idea definitely had merit and he was musing just how he could approach the whole thing with Violet as he pushed open the study door. Inside, Celine was standing over Holly, holding the little girl's arm, the other hand raised as if she was about to strike her.

'What the hell do you think you're doing? Let her go now!'

Celine released Holly and spun around, her face furious.

'When I came in here to check on things, this child was opening the party favours for the dinner and ruining them with her dirty little hands. Honestly, I don't know why she's even here!'

Holly ran around Celine and hurtled herself into Mac's outstretched arms.

'I don't give a damn about your decorations. If you ever lay a finger on Holly again, I'll forget how my parents raised me. Do I make myself clear?'

'All children need to be disciplined. Look what she's done!' said Celine, pointing to one little glittery chiffon bag. It was open, and a couple of the pale-pink sugared almonds and one silver-wrapped chocolate heart lay next to Holly's colouring book. The rest of the favours were still stacked in a box on the desk, untouched.

'I only took one, Mac,' said Holly, tightening her hold around his neck as she buried her head into his shoulder. 'I shouldn't have done it but Mummy always makes extra, and they looked so pretty.'

'Shhh, it's alright, Holly,' said Mac as she trembled with fear.

Then he looked towards Celine. 'Once this wedding is over, you are not welcome in my house. Stay away from Holly and stay away from Violet and me.'

Celine nodded.

'Now get out and don't ever try to step foot in this room again,' Mac said as he turned his back.

'She's scary,' said Holly, once Celine was gone.

'It's okay, honey. Did she hurt you?' Mac asked as he sat Holly down on his office chair.

She shook her head. 'No, but I think she wanted to.'

'Do you want me to go and get your mum?' asked Mac.

'No, she'd be really cross,' said Holly.

'Yeah, she would. How about we find my mum and go and play with the kittens? It was the reason I was coming to see you in the first place. See what I've got?' said Mac pulling out from the drawer in his desk some toys that Holly could use to play with the kittens.

Holly's eyes lit up as she picked up a small red ball and shook it. 'The ball has a bell in it and there's a toy mousey.'

'Uncle Dan's bringing dinner in a little while. I reckon you can hang out with Mud and her kittens until then. What do you think?'

'That'd be great, Mac. I haven't seen the kittens for ages.'

'Hah, don't give me that. It was only a couple of days ago.'

'That's *ages*!' said Holly with a serious expression on her face. 'They'll forget who I am.'

'Nah, sweetie, that'll never happen. I promise.'

Chapter 30

Violet straightened the elaborate centrepiece before standing back and surveying the whole room. Everything looked perfect for tomorrow's wedding.

The silence of the room was shattered as a slow song filtered through the sound system. Violet turned around as she heard footsteps across the wooden floor.

'Beautiful.' Mac ambled towards her, holding out a glass of wine. 'Just beautiful.'

'Thanks, Mac,' said Violet as she accepted the glass with a smile. 'I think everything is in place.'

Mac's eyes locked onto hers as his fingers closed over the back of her hand. Her heart did that quaking thing as he took one more step closer. He leant over and whispered in her ear, 'I meant you, Violet. You're beautiful.'

Her skin tingled under his breath. 'Mac?'

'Yes, Violet?'

'I should just check everything once more. I'll need one of the guys to move the crates away from the kitchen door and make sure Dan knows about the three last-minute guests who telephoned earlier to say they were coming after all,' said Violet.

'Everything's perfect and if you hadn't noticed it's late and everyone has gone home.'

'They have?'

'Yes.'

Mac took the glass from her hand and set it on the table before tugging her towards him. Violet let him. She needed a hug, she needed to feel that sense of protection he imbued in her. Mac stepped in even closer and she felt his hand splay across the small of her back. Slowly they began to move with the music.

Violet relaxed in his arms and rested her head on his shoulder. All the stress of the last month seemed to melt away and she was only aware of Mac. She was acutely conscious of the strength in his arms, his cool scent, and the hardness of his body.

'When was the last time we danced together?' he asked as he dipped his head next to her ear. The warm of his breath made her shiver. She'd forgotten what it felt like to be slow-danced around a floor. No, that wasn't right. She'd forgotten what it was like to dance with Mac.

'That party you had at the end of Year 10 before Jason went away to uni.'

'You remember that long ago?'

'I remember dancing with you.' Violet leant her head against his shoulder. This felt so right. 'We danced out in the court-yard, you whirled me around in the starlight and held me.'

His hands ran up and down her spine. 'I remember too, oh, I remember. But all you could think about was Jason. God, I envied him.'

'Well, we're here now.'

'I've been wanting this since the minute I set eyes on you again,' said Mac, his mouth hovering just above hers for a moment, teasing and tempting her. She raised herself on tiptoes and kissed him.

At first the kiss was soft and gentle as silk, Violet sighed into him as her hand crept behind the back of his neck. Mac ran his hands through her hair, his kiss changing from sweet to demanding.

Violet sucked in a breath as her lips parted. Her nipples hardened and brushed against his chest as his tongue rubbed against hers. Violet ran her hands over his broad shoulders, his skin was hot beneath the cool cotton of his shirt. They kissed each other long and hard, her body calling out for more.

Mac unfurled his fingers and slid his hands down her back. Violet's heart picked up the beat as both his hands clasped her bottom—caressing, kneading and then without warning, lifting her up. To steady herself, she locked her legs around his waist.

'Hurry, Mac,' Violet said between kisses. 'Get us to the couch.'

'No babe, we're going where I've wanted you for so long,' Mac said as he carried her out of the room.

Violet drew back and raised a delicate brow. 'And where exactly is that?'

'My bed.'

* * *

Somehow they made it up the stairs, although they did pause on the landing to kiss each other wildly, full of passion and desire. Violet released all the longing she'd been suppressing. She was free of the doubts and the fears which had shackled her to the past, and Mac's love had done that.

A fire sparked within her. She wanted to feel his skin against hers. She *needed* him.

He leant her against the door; the hard wood felt cold against her back while he fumbled with the door knob. Mac never broke their kiss but a frustrated growl came from the back of his throat as he jiggled the uncooperative handle. Finally, after an infuriating moment, the door swung open and they stumbled towards the bed.

Mac put her down. 'I can't stop touching you.'

'Then don't.' Violet's hands moved to the side of her waist and she slowly began to undo the tie of her wrap dress. She watched Mac's eyes darken as she let the dress pool at her feet.

'You're killing me, sweetheart.'

She smiled, panting. 'Believe me, I don't want to kill you, I want to love you.'

'You're so beautiful, Violet.'

'You're totally wonderful, Mac,' breathed Violet reaching up to unbutton his shirt. Her hands skimmed over his chest as the shirt fell away. Violet leant in close. She could feel the strong beat of his heart beneath her palm and the faint scent of his woodsy aftershave.

'I want you, Mac. I need you to touch me, I need to feel you inside me.'

'God, Violet,' said Mac, crushing her to his chest. 'I've wanted you for so long like this!' His hands ran over her back and unhooked her bra, slipping it from her. He pushed down her lacy black knickers, the look on his face full of love and desire.

'Perfection,' he murmured as he slowly moved his hands down her body.

The warmth within Violet unfurled, as Mac's mouth clamped over her hardening nipple. She was naked in his arms and Violet knew she was right where she was meant to be.

'Mac.'

He manoeuvred them towards the bed and laid her down. He lingered above her as he kissed a trail from her breasts, all the way along her neck.

'Hang on a sec.' He pushed off the bed and Violet almost cried out at the loss of his touch.

Violet's mouth went dry as she watched him shed the rest of his clothes. She stared at the male perfection in front of her. 'You're beautiful.'

Mac reached over and opened the small drawer on the night stand and took out a condom.

'I could—' said Violet.

Mac shook his head. 'Next time, sweetheart. I'm about ready to burst.'

Mac climbed onto the bed and pulled Violet down into his arms. Violet let him, feeling full of desire for him.

Mac's hand started to meander over her skin—circling, skimming, teasing as he nuzzled the side of her neck. Violet arched towards him as his hand cupped her.

Violet gasped as he slipped his finger into her. The fire within her burned hard and fast, her breath quickened, her every nerve ending engaged. He gently moved his hand until Violet was brought to the edge. She looked at him through half-closed eyes as the pleasure of his touch washed over her like a wave.

He settled between her thighs and slid into her, inch by inch, until Violet bit back a moan. He stilled for an instant, and he looked into her eyes. 'I love you, Violet Beckett.'

She reached up and ran her fingers along the side of his face. 'I know.'

'This is forever, Violet. I can't ever let you go.'

'I wouldn't want to be anywhere else, Mac. Not ever.'

* * *

Afterwards Violet linked her fingers through Mac's, her face serious.

'Sometimes I never thought I'd say this to anyone, but I love you so much. I want us to be together. You, me and Holly.'

Mac pushed himself up on his elbow and leaned over to kiss her.

'I'm sorry it took me so long to say it,' said Violet. 'I guess in the beginning I was afraid that this could never happen and then I didn't want anything to jinx it.'

'Never thought you were the superstitious kind.'

'Only where love is concerned,' said Violet smiling. 'I suppose I never really thought I could, or even deserved to be, this happy. Sometimes I think I'll wake up and all of this, all of us, will have been a dream.'

'It's no dream, Violet, and I'm sure as hell not going anywhere.'

'I know that now,' said Violet.

'I love you, Violet Beckett. You're the only woman I've ever really wanted, the only one I'll ever want.'

Chapter 31

Violet's eyes fluttered open and for an instant she didn't know where she was. But then the mattress moved and Mac's arm snaked around her waist and pulled her close. She smiled, this was a good way to wake up, and one she could get used to. Through the open window, Violet could see the dawn break over distant hills. A cool breeze filled the room but she was warmed by Mac's body. She should be tired, as Mac's lovemaking had kept her up most of the night, but she wasn't. Instead there was a buzz running right through her body.

The morning air was still but Violet could feel the potential in it. Anticipation bubbled through her; it was going to be a good day. Everything to do with the wedding was pretty much under control, though there were still a few things to do, but first she needed some coffee and then Mac.

Gingerly, she moved Mac's arm just enough so she could slip out of bed. The air was chillier than she'd expected and it was all she could do not to jump back into bed and snuggle into Mac. She shivered, then grabbed Mac's shirt from the chair, slung it on and headed downstairs.

After flicking on the switch to start the coffee machine she hunted around the kitchen for some cups. She'd just have enough time to wake Mac up with coffee, kisses and maybe a little bit more. Yeah, it was going to be a good morning.

'Did you really mean what you said?' came a voice from behind her.

Violet swung around to see Jason hunched over at the end of the long kitchen table.

'Jason, you scared me. I didn't hear you coming in,' she said.

'Did you mean what you said, Violet?'

'What are you talking about?' she asked.

'The other night. Do you really believe I'm still a good man?'

The question hung in the air awkwardly as Violet turned and busied herself making the coffee. 'I think you've lost sight of him, Jason. But he's still there,' she said after a while.

'I'm sorry, about the other night. The kiss, I mean. I was way out of line,' he said, as he raised his head for the first time.

'It's okay,' said Violet, noticing Jason's eyes were red-rimmed and he looked as if he hadn't slept. Not a great way to begin your wedding day.

'So, you and Mac, huh?'

'Yes, me and Mac,' she answered as she walked over and placed a coffee in front of him. 'Here, you look as if you could use it.'

'Thanks,' he said simply. 'I'm not trying to push in, I don't have the right. I know I didn't support you all those years ago and that's something I have to live with. I'm just curious about Holly. Does she know I'm her father?'

'No, she doesn't.'

'Are you ever going to tell her?'

Violet leaned against the kitchen bench and looked out the window. 'Yes, Jason, but I want to wait a while. She's just had Mac come into her life.'

Jason took a gulp of his coffee. 'Thank you, that's more than I could really have hoped for, all things considered.'

'It's not just about you, Jason. Eventually Holly will want to know the truth.'

'And what will you say about me. About us?'

'That we were once, long ago, in love and had a few unforgettable summers. But we couldn't last, it was all too much, too soon and we were so young and just starting out in our adult lives. No matter how much I might have wanted it at the time, we didn't have a future together,' Violet said as she stared out the window. 'And that she's a lucky girl because she has two great fathers—one who made her and one who chose her.'

'Thanks,' said Jason, his eyes looking a little misty. 'Mac will do a good job. He loves you both. I just wish—'

'You can't live in the past, Jase. Let it go. It's okay.'

'I have to start putting things right.'

'It's your wedding day, Jason. Cheer up and look to the future. It's about to change.'

'Yes, it is. Are you happy? I mean are you happy with Mac?'

'More than I thought possible,' Violet answered as she picked up the other two coffees she'd made and took a step towards the door. 'Now, I'm going back to bed. I'll see you later.'

'I'm glad you're happy. You deserve to be,' said Jason as she walked out of the kitchen.

Violet tried to put the conversation out of her head as she walked back up the stairs to Mac's bedroom. She lingered in the doorway and stared at Mac. His hand was thrown up near his head, his wide shoulders spread across the white sheet and his jaw was shadowed by stubble. Violet's fingers itched to touch him.

She put the cups down on the bedside table and slid back into bed.

'Hey, Mac,' she said before giving him a series of kisses along his jaw.

Mac opened one eye. 'Hey, yourself. Are you wearing my shirt?' he said, moving his head and gently catching her bottom lip with his teeth. He wrapped his arms around her and kissed her, and she could feel him getting hard.

'Ah huh. I borrowed it,' she said between kisses.

'I like that you did. You look good in it.'

'Charmer.'

'I like waking up with you in my bed. I can't wait until it's happening on a regular basis,' he said with a grin.

'I might be persuaded.'

Mac reached up and in one fluid movement pulled Violet beneath him.

'Mac! What do you think you're doing?'

'Persuading you, sweetheart,' he said with a grin as he settled between her thighs. 'Persuading you.'

* * *

Violet stepped into the shower and smiled with pleasure as the steamy water ran over her body. It was amazing to make love to someone she totally cared about and who loved her.

Was it wrong to feel this happy? She was in love as an adult woman for the first time—really truly in love. It came from somewhere deep inside her and it felt strong, dependable and profound. Comparing it to what she'd once felt for Jason seemed almost laughable. She'd been so young and naive and though their love affair had been bright, hot and exciting, it had burnt out as soon as the realities of life encroached on them. But this feeling with Mac was something different altogether. Already she could imagine a future together. Yeah, how about that? Life sometimes did end up happily ever after and there was the odd rainbow.

She hadn't meant it to happen but Mac had wound his way into her heart. And she was so very glad he had.

Violet squirted shower gel onto her palm. It smelt of Mac—cool and clean. She lathered herself with the foaming bubbles and started to hum. All she wanted to do was go back to Mac's bed—again. After prevaricating for so long, she couldn't get enough of him.

Her cheeks flushed with heat as she remembered last night. It was in the way he held her and the way he'd made love to her until her body trembled. If she closed her eyes she could almost feel his lips on her nipples, feel him entering her so gently, their orgasms shuddering together and, just as beautiful, Mac holding her in his arms and stroking her afterwards, kissing her neck and telling her how much he loved her.

She ducked her head under the stream of water. Enough! She had to make sure the wedding went off without a hitch. She'd have to leave fantasising about Mac till later. With a little luck, maybe tonight after the wedding was over and Holly was in bed, then they could have a few moments relaxing together.

Savouring the thought for a while, she finally turned off the water, stepped out of the shower and snatched up a fluffy towel. She walked back into the bedroom and suppressed a pang of disappointment when she saw the bed was empty and Mac was gone.

Violet picked up her watch from the nightstand. It was 7.32 so she was already running behind. She slipped back into her clothes and hunted for her shoes. One she found rammed under the bed while the other was halfway down the hallway. She bit back a smile. How had *that* happened?

She could smell bacon cooking and the heavenly scent of coffee and smiled, realising Mac hadn't had a chance to drink the one she'd brought to him. Following her nose, she headed downstairs to the kitchen.

Mac was standing with his back to her as she walked through the door. He looked over his shoulder and gave her a grin which melted her heart. His hair was still damp from the shower, it was slicked back, except for one lock that fell forward towards his eye.

Did any man have the right to look that sexy at seven-thirty in the morning?

'Hey, sweetheart. Sit down and I'll grab you a coffee,' he said.

Violet walked over and placed her hand on his shoulder. 'Thanks,' she said, reaching up and giving him a kiss on the cheek.

In a fluid movement, Mac moved the frypan off the heat and pulled her to him, kissing her as if he could never get enough.

With each heartbeat, his kisses became more demanding, until finally Violet gasped. Heat travelled through her body. God, she wanted him *again*. She clung onto his broad shoulders and kissed him back.

By the time they broke apart both of them needed to catch their breath.

'Now that's what I call a good morning kiss,' Mac said as he rested his forehead against hers.

'Yes, yes it was,' said Violet, smiling.

Mac released her. 'Go and sit down and I'll get your breakfast. Although, I have to admit it isn't my best work. I got distracted.'

Violet sat down and a couple of minutes later Mac placed a plate of bacon, eggs and toast in front of her.

'Are we sharing this?' she said, staring down at the quantity of it.

'Nope. I already had mine. I have to stop by the shearing shed now and then there are a few other things I've got to clear out of the way. I'll be back by lunchtime in case you need any more help with the wedding.'

Violet swallowed a mouthful and put her hand up to her mouth and said, 'This is good.'

'I'm glad. So what are you doing this morning?'

'What, other than the walk of shame, only about a hundred things.'

Mac placed a coffee down in front of her and frowned. 'What the hell are you talking about?'

'Oh you know; arriving home in the same clothes I wore the day before, after spending a night in a sexy man's bed.'

'There's no shame in that, honey,' said Mac leaning over and kissing her on top of the head. 'None at all.'

'Well, I do have to change and pick up my clothes for the wedding. After that, I better go over to your mum's place and see how she and Holly are going.'

'I wouldn't worry. You know Mum loves her.'

'Yes, I know. She also knows about Jason being Holly's father.'

'I think she's had her suspicions ever since you returned home. I know Holly looks like you in just about every way except she does have Jason's eyes. I guess Mum probably has a few questions she'd like to ask. Maybe you should sit down and have a bit of a chat with her?'

'I will, I promise. But only after the wedding's done and dusted. Anyway, I still have to double-check everything is set for this afternoon. We have hair and makeup arriving at one o'clock, so that will keep Celine and her bridesmaids busy. The photographer will be here a bit after that. Celine wanted everything documented before the ceremony as well as during it and at the reception.'

Mac shook his head. 'Everything?'

'Pretty much.'

'I've said it before and I'll say it again—bat-shit crazy. I wish they'd bloody eloped.'

Violet leaned back on her chair and smiled at him. 'If they'd done that, we may not have got together.'

'No way, I would have found you soon enough,' said Mac, a grin spreading over his face. 'No matter how insane today gets, it'll be worth it because once it's all over, I'll still have you,' Mac said as he picked up his hat and headed to the door.

'The things you say, Mac McKellan. I'll see you later, then?'

'You can count on it, sweetheart.'

Chapter 32

There just didn't seem to be enough time. No matter how fast Violet moved, unexpected things kept being thrown at her. She'd already comforted a distraught bridesmaid who was convinced she looked like an overblown stick of fairy floss in her pink dress. Plus, the box of spare candles had vanished and then she was busy trying to track down the missing makeup artist.

She was just moving a large crystal bowl of roses on the entryway table to allow room for the guestbook when she heard a car rolling up the drive.

Violet glanced at her watch and headed over to the window, hoping against hope it was the makeup artist, who was already two hours late and not answering her mobile. Violet made a mental note as soon as she got back to her office that she was removing Katie's Professional Makeup Artistry from her contacts list. Looking out she watched as the car sped to the front of the house and screeched to a halt. A tall man in an exquisitely tailored suit stepped out of a blue BMW.

Violet frowned, so not 'Katie' the makeup artist then. From his bone structure and the harassed look on his face, he had to be Celine's father.

She looked around the almost wedding-perfect area, there was no sign of Mac or Sarah, and as far as she knew Celine was upstairs with all her bridesmaids. There was nothing for it, she'd have to get the door.

Violet readjusted her messy updo as she headed to the front door, opening it just as the man knocked on the other side.

'Hello, and welcome to McKellan's Run,' said Violet with a cheery smile.

There was a slight smile on his lips but it didn't reach his eyes as he studied Violet's shirt and jeans-clad form.

'Is Celine here?'

'Yes,' said Violet, thinking he was as rude as his daughter.'

'Laurie Thornton, father of the bride,' he said, looking past her.

'Please come in,' said Violet, swinging the door open wider and standing to one side. 'I'm Violet Beckett, the wedding planner. Celine is upstairs with the bridesmaids. It's the first door on the left.'

Violet felt the room temperature drop suddenly as an invisible frost wall crashed down between them.

'So you're Violet Beckett?'

'Yes.' Violet pushed back her shoulder and stood a little straighter.

'I've heard a lot about you.'

'All good I hope,' said Violet, smiling innocently. 'I have a lot of things to do. Celine is upstairs on the left.'

'I told her to be wary of you. We thought—'

'I'd be very careful about the next words out of your mouth,' Mac said as he walked through the doorway and next to Violet, draping his arm around her. 'It's your daughter's wedding but this is my house and my land.'

'So you're Jason's famous brother?' said Laurie.

'That's right. Now as Violet said, Celine is upstairs. Don't let us keep you.'

Thornton nodded, before walking to the stairs, his back stiff and unbending.

With a pang of regret Violet wriggled out of Mac's arms. 'I've still got some stuff to finish up. What do you have to do?'

'Kiss you again.'

Violet reached up and kissed his cheek.

'Seriously, that's all I get?'

A grin tugged at her lips. 'Yep, that's it. Now go and do whatever it is you have to do.'

'I'm heading up to get changed in a minute. What about you?'

'I just want to do the last minute run-through to make sure everything is perfect.'

'Okay, I'll see you soon,' said Mac, kissing Violet on the top of her head before heading upstairs.

Violet stood there for a moment thinking how much she loved him and how well he wore a pair of jeans.

* * *

Violet tapped on the door as she pushed it open. The room was filled with women, including the errant makeup artist, bridesmaids' tulle and the air smelled of French perfume and roses. Celine turned her head towards the hairdresser, who was just pinning in the tiara and wispy veil and gave Violet a slight smile.

No matter how Violet felt about Celine, she had to admit she made an absolutely stunning bride.

'You look beautiful, Celine. Absolutely breathtaking.'

For once the smile on Celine's lips reached her eyes. 'Thank you, Violet,' she said as she stood up and walked over to the full-length mirror hanging on the wall.

The gilt-edged mirror was ornately carved with flowers and cherubs. Violet glanced at the reflection. For a second, Celine looked like a serene princess from a fairytale. The moment vanished as Celine looked over at Violet.

'The Cassidys have just messaged me. They're going to be able to make it after all. So, that's another three for the reception and dinner. You'll let Dan know, won't you?'

Violet bit her tongue. 'Yes, of course,' she said as she went to leave.

'Oh, and Violet, Marina Cassidy is gluten-free and young Amelia doesn't like orange food.'

'Orange food?'

'Carrots, oranges, pumpkin; anything orange in colour.'

Violet wanted to say that at this late notice Amelia should be grateful for whatever she could get, but Celine had already turned back to admire herself in the mirror a little longer.

Violet checked her watch as she sprinted back down the hallway. There was less than two hours before the wedding started and she had to squeeze in another three dinner settings to her finished reception space. Even worse, now she had to break the news of more guests to Dan.

She stopped outside the master bedroom and knocked on the door. It swung open and Mac seemed to fill the space.

'Hey, sweetheart,' he said before he swooped down and laid a kiss on her mouth.

It would have been so tempting to give in to it but Violet placed her hands on his shoulders and gently pushed him back.

'Have you seen Dan?'

'We're really going to have to work on how you greet me. I swear I'm beginning to feel unloved.'

Violet let out an exasperated sigh. 'I love you, Mac McKellan, but at the moment I need your brother.'

With a shake of his head, Mac stepped aside and opened the door to reveal Dan in the centre of the room.

'Mac, I can't get this tie to work. Oh, hi Violet.'

'Forget the tie, we have a little problem,' said Violet. 'There are another three guests coming. One is gluten-free and one doesn't like orange food.'

'You're messing with me, right?'

'Nope, I'm serious. Apparently there shouldn't be any orange food on the plate. So no carrots, mangoes or pumpkin. I'm about to try and fit in another three table settings. God only knows where.'

'Shit,' said Dan. 'This bloody wedding's going to be the death of me.

'My sentiments exactly. I've got to run,' said Violet.

Violet turned to leave but paused just long enough to rise up on tiptoes and give Mac a kiss on the cheek. 'I'll see you later.'

'We are so working on this,' he growled as he tried unsuccessfully to catch her.

'Tomorrow, Mac, I promise we'll start working on it tomorrow,' Violet said with a smile as she headed down the hallway.

'Mac, did Violet Beckett just say she loved you?' came Dan in a booming voice.

'You bet your arse she did,' said Mac, beaming.

* * *

Violet scrutinized the table where she'd fitted in another three settings. She'd had to move everything around and it was a pretty tight squeeze.

'Well, that will just have to do and if anyone else turns up they'll have to eat their dinner in the kitchen,' she muttered to herself.

'You know, darling, talking to yourself is the first sign of madness,' said Sarah, standing in the doorway hand in hand with Holly.

'The first sign? This wedding has definitely sent me around the bend. I think I can safely say I've been there, done that and bought the t-shirt. You look beautiful by the way, Sarah,' said Violet smiling at her. The periwinkle blue of Sarah's dress accentuated her eyes and showed off her figure to its best advantage. 'Fab dress! I love it.'

'Oh, so do I, but you don't think it's a bit too much? Is the colour too bright?'

'No, absolutely not! You look terrific, you really do. As

do you, sweetie,' Violet said as she scooped Holly up in her arms. 'That's a very pretty dress you're wearing.'

'Thanks! Nana Sarah bought it for me.'

'I hope you don't mind, Violet. It's just that we were out shopping and we both fell in love with it.'

Violet looked down at the creation in soft pink and tiny rosebuds. 'Of course I don't mind. Thank you.'

Violet gave Holly a quick squeeze before she put her down. 'Now, what are you two up to?'

'Nana Sarah said I shouldn't go and see the kittens just yet in my new dress so we're going to see if we can help in the kitchen,' said Holly as she twirled and swished her skirt.

'What she really means is, we're going to see if we can snag something to eat before the wedding starts,' said Sarah.

'Mind that Dan doesn't catch you.'

'What can he do? I mean, I am his mother.' Sarah laughed and held out her hand to Holly. 'Let's see what yummy things we can find. Shouldn't you get changed, Violet? It's almost time.'

Violet glanced at her watch. Damn, where had the last half an hour gone?

'I sure should. I'll see you both at the ceremony.'

'Bye, Mummy,' Holly said, blowing her a kiss.

Violet made a great show of catching it in mid-air before she blew one back. 'Be good.'

'I'm sure she's always good,' Sarah answered.

'But I was talking to you, Sarah,' said Violet, laughing as she hurried towards the door.

'Your mummy is very cheeky,' said Sarah to Holly.

'Yep, she is,' Holly said with a laugh.

Chapter 33

Violet brushed a thread off her slate-grey jacket as she made her way down the hallway. Mac appeared and wrapped his arms around her waist as she walked past the study.

'Not so fast, Ms Beckett,' he said, pulling her close, his lips nuzzling the side of her neck. 'Did I ever tell you just how sexy you are in a suit?'

'No, but I'm listening,' she said, looking up and wrapping her arms around his shoulders. 'You scrub up well. You're pretty damn hot in a tux.'

'Just in a tux?'

'Nah, I'd have to say all the time.' Violet stood on tiptoes to kiss him just as someone knocked at the door.

'Sorry but, um, Mac, I need to talk to you for a minute,' said Jason, standing in the doorway, looking serious.

Mac let go of Violet's hand and kissed her. 'I'll be right back.'

Violet reached up and wiped a tiny smear of lipstick from the edge of his lips. 'Okay,' she said with smile. 'The ceremony is going to start soon. Are you alright? Is there a problem?' she said to Jason.

Jason shook his head. 'No, Violet, it's all good. I just need to speak to Mac for a second. I won't take too long, promise.'

'Okay, I'll see you both shortly,' said Violet.

* * *

'What's up?' Mac asked with a frown.

'I need to speak to you privately,' said Jason. 'Can you come in here?'

Mac stepped inside the study, shut the door and waited for Jason to speak. Jason was staring out the window into the late afternoon sky.

'I spoke to Violet this morning,' he said without looking up.

'When?' Mac felt a knot in his stomach. Something was very wrong; he'd never seen him this pensive.

'This morning she came down to make coffee. We had a talk about the other night and what she said got me thinking. I know I should have done some more thinking a long time ago.'

'I don't understand, Jason. What's the problem?'

Jason looked up and slowly shook his head. 'Probably way too many problems to deal with in this conversation. Let's just say, some of the things Violet and I talked about hit home.'

'Like what?'

'That I've been jealous of you since we were kids. When Mum married your Dad, I didn't like it. I felt I was being forced to share her with you.'

294

Mac wandered over and sat in the nearest chair. A silence lingered between them. 'Yeah well, to tell the truth I wasn't very happy about having a stepmother and an instant brother, either.'

'Sorry, I wasn't the best brother. I thought if I competed with you and won, Dad would love me.'

'But he did love you, you must know that?'

'Yeah, I do. But maybe I just wasn't so sure about it when we were kids. I mean, you were his "golden boy" and well, I guess I was more jealous of you than I wanted to admit. I thought you should know.'

Mac was silent for a minute, while a string of old hurts and rivalries flashed through his head. Jason was offering an olive branch and maybe it was time to put the stings of childhood behind them.

'It's fine, you used to annoy the shit out of me but some-times I was jealous of you as well. Just forget it, Jase. We're brothers and that's all that matters.'

'I always wanted to prove myself which is why I left here and followed the law. Violet said to me last night that I'd lost the man I used to be, or the boy she fell in love with, and I've realised she's right. I was so focused on chasing my career and becoming the best corporate lawyer in the business that I lost sight of myself.'

'Jason, everything will be fine,' said Mac.

'Yes, it will, but only once I put it right. I don't know if I even deserve to ask this but I want your support, Mac.'

'Of course,' said Mac. 'Whatever you need.'

'What I need is for you to stand next to me when I go out there and tell everyone the wedding is off.'

'What?' Mac jumped out of his chair and headed to the window next to Jason. 'Are you serious?'

Jason nodded his head. 'Yes, the wedding is a mistake. I realise I'm getting married to Celine for all the wrong reasons. Her father introduced me to a lot of my most important clients but I don't share her values and we don't have the same dreams. Coming home has made me realise that.'

'What are you saying? You were using her to help further your career?'

Jason's head snapped up and he looked Mac in the eyes. 'Believe me, the whole "using" thing is mutual. Celine needs a stable income, one that will allow her to carry on living the way she always has. Her father has pretty much lost the family fortune through a series of bad investments. He's already sold a lot of assets and he faces losing his house, but I can't keep lending him money because I can't see it changing.'

'So, why has it taken so long to realise the difference in your values?'

'I'm a very good corporate lawyer but marrying Celine would help me move even further up the food chain. Celine is well-connected and marriage would give me the opportunity to network and enlarge my client base with some very influential firms.'

'That's pretty cold, Jase.'

'Yeah, I know. Don't get me totally wrong, I did think I loved her, she can be a lot of fun and deep down there's a good person there. You haven't seen her at her best. She's been truly awful since she's been here but she isn't always that way. She's worried about her dad and the wedding just seems to be doing her head in. As I said, I don't think I . . .'

'Love her?'

Jason nodded and stared back out the window. 'I thought we could have a perfect life together, that having the same sort of goals would plaster over the things I didn't like so much about her. But after seeing how she's behaved and how she was prepared to blackmail you and give Violet a hard time, I don't feel confident it will. And that's what I have to go and tell Celine. After that I need to go and get my priorities right and find something deeper—something closer to what you and Violet have.'

'I can tell the guests if you want.'

'Nah, it's my fuckup, so it's my responsibility. I'll do it. I'd just appreciate it if you were standing next to me while I did.'

Mac placed his hand on Jason's shoulder. 'Don't worry; I've got your back.'

* * *

Jason knocked on the door and waited until one of the bridesmaids cracked it open.

'What are you doing here, Jason? It's bad luck to see the bride before the wedding—you know that,' said Tracey, Celine's best friend.

'I know Tracey but I have to speak to Celine. It's important.'

Tracey gave him a nervous look. 'Is everything okay?'

'Yes, it will be, but I have to talk to Celine.'

'Alright, I'll tell her you're here.' Tracey slipped back into the room and closed the door.

There were a few muffled voices before Celine opened the door. She was standing behind it so all Jason could see was a fluffy cloud of white tulle.

'Jason, we're getting married in a few minutes. Can't this wait?'

'No, I really need to talk to you in private,' said Jason, his face tense.

Before Celine could respond, Laurie Thornton stepped into the hallway.

'Hello son,' he said as he shook Jason's hand.

'Laurie, I didn't know that you'd arrived,' said Jason, smiling awkwardly at him.

'Yes, I've been here for quite some time. The *wedding planner* let me in,' said Thornton.

'Violet is an old friend of the family and very close to my brother's heart.'

'Well, Celine told me all about her and how she turned up with a child, claiming it was yours,' said Thornton.

'The child *is* mine and Violet never wanted or asked for anything. But that's beside the point. I need to speak to Celine privately.'

'Now what's all this about?' Thornton asked with a deepening frown. 'Is there something wrong?'

Jason ignored him, pushed open the door and walked into the room. With a forced smile he greeted the bridesmaids.

'You all look beautiful but if you could just excuse Celine and me for a few minutes, that would be great,' he said as he gestured to the door.

The room fell silent as the bridesmaids filed out with worried looks. Laurie Thornton went to walk back in but Jason shook his head, closed the door in his face and turned to face Celine.

'What's the matter, Jason?'

'Before I say anything, Celine, I have to tell you just how bloody breathtaking you are. You look beautiful, you really do.' There was an awkward pause, before Jason added, 'I'm sorry Celine but I can't marry you.'

Celine sucked in a breath and leant against the dressing table. 'Wow, you waited until *now* to tell me?'

'I'm sorry. I thought we'd be good together since we wanted the same sort of things, but it's not enough. We both deserve more than just settling for a comfortable life. There should be passion and—'

'And what? Love?' Celine snapped.

'Yes. I don't love you anymore.'

'Do you love Violet? Is that what this is all about? You're throwing me over for her?'

'No, I've just come to realise that I want someone to fall in love with and really share all the same values, and back each other in everything.'

'You're unbelievable!' Celine snapped as she reached out and grabbed the nearest object, which happened to be a heavy silver-etched hairbrush from the dressing table. With a shriek she threw it at Jason. 'How could you humiliate me like this?'

Jason managed to dodge the brush before it smacked against the door. He held his hands out in front of him—whether it was in order to placate her or surrender, he wasn't sure.

'Celine, I can't tell you how sorry I am. I do love you but not enough to believe we can share a future together.'

Celine shrieked as she launched another handful of missiles at him.

He rattled the handle and managed to open the door just as a crystal bottle of perfume shattered next to his head. He wasn't that lucky with the hot curling iron—it managed to hit him on the thigh as he dived through the door.

Chapter 34

Violet slipped out the French doors for a last-minute check. Two rows of scattered rose petals defined the bridal aisle which led all the way to the rostrum.

The aisle was flanked on either side with rows of cream vintage chairs. Each chair was different but they were pulled together as a whole by the colour. Tall, freestanding candelabra were dotted down both sides of the brick walls of the courtyard. The day was beginning to dull and the light of the fat candles became stronger. By the time the ceremony began they'd give a soft ambience to the space.

Two large floral displays sat at the front of the arched rostrum. She'd managed to get some latte-coloured roses as well as others in shades of cream, pale pink and dirty pink, which cascaded from their vases and filled the air with a heavenly scent.

There was an old-world romantic 'classical elegance' feel to the space without being too fussy.

Violet frowned as she looked up at the sky. Celine had wanted the ceremony to take place at sunset. Time was running out. They needed to get this show on the road.

She opened up the French doors and went in search of

301

the string quartet. Perhaps if they started playing, the guests would drift into the courtyard.

Violet found the young musicians gathered around one of the trays of hors d'oeuvres.

'Hi, I'm thinking we should get things going,' she said with a smile. 'I'm sure if you start playing, the guests will begin wandering in to take their seats.'

'Sure thing, Violet. It'll only take us a couple of minutes to get ready,' one of the quartet said before he popped a canapé into his mouth. 'These are great.'

'I'm glad you like them,' Violet said as she turned away. 'I'm off to check on the bride.'

She walked out of the great room and towards the stairs, her heels clicking across the wooden floors as a muffled shriek came from upstairs causing Violet to break into a run. Mac stepped out from his study and stopped her.

'Don't go in there,' he said.

Violet stared up at him questioningly. 'But I think I heard someone scream.'

'It's fine, Jason is just having a word with Celine.'

Mac pulled her a little closer and she relaxed in his arms.

'It sounded more than a word, Mac. She shrieked. He's finally snapped and is murdering her for being such a cow?'

Mac let out a laugh as he shook his head. 'No, I have to tell you something, but don't freak out, Violet.'

'You're scaring me.'

'Jason is calling off the wedding.'

'*What?*'

'It's true, apparently it was something you said. Whatever it was, it got him thinking that he was settling for a life that wouldn't make him happy.'

'Poor Celine,' Violet whispered. 'I can't stand her, but I wouldn't wish that on anyone.'

'Seriously, the woman has been nothing but mean and vicious to you and you feel sorry for her?'

'But imagine being jilted on your wedding day. That's awful,' said Violet, looking stricken.

'Yes, I suppose it is, but better to break it off before the honeymoon.'

'So what happens now?' asked Violet.

'I'm going to support Jason while he tells all the guests and then, I don't know. What's the protocol on this? Feed some people and send them on their way?'

'How can I help?' asked Violet.

'Stay close,' he said as he bent down and kissed her.

'The guests will be making their way to the courtyard by now, shall I send them back inside?' she asked in a hushed voice.

'No, Jason can break the news out there. At least they'll all be sitting down. You might want to keep a low profile though, who knows what the reaction is going to be.'

'You don't expect trouble do you?'

'No, I just want you out of harm's way. Go find Holly and we'll be out in a minute. If you see Dan and Mum on the way, could you get them to come in? Oh, Flynn too, if you happen to see him.'

Violet put her hand on his chest. 'Of course.'

'Thanks. I'll see you soon.'

With a nod, Violet turned away and hurried towards the courtyard. She headed down the makeshift aisle right up to the front. Sarah was already seated in the first row with Holly next to her. Violet knelt down and whispered in Sarah's ear.

'Jason is calling the wedding off. Mac wants you, Dan and Flynn inside.'

Sarah gasped, her face suddenly pale.

'Are you alright?' asked Violet.

Sarah nodded as she stood up. 'Of course. I'd better get in there straightaway.'

Violet took Holly's hand. 'Nana Sarah has to go inside for a minute and see Mac. So, you better stay with me.'

'Okay, Mummy,' said Holly.

Violet and Holly walked back down the aisle and headed to the kitchen. There was the rhythmic sound of the clatter of a busy kitchen as Dan and his staff geared up to feed the wedding guests.

Flynn was snagging a cheese tart off one of the serving trays as Violet walked through the door.

'Ah, you caught me,' he said with a grin.

'So it seems,' Violet said with a smile. 'Listen, Jason needs you up in the study.'

Flynn frowned. 'What's going on, Violet?'

Violet took a step and lowered her voice. 'Jason has called off the wedding. He wants his brothers and you to stand by him as he makes the announcement.'

'Shit!' said Flynn, his face totally serious for once. 'I better get in there.'

'Yeah, they're going to make the announcement any minute now.'

Violet watched as Flynn hurried away before she nicked a cheese tart and handed it to Holly.

'I want you to stay in here until I come and get you, okay?'

'Alright.'

Violet looked up, her face grave as she beckoned Dan's head waiter over.

'Hi Tom, I know you're incredibly busy but can Holly stay in here with you for a few minutes? There's a few problems I need to take care of.'

'Sure thing,' said Tom with an easy smile before turning to Holly and saying, 'Why don't you come and sit up here in my special hidey hole and fold some napkins for me? It would be a big help. Hey, do you want a ride?'

'Sure.' Holly lifted up her arms and waited for Tom to kneel down so she could climb on his back. He carried her over to the end of the kitchen.

'There you go,' he said as he put her down. 'You'll be fine here, won't you?'

Holly nodded and gave him a thumbs up.

Tom handed her a small stack of serviettes. 'Here, can you fold them like this?'

'Yep,' said Holly as she started folding the dark cream serviettes.

'Good job, Holly. That's brilliant.' Tom turned to Violet. 'You head on. I'll keep an eye on her.'

'Thanks, Tom, I'll only be a few minutes. Hey, sweetie, I'll be back in a tick,' said Violet, giving Holly a hug.

Holly nodded but she was too engrossed in napkin folding to look up.

Chapter 35

As Violet walked out of the kitchen she noticed that several of the candelabra weren't alight.

She frowned; a gust of wind from the open doors must have blown them out. Violet hurried over to grab the long matches from the fireplace. She knew that it was probably silly as the wedding wasn't going ahead but she really wanted to see how the candlelight would transform the room. She had imagined the design and she needed to see her vision realised. Violet drew the match across the striking surface of the matchbox. After a raspy sound the match burst into life and she lit the first tall cream candle which was scented with French Pear. Just as she was beginning to light the last one a loud voice from the doorway made her start with fright.

'You! This is all your fault.'

Violet glanced up and saw Celine walking towards her.

'Sorry, Celine, I don't know what you mean.'

'Yeah right, still playing the innocent mealy-mouthed little princess are we?'

Violet straightened her shoulders and stood her ground.

'Seriously, Celine, I have no idea what the hell you're talking about.'

Celine marched forward, her long veil floating out behind her like the wake from a ship.

Too late, Violet realised what she was doing. She took a step back but Celine was too quick and she placed her hands on Violet's shoulders and shoved her hard. Violet stumbled back and landed with a loud thump against one of the open doors which led to the courtyard. She was vaguely aware that the majority of guests had swivelled around and were gawking at her. Anger burned through her, she wasn't hurt, just bloody furious.

'Just back off, Celine,' she snapped, standing up and straightening her jacket then trying to stare the other woman down.

'You've ruined everything.'

'That's enough. Violet has nothing to do with this,' called Jason as he ran into the room.

'She has everything to do with you calling off the wedding. You know it and so do I.'

Hearing the ruckus, the rest of the McKellans filed into the room. Mac pushed his way through and headed over to Violet. He put his arm around her and pulled her to his side. It was comforting to have him near and whatever now happened Violet knew that she could always count on him.

'It's not Violet's fault. The problem is between you and me,' Jason said.

'Oh, don't be an idiot, Jason. Ever since I stepped foot in this shoddy excuse for a town it's all been about Violet and her brat of a daughter.'

Violet stiffened at Celine's words. Celine could call her all the names she wanted but she wasn't going to bring Holly into this. She went to take a step forward but Mac's arm tightened around her and held her back.

Celine stretched her arms out as if to encompass the entire room. 'Not even this was about me. I didn't even have a say in the design of my own wedding. I was pushed into having this blasted wedding here in the arse-end of the country and then I couldn't even have my own way with the wedding decorations.'

Violet glanced out into the courtyard and saw that half of the guests were nodding in sympathy. Perfect, just bloody perfect. Celine was totally playing to the crowd now.

'I had to give way about everything to do with *my* wedding so Violet wouldn't be hurt or upset. Well, what about me? What about my feelings? All I've heard since I've been in Violet Falls is what a wonderful woman she is, what a great mother she is and how talented she is at planning parties. Well, I'm sick of it—you can keep your wedding and the wedding planner as well. But that's what you want to do anyway, isn't it, Jason?'

'Don't be ridiculous,' said Jason. 'Come away from here and we can talk sensibly. I totally understand how upset you are, but—'

'Don't give me that. I know what's going on, you and Mac are both in love with her. The question is which one of you will succeed.'

Violet sucked in a breath at the sting of her words. Celine had cast her eyes down and looked the perfect picture of the wronged bride. Everyone had their eyes on her—just the way she liked it.

'That's not true,' Jason said. 'You know it's not.'

Celine stood there with her eyes filling with tears. 'I just wasn't enough for you, was I?' She addressed the question to Jason but her voice carried all the way through the courtyard.

'You love her, Jason, you always have,' said Celine, sobbing. 'I mean they say you never get over your first love.'

There was a murmur amongst the wedding guests.

'Celine, just stop it,' Violet said. 'This is just rubbish.'

There was a gleam of triumph in Celine's eyes as she levelled her gaze at Jason.

'What's the matter, lover, terrified I'll let the big dark McKellan family secret out of the bag?'

'Celine, for God's sake.' Mac warned as he loosed his grip on Violet and took a step forward. This time it was Violet who grabbed onto his arm and pulled him back.

The tears forgotten, Celine whirled around and said. 'I'm not afraid of you, Mac, I'm not afraid of any of you.'

Celine faced the crowd and said in a clear voice. 'As you may have guessed, Jason and I are calling off our wedding. There's no way we ever had a chance for it to work. You see, he's still in love with Violet Beckett, his ex-girlfriend and the mother of his child.'

Violet winced as she heard an audible gasp from behind her. She turned to see some of the wedding guests looking shocked, while others were shaking their heads in disgust. And every single bridesmaid looked as if they wanted to kill her.

Celine swirled away in a cloud of tulle and perfume. As she passed each of the tables she knocked over as many of the candelabra as she could. Some of the lit candles blew out but others licked the delicate material of the table overlays and sparked into flames.

Flynn and a couple of the bridesmaids dashed forward and started putting out the flames before they could take hold.

Violet felt sick in the pit of her stomach. She hunched her shoulders. The only thing that she was thankful for was that Holly was still tucked away in the kitchen. Celine's dramatic departure had left a vacuum and Violet hoped the whole hideous scene was over—but she was wrong.

Laurie Thornton pushed his way into the room until he was standing red-faced in the middle.

'You've got a hell of a lot to answer for,' he spat as he marched up to Jason and jabbed a finger at his chest.

'Yes, I know I have,' said Jason, looking stricken at the mayhem he'd caused. 'But this isn't the place to discuss it. Let's go upstairs to the study.'

But Thornton stood his ground, seeming to draw power from the spellbound onlookers.

'You've broken my daughter's heart.'

'I know,' said Jason, still looking stricken.

'Bastard. You've thrown my daughter over for that—' he spat as he pointed to Violet.

'It was my decision, Laurie. The blame rests solely with me, no one else, least of all Violet. Now, I think it's time for you to leave.'

'As if anyone here believes that!' Thornton said, his face nearly purple.

'You know what, Laurie, maybe you're right. I do admire Violet; she's a talented woman, a good person and a great mother. Looking back now, probably the stupidest thing I ever did was to end our relationship. What can I say? I was a young idiot who couldn't see true worth when it was literally staring him in the face. Too late now because she's in love with someone else.' Jason turned his head and smiled at Violet and Mac. 'She deserves the best . . . and she's found that in my brother, Mac.'

'I'll make you pay for this, Jason. I'll ruin you, just wait and see!'

'Do your worst.'

'This isn't over,' Thornton snarled as Flynn and Dan clamped their hands on his shoulders.

'Yes, it is,' said Flynn. 'Come on Laurie, you've outstayed your welcome . . . And Celine will need you,' he said leading him away.

* * *

Amidst the hubbub that rose up from the wedding guests, Mac took Violet's hand and pulled her close. 'Jason's going to handle things, and Dan and Flynn will be helping him out. Let's get away from here,' he said.

Mac led Violet out the front door and they walked in silence for a long time. Finally Mac stopped, held Violet close and gave her a tender kiss. 'Hey, are you alright?'

Violet nodded her head. 'I will be.'

'Good.'

Violet looked up at Mac and smiled. 'I love you, Mac McKellan, and I should have told you earlier.'

Mac stilled for an instant. 'Sorry, could you say that again please?' he said, his smile breaking into a grin. 'I'll never get tired of hearing it.'

'I love you,' said Violet. 'More than I could ever have imagined loving anyone.'

Mac dipped his head and kissed her.

Chapter 36

Mac sat by Violet's side with his arm thrown casually around her shoulders. The first few buttons of his shirt were undone and he'd loosened his tie. Violet's eyes travelled down the strong column of his throat. She gazed at his muscular frame from the hard work he'd done around the farm for so long. She hugged Holly closer to her chest.

It felt good just to sit down together and let the world pass them by. As soon as Celine and her father had left, the wedding party had broken up quickly, with none of the guests really knowing what to say.

Jason had stayed awhile, thanking people for coming and accepting their commiserations or the odd hostile glare with as much good grace as he could muster.

There had been a few harsh whispers and pointed looks thrown in Violet's direction but she didn't care. To hell with them, the only person's opinion she cared about was Mac's—and he loved her.

Almost everyone had gone by now, with the exception of some of the staff Dan had organized to help with food service, and the string quartet, who were still eating.

'I think we'd better pay them more,' Violet said as she

gestured towards the musicians. 'They obviously don't make enough to cover their grocery bills.'

'Well, the last thing we're short of is food,' Mac said with a grin. 'Just as well I have a big freezer—I reckon we'll be eating wedding food for at least a month.'

'Just as well your brother is a great chef,' Violet said.

A comfortable silence settled over them for a minute as they watched Dan's staff clear the tables.

Mac absently toyed with a lock of Violet's hair. 'Well, I'd like to say it was a wonderful day but that would be a total lie.'

'I guess we should just be grateful that it's over.'

'Amen to that,' Mac said with a sigh.

'Is Jason still here?' asked Violet.

Mac shook his head. 'No, he took off a little while ago. Dan packed him up some provisions and he headed to his cottage. He said he needed some time to himself.'

'Is he alright? Did he seem depressed or anything when you spoke to him?'

'Dan and I are going over there tomorrow to check up on him. I think that even though it was the hard decision, he knows he's done the right thing. He needs some peace and a bit of quiet just to work things through in his head.'

'I hope so, I have to admit I didn't think my conversation with him would have had such a huge impact.'

'Why, what was his response?'

'He seems to be remembering who he once was.'

'Jason should have re-evaluated his life a long time ago. Despite all the pain he's caused he's made the right decision and it's about time he realised the things he thought he wanted aren't what he needs. He thought he wanted a certain type of successful and high-flying future with Celine. But there's so much more to life. He'll be fine. We'll all make sure he is.'

'I have to admit I'm not going to miss Celine at all,' said Violet.

'She's a witch,' Holly said as she looked up at her mum.

Mac threw back his head and laughed. The sound seemed to echo through the entire room and Violet couldn't help smiling. It was a good sound and one she hoped to hear a lot more of through the years.

'Mummy, did I say something funny?'

'No, sweetie, Mac is just happy the whole wedding thing is over, that's all.'

'Your mum's right. I finally get my house back. But you know this was the prettiest non-wedding I've ever attended,' Mac said with a grin. 'You did a great job, Violet, the house looks amazing.'

'Thanks, but it's a bit of an anticlimax. I mean we did all that work, and now . . .'

'The house feels sad,' said Holly, looking around the room.

Mac leant down and tapped Holly's nose. 'You're right, fairy, the house does feel sad. What can we do to cheer it up?'

Holly shrugged her shoulders and sighed. 'I don't know.'

'I'm thinking maybe we should have a party.'

'Really? With ice cream?' Holly asked.

'Why not? We'll have lots of ice cream. What flavours should we have?'

Holly thought for a second or two. 'We should have chocolate and strawberry and vanilla and . . .'

'And peppermint?' Mac asked.

'Ew no. Peppermint is yucky,' Holly said with a firm shake of her head.

'Right, gotcha. No peppermint. How about coffee or raspberry or caramel?'

'They all sound yummy, Mac.'

'Well, I don't know about you two, but I think I need a rest before planning another party,' Violet said as she sunk back into her chair with a sigh. 'This one kind of wore me out.'

'Don't worry, sweetheart, you'll have plenty of time,' Mac said. 'Well, at least I'll give you a bit longer than four weeks to pull the next one together.'

'What are you talking about, Mac?'

'I'm talking about a wedding, Violet, our wedding,' said Mac taking her left hand and bringing it to his lips. 'I love you and I love Holly. Say you'll marry me. Please Violet, be my wife. We don't have to rush but I just want to know we'll always be together. You, me and Holly.'

'Mac,' Violet swallowed, her vision blurred as tears welled in her eyes. 'Mac.'

'That'd be the *best*,' said Holly. 'I could have all three kittens then.'

Violet and Mac looked at each other, laughing, then Violet said, 'Sure, Mac, I want to be together too—you, me, Holly and the kittens.'

* * *

317

It was a clear spring morning when Mac lifted Violet up and sat her on what was left of the old garden wall at the ruined cottage.

'It's beautiful here, Mac,' said Violet as she settled on the cool stones.

'Yeah, it is.' Mac smiled as he leant against her leg. The sound of the nearby stream was soothing as was the magpie's warbling song from a nearby tree. In what was once the garden, Holly laughed as she played fetch with Razor.

Mac felt blessed. He had the woman he loved and the daughter of his heart on his land. As mushy as it sounded, he was kind of in heaven.

'I've never been here before,' said Violet as she ran her hands through Mac's hair.

'You don't find it sad?'

'Not at all. There's a happy sort of peacefulness about it.'

Mac couldn't work out why but a wave of relief flooded through him at what Violet had just said. Somehow what Violet thought about the ruined cottage was important.

'I'm going to restore it with Johnno's help. It's going to take some time, because Johnno and I will only be working on it when we can. I'd love it if you can take over when it comes to designing the inside.'

'That's a great idea,' Violet said, looking thoughtful. 'I can almost see what it will be like. What are you going to do with it?'

'Well, I thought it could be your new office.'

'Really?'

'Yeah. You could run your business from here. I know you already have an office at your place but once we're married, I thought you might like one closer to home. Besides, I have an ulterior motive,' he said with a smile.

'Oh and what's that?'

'If you were here it would be a whole lot easier for me to drop by and visit each day,' said Mac. 'Anyway, it was just an idea.'

Violet bent down and dropped a kiss on his head. 'It's a fantastic idea and it means a lot to me.'

Her happiness caught Mac up in the enthusiasm of the new project. 'I'll be great, I promise. We'll restore it to its former glory and throw in all the normal utilities along with WiFi. Whatcha think?'

'I love it and it will still be a lovely reminder for your family.'

'I know we have to look to the future but I reckon remembering the past can be a good thing too.'

'You're right. It reminds us where we came from and just how much it took to get us here.'

'Mummy, Mac, look how fast Razor gets the stick!' Holly called out.

Mac watched as the little girl hurled the stick and Razor darted after it. Grabbing it in his mouth, he trotted back and dropped it at Holly's feet, before sitting down and eyeing it off. As he waited expectantly for Holly to throw it again, his tail thumped against the earth.

'That was super fast!' Violet called out.

'It sure was,' Mac added.

Holly grinned as she picked up the stick and threw it again.

'I wonder which of them will get tired first,' Violet whispered as a smile tugged at the corners of her mouth. 'So, is there a reason you brought us here today?'

'No, well maybe. I guess I just wanted to show you the cottage where our family began. I suppose I needed to show you that just like the land, you can depend on me, Violet. I won't let you down. Just like this place, I promise to build us a life that lasts and endures,' Mac said as he looked up at her. 'This was where Angus and Bridie started a life together. It just seemed like the right thing to do, bringing you here, I mean—since we're just starting out too. I want you to know that I love you, Violet, with all that I am.'

Violet wriggled off the fence into Mac's arms.

'Ah, the things you say,' she said kissing him on the lips. 'I love you, Mac McKellan—more than I ever thought possible and I can't wait to spend the rest of my life with you.'

Mac tightened his arms around her and kissed her with all the love he felt.

Yep, he reckoned he was a lucky man, and it was a damn good day on McKellan's Run.

Acknowledgements

A huge thank you to Louise Thurtell, Siobhán Cantrill and the whole Allen & Unwin team.

I would also like to thank Noel Flanagan for his insights into farming, shearing and wool classing, and Tom Chippindall, who escorted me through numerous paddocks, sheep pens and shearing sheds.

And finally, thanks to Ciandra, Conor and Alannah for their support, humour and general awesomeness.